RedHook

red Hook

GABRIEL COHEN

THOMAS DUNNE BOOKS
ST. MARTIN'S MINOTAUR
NEW YORK

This is a work of fiction. All the characters and events portrayed in this novel are either fictitious or are used fictitiously.

THOMAS DUNNE BOOKS.
An imprint of St. Martin's Press.

RED HOOK. Copyright © 2001 by Gabriel Cohen. All rights reserved. Printed in the United States of America. No part of this book may be used or reproduced in any manner whatsoever without written permission except in the case of brief quotations embodied in critical articles or reviews. For information, address St. Martin's Press, 175 Fifth Avenue, New York, N.Y. 10010.

www.minotaurbooks.com

"That'll be the day." Words and Music by Jerry Allison, Norman Petty, and Buddy Holly © 1957 (Renewed) MPL COMMUNICATIONS, INC. and WREN MUSIC CO. All Rights Reserved

Map of Brooklyn by Jeffrey L. Ward

Library of Congress Cataloging-in-Publication Data

Cohen, Gabriel.
    Red Hook / Gabriel Cohen.—1st ed.
        p.   cm.
    ISBN 0-312-27458-0
    1. Police—New York (State)—New York—Fiction. 2. Brooklyn (New York, N.Y.)—Fiction. I. Title.

PS3603.O47 R43 2001
813'.6—dc21

                                                    2001037185

First Edition: October 2001

10 9 8 7 6 5 4 3 2 1

For Monroe and Miriam Cohen,
with love and thanks

acknowledgments

I'd like to thank the many people who helped me research this book. They include Buddy Scotto, Sonny Balzano, Adam Cohen, Kevin O'Leary, Chino Suarez, Ivor Hansen, NYPD Detective Sergeant Christopher Jackson, former NYPD Detectives James J. Conaboy and Bill Clark, and several kind detectives from the 76th Precinct. (Any factual errors are mine.) Several fine readers gave me invaluable advice: Miriam Cohen, Tim Cross, Chris Erikson, and Elana Frankel. Important support or encouragement came from Michael Epstein, Naomi Ayala, Roxanne Aubrey, Todd Colby, Thom Garvey, Lee Sherratt, Phyllis Rose, James Wilcox, Jared Cooper, Mary Beth Lewis, Edward Scrivani, Dr. Ian Canino, and Paul Griffin (a.k.a. The King).

Thanks to Michael Ackerman and Eric Wolf for the photos. Very special thanks to Jen Bervin. I'm deeply grateful to my agent, Paul Chung, and to Ruth Cavin, Pete Wolverton, and Julie Sullivan at Thomas Dunne Books.

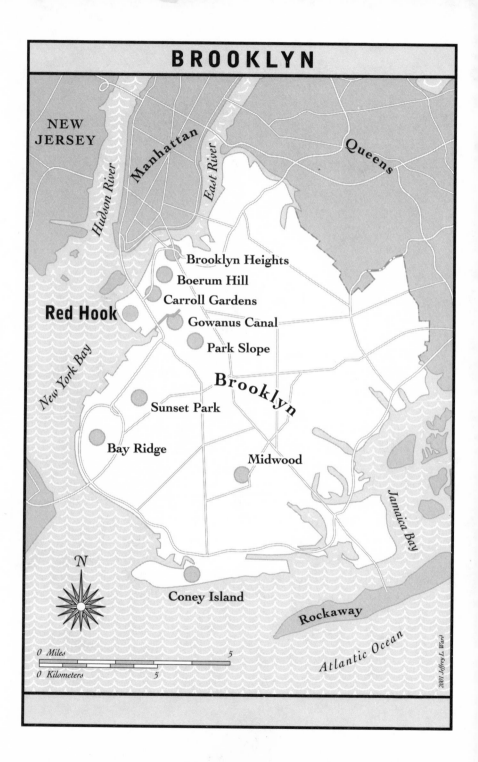

BROOKLYN

NEW JERSEY

Manhattan

Hudson River

East River

Queens

Brooklyn Heights

Boerum Hill

Carroll Gardens

Red Hook

Gowanus Canal

New York Bay

Park Slope

Brooklyn

Sunset Park

Bay Ridge

Midwood

Jamaica Bay

N

Coney Island

Rockaway

Atlantic Ocean

0 Miles   5

0 Kilometers   5

2001 Jeffrey L. Ward

Red Hook

prologue

Tomas Berrios pulled his Yankees cap out of his pocket and set it backward on his head, then ran his hand along his thigh, enjoying the smoothness of the nylon cycling shorts and the tautness of the muscle underneath. Good to be alive, yo. Good to be young.

He pinched the tuft of hair under his bottom lip and surveyed his crew, gathered under the street lamp in front of his apartment: Felix, Ramon, Dionicio. Only Hector the BigHead was missing, late as usual.

Upstairs, his little son's head peered over the windowsill. "Get back inside," Tomas said, but he smiled fondly at the boy.

"Okay," he said, bumping his bicycle down over the curb. "Let's roll." He didn't look back — he knew that everyone would follow. And they did, pursuing the glowing taillights of a taxi as they pedaled off into the hot Brooklyn night.

Just as they reached Fourth Avenue, a shout came from behind.

"Yo! Hold up!"

As Hector came pedaling, the crew waited outside a bodega. Melon-breasted women smiled at them from the malt liquor posters in the window. Across the street, a robed monk on a billboard beamed up at a bottle of Frangelico. "Tomarlo No Es Pecado." To drink it is not a sin.

"What the fuck is that?" said Ramon, laughing at Hector's banana-seat bike with its high handlebars.

"What happened to your for-real bike?" Tomas said.

"Somebody stole it," Hector mumbled, his oversize, pale head shadowed by the hood of a ratty sweatshirt.

"You gonna make all of us look bad, riding that thing," Tomas said. "How you gonna keep up?"

"I be all right."

The group swerved onto the avenue, its four lanes divided by a concrete median. The first forty blocks were industrial, a strip of fix-a-flat shops, muffler-repair garages, auto parts warehouses. The breeze smelled of stale oil and fresh gas. Tomas hunched over the handlebars, shoulders straining over his pumping knees. His arm itched: he'd had the tattoo on his right tricep re-inked and the scab was almost ready to peel.

They rode a wave of changing traffic signals, red winking to green as they blew down the avenue. Little bright bodegas whipped past, signs and smells announcing Cuchifritos, Comidas Criollas. They picked up speed, pouring faster and faster into a long V of streaming light, along the dark wall of a cemetery, through silent sleeping Sunset Park, past the somber basilicas and lumbering brick buildings of Bay Ridge.

At the corner of Seventy-third Street, a red Camaro roared past. The passenger window rolled down. "Nice wheels, greaseballs!" shouted the shirtless Italian kid riding shotgun.

Tomas's heart shifted gears. He called to his crew, "Let's get those guinea bastids!"

The Italian leaned out of his window, laughing as he checked their progress.

Maybe they'd catch him at a light. Concentrating on the Camaro two blocks ahead, Tomas rode close to the cars parked along the avenue, straight into a suddenly opening driver's door. He flipped over the metal, flew tumbling twenty feet across the asphalt, thudded onto the hood of a parked Chevy Nova, and landed on his back in front of an Italian restaurant. The diners stared out the window in horror.

His homies screeched to a halt, dropped their bikes, ran to him. "Jesus, guy, I'm sorry," said the anxious white driver. Tomas raised a hand weakly, all his wind knocked out.

After a minute he sat up, brushed some grit off his riding shorts, staggered to his feet. Little bits of gravel were embedded in his palms. He took a few tentative steps, stomach heaving: everything seemed to work okay. A miracle. He laughed. He was okay. Fucking *invincible*.

While the crew regrouped in the street, the driver took advantage of Tomas's good humor to retreat into the restaurant. Tomas picked up his bike, which had also survived with just a toe clip torn away. He turned. "Where's Hector?"

Felix unclipped the water bottle from his crossbar, spit. "I think he stopped off at the McDonald's back by the cemetery."

"We'll give him one minute," Tomas said. "That's it."

"Forget his ass," Ramon said, the sharp angles of his face made starker by the streetlight overhead. "Let's go."

The others waited to see what Tomas would do. For years he'd been the leader of the group, but in the past several months, for some unknown reason, Ramon had taken it upon himself to test his authority.

Tomas pretended not to hear. After a minute, he led the crew off again, spreading out in a line for the last lap before they reached the water. The night air was sweet. Now and then a flash of gleaming metal, a silver-blue arch of the

Verrazano-Narrows Bridge, rose over the rooftops like some improbable element of a dream.

At the end of Fourth Avenue, they crossed the Shore Parkway to a grassy strip bordering the harbor. They hit high gear now, gliding single-file on the smooth path along the river, a squadron of Stealth bombers under the moonlight, coursing between the bay on the right and the Shore Parkway's river of lights on the left.

Tomas braked to stand exhilarated under the bridge, which rocketed across a lake of molten pewter toward the dark mass of Staten Island. Unlike the Brooklyn Bridge, with its spiderwebs of cable and comfortable stone towers, the Verrazano was Space Age, stripped for speed, an expressway hung from two grand but simple strings of light. From under the bridge, a barge glided by like a half-submerged submarine, bucking powerful currents rippling silver around the bend.

Tomas moved away from the others and stood on the path along the water's edge. Finally, a moment alone. Always, there was his wife, and his mother-in-law, who never left the house. Sunday morning, when a man deserved a few moments of peace and quiet, the kids pounced on him in bed, squealing like puppies. At rush hour in the subway he was packed in with a bunch of other wage slaves in an airless sardine can. The only time he was by himself was when he was on the john or riding up and down in the service elevator at work.

This, now: here was a place of power. Under this eerie manmade object built to such an immense scale, a floodlit arc reaching out into the sky, the night hummed with something great, some invisible electric force. Funny, he thought: that he should be dwarfed by the bridge, yet feel his heart expand.

It bothered him that none of his crew could appreciate

the scene right in front of their eyes. Except Hector the BigHead, who finally caught up, swerving next to him. In the background, the others grumbled about getting under way, but Hector stood silent, showing the proper reverence. He felt it too. Maybe that was why Tomas put up with him, touched in the head as the kid was.

Across the harbor, the Statue of Liberty held up her torch like a cigarette lighter in the night. *Give me your tired, your poor* . . . Fuck that, Tomas murmured to himself. You weren't really an American until you had money —you were still just a Dominican or a Puerto Rican or a Pole.

Five miles back, just across from the southern tip of Manhattan, lay Red Hook, his lucky neighborhood, where soon he would make the score that would change things forever. Tonight he was on one side of a great wall, a wall built to keep people like him out, but in just twelve hours he would stand on the other side. He was glad for his children, glad for his wife, but most of all, in his deep heart, he was glad for himself. Tomorrow his life would begin.

one

The Gowanus Canal was a bilious green. Long ago, Brooklyn kids had jumped in off its narrow banks to shout and splash around, but more than a century's worth of raw sewage and pollution from the adjoining factories had rendered the water unfit for every living thing except some algae and a tiny perverse species called killifish. Its opaque depths kept many secrets, but by a stroke of luck this corpse was not one of them.

The body lay in a scrub of sun-dry marsh grass at the top of the bank. As Detective Jack Leightner made his way up, his hamstrings strained, but he told himself he was still in good shape for a fifty-year-old. As a member of the elite Brooklyn South Homicide Task Force, he'd been called in to aid the local precinct with the investigation.

A team had already fanned out around the corpse, stooped over like migrant workers as they searched the ground for evidence: a scrap of clothing, a clump of hair, maybe just a cigarette butt with DNA evidence smooched on the filter . . . A Crime Scene Unit photographer shifted around, snapping pictures.

One of the locals, a massive man with a bear's ponderous

gait, straightened up and smiled as Jack approached. "Hey, whaddaya know?" he said. "The cavalry's here!"

At thirty, Gary Daskivitch was the youngest detective in the Seven-six Precinct. He and Jack had worked together the year before on a murder in the nearby Gowanus housing projects.

"You catch the case?" Jack asked.

"Yeah. Looks like we're partners again."

At four o'clock the August sun should have been high, but a bank of scudding dirty-cotton clouds dimmed the light. The air bore the heavy, metallic tang of an approaching storm.

"Hey, you see the Mets play last night?" Daskivitch asked.

Jack snorted and looked up at his partner, who stood a full head taller. "I saw it. Almost made me ashamed to be a New Yorker."

He tugged the knees of his slacks and squatted down. Baseball was fun, but not nearly as interesting as a fresh murder. The vic lay on his left side, splayed out in the grass in front of a chain-link fence. A beefy young man, he wore a pair of cheap gray dress slacks and a T-shirt beneath a red plaid shirt. Hispanic, probably mid-twenties. Several nasty bruises mottled his face but the cause of death was not apparent. The kid stared out, his eyes gray as the sky above; they glinted silver in the photographer's flash.

A chain joined two cinder blocks to his ankles. The fence, which marked the rear boundary of a lot filled with abandoned delivery trucks and a rusted black crane, curled up at the lower edge; a rusty spike had pierced the cuff of the victim's pants. The cloth was bloodsoaked: closer inspection revealed that the wire had also pierced the vic's calf.

Jack duckwalked around to look at the corpse's back. The man's well-muscled arms were tied behind him with rope and his legs were similarly bound. "Hey, Dupree," Jack called out, "you get a close-up of these knots?" A particular knot could be a signature, linking this case to other murders.

"Got it," the photographer said curtly, annoyed by this questioning of his expertise.

The vic's T-shirt was raised above his belly, which hung to the side like a sad, soft gourd. If Jack didn't know better than to touch a corpse before the Crime Scene guys finished their job, he would have reached out to pull the shirt down.

"Who found the body?" he asked the young detective.

"We got an anonymous call early this afternoon."

"You ID him yet?"

"Nope."

"Okay," Jack said, rising. "Why don't you make a sketch while we wait."

Daskivitch took out a steno pad and began to draw the position of the body in relation to the fence and the canal.

Down on the water, a breeze jigged the reflections of the sky and the straggly trees and bushes that managed to cling to the banks. Across the way ran a long factory wall with no windows. Farther along, the canal was bordered by warehouses and industrial lots. A drawbridge crossed the water seventy yards to the north, but the sightlines were obscured by trees and tall grass. Whoever killed this man had picked a spot so isolated you could dump a body there in broad daylight.

Half a mile to the south, the F train shuttled across the skyline, a centipede on its elevated track. A mile over the horizon the canal would pass through Red Hook—where Jack was born, where his father had worked the docks—and then open into the Gowanus Bay and New York harbor.

Jack sidestepped down the bank. He watched a Clorox bottle and a potato-chip bag float south on the oil-slick water. Which would reach him first? He put his money on the Clorox bottle.

A minute later the chip bag slid by in first place.

"Hey, Jack!"

He turned and clambered back up, pleased to see that Daskivitch had been joined by Anselmo Alvarez, the head of the Crime Scene Unit, a short Dominican man with ramrod posture. A few strands of hair were combed carefully across Alvarez's bald pate, in tribute to what his ID photo revealed had once been a proud pompadour. The investigator was the best forensics man in Brooklyn — he took seriously the responsibility of standing up for the dead.

"Let's start," Jack said.

Daskivitch shut his notepad. The men pulled on white latex gloves and crouched down.

First Jack checked the victim's pants for identification. Due to the execution-style disposition of the body, there wasn't much chance of finding any, but he had to check. Even after twelve years in Homicide, it still felt odd to reach his hands into someone else's pockets. They were empty.

The victim's kinky black hair was pressed out awkwardly against the dirt.

"We can surmise one thing right off the bat," Alvarez said. "The deceased is having a very bad hair day."

Jack smiled. Alvarez himself could not really be said to have hair days at all anymore, but he kept the thought to himself.

He noted the soul patch, the tuft of beard under the vic's bottom lip, and the tattoo of a jaguar on the right tricep. The red and green lines of the tattoo were crusted over — it was either fresh or had just been renewed. Jack had never gotten a tattoo, even during his time in the Army: a tattoo would brand you forever. He avoided bumperstickers on any car he owned for the same reason. It was better to go through life unmarked.

"What should we do next?" he asked Gary Daskivitch. When it came to murders, the kid was a rookie. (With only four homicides in the past year, the Seventy-sixth Precinct was hardly a crisis zone.) He'd learn better if he was pushed to do more than just watch.

The young detective frowned in concentration. "How about we check to see how long he's been here?"

"Okay. How we gonna do that?"

"I guess . . . first we need to get him off the fence." Daskivitch took a breath, then reached out and hesitantly prodded the corpse. Jack traded a subtle wink with Alvarez; the rookie hadn't yet seen enough bodies to be comfortable with the task. Hell, the kid didn't even look comfortable wearing a suit.

It took the men several minutes to disengage the victim's leg and pants cuff from the rusty chain-link.

Daskivitch rolled the body forward; he noted that the weeds underneath had not had time to brown.

"You're doing good," Jack said.

Alvarez took out a flashlight and shone it into one of the victim's eyes: the cornea was clouded over. The forensics man pressed his hands against the face, arms, upper body. Jack followed his example. The body was rigid until he reached the thighs, where the flesh still rolled under his palm.

"Feel this," he told the young detective.

Daskivitch winced as he patted the body. Other veterans would have baited the rookie with wisecracks, but Jack refrained. He liked the young detective. The kid was brash — he'd recently come from several years of playing cowboy with a narcotics squad, leaping out of vans and making tough with crack sellers — but he took his new job seriously and was eager to learn.

"What do you think?" Jack said.

"Rigor mortis hasn't set in all the way down."

"Correct. How many hours since the lights went out?"

"I dunno." That was another good thing about the kid—he didn't bullshit. "Less than twelve?"

"I'd say six."

Alvarez nodded. "I'll have to take an internal temp to make sure, but that sounds about right."

The back of the dead man's neck was purple, a different tint from the bruises. Jack pushed a finger into the flesh and pulled it back. The spot momentarily whitened. He knelt down and pulled the back of the T-shirt up: same purple discoloration, same white spot when pressed.

"The body was moved postmortem," Jack said. "How do I know?"

Daskivitch frowned again. "Uh, lividity, right? After the blood stopped circulating, it would have pooled in the lowest parts of the body. That should be his side, not the back."

"Good." Jack turned to Alvarez. "Could these blows to the face have done him in?"

The forensics man stared down thoughtfully. "I think that was just a warm-up."

"Help me here," Alvarez said to Jack. They rolled the body over and Alvarez pulled aside the plaid shirt. The T-shirt underneath was stained with a big patch of rust-colored blood. There was no blood on the ground, confirmation that the body had been moved.

Alvarez rolled the T-shirt up the victim's chest. "There you go."

At first Jack didn't see what he was talking about, but then Alvarez pressed down on the corpse's side, opening the thin ugly slit of a stab wound. Jack pressed his hands against the spiky grass and squeezed his eyes shut. Sweat beaded his upper lip.

"You okay?" Alvarez asked.

Jack nodded, but swallowed, fighting the bile rising in his throat. His head swam and he was afraid he might black out.

"Jack?" Daskivitch said.

Weakly he shook his head, lurched to his feet, staggered a few yards away, and heaved up his guts.

He took a deep breath and wiped his mouth with a handkerchief, ashamed to turn around. A veteran getting queasy over such a well-preserved corpse—it was as pathetic as a surgeon fainting over a nosebleed.

He patted the sweat from his forehead, straightened up, and turned back to the other detectives. They seemed to have trouble meeting his eyes.

"Whew. Must've been something I ate. Bad shrimp, maybe."

"What is it with you and the stabbings?" Alvarez said quietly.

Jack looked up sharply. "Why don't you mind your own fucking business!"

"*Whoa.*" Alvarez raised his hands.

Daskivitch's eyes widened. The kid had seen the veteran lose his lunch; now he was losing his cool. Jack cleared his throat. "Sorry. I just got a little dizzy, is all. I'll be fine."

The forensics man shrugged, then knelt down by the corpse and started doing something unpleasant with a thermometer.

Jack turned away, queasy again. He glanced at Daskivitch, alert to any condescension or contempt.

The kid just looked concerned. "You sure you're okay?"

"Yeah. Let's just drop it, all right?"

Daskivitch nodded and looked away.

"Okay," Jack said, taking charge again, "the vic died

12

somewhere else and was shlepped here. He could have been carried from the bridge, but that's a long way and there's no stairs. I think they just chucked him over the fence, and he got snagged on the other side."

"They?"

"One guy could never have gotten him over. So—first of all, they would've had to untangle him from the wire. Then they'd have to carry him down to the water. The question is, why didn't they finish the job?"

"You think somebody eyeballed them from the bridge?"

"Too far. The sightlines are crap."

He looked down at the water. "At least the scubas will be glad they don't have to go in." Once he'd seen a couple of miserable Harbor Scuba Unit divers kneeling by a hydrant near the canal as they hosed off a thick layer of scum and muck. Perhaps they were remembering a scuba whose mask had slipped off while he was down: the poor bastard inhaled a mouthful of typhus and cholera and ended up in intensive care.

Daskivitch grimaced. "A few minutes in that poison would strip a body like frikkin' piranhas."

Alvarez pulled out a couple of paper bags and taped them over the victim's hands. If the man had died fighting, he might have tissue from his murderer under his nails. Unfortunately, they'd have to wait until after the autopsy to take fingerprints.

Jack and his partner took a walk along the canal, discussing the possibilities. A few yards on, they came upon the first officer on the scene, a young uniform anxiously checking the yellow tape he'd stretched between the fence and a tiny tree. In one hand he held a clipboard, his log of everyone who entered the perimeter. He coughed awkwardly as the two detectives approached, unsure whether to look at them or away.

"How's it going, kid?" asked Daskivitch. That he was only a few years older than the patrol cop didn't matter — a detective's shield hung on the pocket of his jacket.

"Very good, sir," the uniform replied. "Do, um, did you find out what happened?"

"Yeah," Daskivitch said. "The vic was offed by a big guy, probably an American Indian, left-handed, wearing a blue-jean jacket and Air Jordans."

The patrol cop's brow furrowed.

Jack remembered his own days walking a beat. Half the time, dealing with the public, you felt like a big wheel; the other half your superiors made you feel like shit. "Don't worry about it," he told the young cop. "He's just busting your chops."

A deflated soccer ball drifted downstream. Jack watched it for a moment, then turned to his partner. "The canal."

"Huh?"

"Someone was sailing down the canal."

"What, are you kidding? It's a cesspool — nobody's sailed here in a hundred years."

On the bridge, a knot of gawkers had already assembled, drawn by the Crime Scene truck and the flashing patrol cars. Jack and his partner pushed through and made their way to the bridgehouse, a squat brick tower rising next to the far end. They peered over the side of the bridge. A crusted metal ladder descended to a half-open door. The detectives climbed over the railing and made their way down.

"Hello?" Jack called.

Inside the tower, a musty stairwell brought them up to a small office, where an old man sat facing a gleaming metal control panel covered with knobs and gauges. In front of him, a picture window offered a broad view of the canal and the metal-grated roadway. He wore headphones over greasy gray hair and flipped through a copy of the *Post*, whistling tunelessly with the music inside his head. 'If you wanna be my lover,' he suddenly sang, falsetto.

Jack rapped on the door and the bridgekeeper spun around. The detectives badged him, then explained their disagreement about canal traffic.

"Well," the man said, "nobody *sails* on the Gowanus, but we get some barges. Did you know this used to be the end of the Erie Canal? Back in the eighteen-eighties —"

"How much traffic do you get?" Jack said.

"I lift the bridge a couple times a day."

"How many people on the barges?"

"They usually run with a crew of two — they trade watches, six hours on and off."

"They have radios?"

"Yeah. These days some of them carry portable phones too."

"You keep a log?"

"Of course I do. It's the law." The keeper lifted a large open notebook from a desk and handed it over.

The *Volsunga*, captained by one Al Perry, had passed by at 9:47 that morning, and the *Chem Trader*, captained by Raymond Ortslee, had passed at 12:40 that afternoon. The anonymous call to the Seven-six had come in five minutes later.

Jack lit a cigarette as he and Daskivitch stepped out the bridgehouse door. Across the canal lay a squat grass-covered berm, an oil company depot, surrounded by coils of barbed wire. Along the front of its loading dock No Smoking was painted in red letters six feet high.

"Jesus, don't drop that cig," Daskivitch said. "Don't worry about the oil — the canal itself'll catch and we'll have a river of fire all the way to Red Hook."

As the detectives climbed back onto the roadway, raindrops

spattered down out of the leaden sky. Jack hunched his shoulders and lifted the collar of his sports jacket. "It's Murphy's Law — on rainy days, the bodies are always outside."

The windshield of the young detective's unmarked Grand Marquis fogged up quickly. Jack rubbed his handkerchief across the glass and watched the thundershower scatter the audience on the bridge. Down by the canal, the Crime Scene Unit was scrambling to spread plastic tarps inside the perimeter.

He reached into his pocket and pulled out a little white packet.

"What's that?" Daskivitch asked.

"It's a hand wipe. You want one?"

"No, thanks," his partner said, amused.

Jack ripped open the packet and wiped down his hands, pleased by the familiar stinging scent of the alcohol. He knew the gesture was mostly futile — the world was teeming with hostile bacteria — but it made him feel better.

The ugly little mouth of the victim's stab wound opened in his mind and he shivered.

Daskivitch looked glum. "I wish I didn't catch this one. I'll take a grounder any day. The jealous wife — you get to the scene and she's standing there with the Ginsu knife in one hand and her husband's stones in the other. Baddabing: case closed."

Jack didn't answer. He wished his partner would stop talking, and especially that he'd stop talking about knives.

"Why do you think the barge captain phoned it in anonymous?" Daskivitch asked.

Jack shrugged.

His partner answered his own question. "The guy's probably shitting bricks. He thinks he witnessed the end of a Mob hit, and the guys who did it saw him, and he's gotta pass by here every day. You think it was Mob?"

"I doubt it." Though the side streets of nearby Carroll Gardens were home to a number of known Mafia *soldieri*, the neighborhood was quiet—they didn't do business where their wives and children lived. Mobsters would have taken the body out and dumped it in the harbor, or by some distant parkway. Secondly, the victim was Hispanic, and stabbing was a Hispanic MO. A knife was often associated with domestic violence—the first weapon handy—but Jack couldn't see some angry woman beating the shit out of this guy and then hoisting his body over a fence. He lacked the patience right now to discuss all this, so he just said, "If it was a Mob hit, they'd probably have just shot the guy."

Daskivitch pondered the matter. After a moment, he chuckled. "How'd you like the look on that rookie's face, huh? 'Blue-jean jacket and Air Jordans'!"

Jack didn't answer. He pictured the hilt mark next to the wound, indicating that the knife had plunged all the way in.

His partner drummed on the steering wheel with his index fingers, a habit Jack remembered from the last time they'd worked together. "You *like* the mysteries," Daskivitch said, his tone a mix of admiration and annoyance. "You're the only detective I know who doesn't mind a dump job." Nearly impossible cases sometimes turned up in car trunks or Dumpsters, decomposed, without ID, without witnesses. Jack had a reputation on the task force for pursuing such cases as far as he could. It wasn't always a good reputation: spending too much time on a few hopeless cases could drive down the team's clearance rate.

A slight tightening of his face was Jack's only response. He looked out the side window. A CSU man's red umbrella bobbed alongside the canal, a small splash of color against the unrelenting gray of the scene.

He loosened his tie, tilted his head back, and closed his eyes. Rain rattled on the roof.

The stab wound was directly above the heart. The victim might have bled to death, or the trauma might even have stopped the muscle directly. Sweat beaded Jack's lip again.

Daskivitch drummed his fingers on the wheel. "What do you say we go find the barge captain? I know the shift's almost over, but we could pick up some good OT."

Jack opened the door and stepped out. The red lights of a patrol car parked on the bridge slapped him repeatedly in the face. Cars slowed as they neared the bridge, their tires making a sound on the wet asphalt like tape being pulled up. He bent down to speak through the window.

"I'm gonna head home. We can do it first thing in the A.M."

He turned away from Daskivitch's look of surprise. They had a hot murder; the rookie was excited to pursue it. And here was the infamously dogged Detective Leightner, ready to call it a day.

Daskivitch shrugged. "All right, bunk. You okay?"

Jack was already walking toward his car.

two

Half an hour later, he arrived home in Midwood, a quiet Brooklyn suburb of stucco and brick. The houses kept close company; tulips filled small front yards often marked by one special tree — a weeping willow, a Japanese maple, an exotic pine. When he moved there after his divorce, Jack knew nothing about the neighborhood save that it was populated largely by Orthodox Jews and had a very low murder rate. He was Jewish himself, but the religious makeup of the neighborhood didn't matter to him — he just needed to live somewhere he didn't have to worry about what was happening in the streets.

He worried about his landlord, though. As he entered the front hall, he cocked his head for sounds of life upstairs. At eighty-six Mr. Gardner was alert and active, but his wife had died the year before and now he lived alone.

Radio voices, a clanking of dishes — thank God, the old man motored on.

Jack stooped to lift a bundle of mail from the Astroturf-carpeted floor. (Mr. Gardner was a big fixer-upper, but he improvised with found materials.) He sensed that he was not alone — an orange cat sat on its haunches at the top of the stairs, regarding him coolly. The cat belonged to his landlord, as much as it belonged to anyone. Jack respected its self-sufficiency: the old man fed it once a day, but otherwise it took care of itself.

Inside his apartment, a floor-through with faded wallpaper, he hung his jacket neatly in a closet and fished his NYPD paycheck out of a stack of junk fliers and credit card offers. In the kitchen, he scrubbed his hands and turned on a radio for background noise while he gathered a makeshift dinner: a can of sardines in mustard, creamed spinach in a boilable pouch, a packaged microwaveable potato. Bobby Darin crooned "Beyond the Sea."

While he ate, he read the back of a cracker box, which suggested accompaniments, including a slice of cheese. What kind of moron, he wondered, needed to be told that cheese went well with a cracker? The answer bounced back: the same kind of moron who couldn't bake his own potato.

The food sat heavy in his stomach while he washed the dishes. As he rinsed the sardine can, he nicked his finger on the sharp rolltop. A knife wound—ugly little mouth— opened in his mind's eye. He flushed with shame. *Indigestion.* That was the reason he'd gotten sick that afternoon. To hell with Alvarez.

He wandered into the living room and picked up the newspaper. Dropped it. Wandered back into the kitchen. The evening stretched ahead. He regretted turning down Daskivitch's suggestion that they work late, but he hadn't felt up to dealing with the kid's concern.

Mr. Gardner's footsteps clomped across the ceiling.

Jack reached into the fridge for a couple cold cans of beer. Several nights a week he went upstairs to keep the old man company. Sometimes the favor was mutual.

• • •

When Mr. Gardner opened the door, Jack half expected to look over his shoulder and see Mrs. Gardner in the kitchen, bending down to pull something from the massive old stove. She would reach a hand back to support the base of her spine, turn, hold up an angel food cake. She'd smile a crinkly big-toothed smile and her dentures would shift, click. Hair white as sugar. "Siddown," she'd say. "Have a piece a cake." Her voice deep, husky, kind. But Mrs. Gardner was gone.

"Hey, Jackie, come on in." Age had brought stocky Mr. G. even closer to the ground. He wore a time-grayed white shirt, faded chinos, cracked shoes. His eyes peered big and droopy through thick black-framed glasses. Leaving the door open for Jack, he reached up into a cabinet and pulled down two delicate china coffee cups. He set them on the kitchen table next to a Tupperware container filled with coupons and reached for a bottle of cheap bourbon.

"Here's how!" he said; they downed the warm liquor.

This ritual dispensed with, Mr. Gardner invited Jack into the living room. "You're just in time," he said, easing back into a duct-tape-repaired La-Z-Boy recliner. Jack handed his landlord a beer, then settled into a nubby brown armchair. They sat before the TV in silence, the muteness of men.

On *Wheel of Fortune*, Vanna White was still going strong, waving at all the lovely prizes. The empty white tiles of a mystery phrase appeared on screen. Players bought letters, Vanna flipped tiles. *A _ _AST F_ _ _ T_ _ _AST.* Jack glanced at Mr. Gardner. The old man rarely ventured a guess, but that didn't stop him from chuckling and nodding in satisfaction at the solutions. Aside from his grief over his wife's death, the man seemed complacent about his life. At least, he never complained.

Most nights Jack would have been content to relax and

sip his beer too, but tonight he was restless and the endless commercials didn't help.

During an ad for Maxi-Pads, Mr. Gardner muted the volume. "Have you heard from the Gangbuster?"

Jack had discovered the apartment through the old man's son, a file clerk at the Sixty-first Precinct. Neil Gardner rarely came by the house, or even called. His father had somehow gotten — or been given — the impression that the guy was busy with critical departmental affairs.

"He's doing great," Jack said, to make the old man feel better. "How was your day?"

Mr. G. shrugged. "Not too exciting, but what are ya gonna do? You can't fight City Hall." One of his stock sayings, applicable to bad weather, ill health, even wars. He said no more and Jack didn't follow up. To be so old, to have so much time for reflection, for regret . . . He was struck by the musty, old-butter smell of the man's skin.

The show returned and Mr. Gardner clicked up the sound. A second contestant bought more letters. $A\ B\_AST$ $F\_\_\_\ T\_\_\ PAST$. An L in the first open slot should have ended the game, but the contestants remained mystified. Mr. Gardner stared at the screen through his thick glasses, waiting placidly for the answer.

Jack imagined finishing his days that way. He downed the rest of his beer and stood up.

"What — goin' so soon?"

"I got some work to finish up," he lied.

Downstairs, before he left the house, he double-checked that the stove was off, the microwave unplugged, the windows all locked.

Monsalvo's was the kind of place where the old men lined up along the bar in mid-afternoon. Not the Orthodox Jews, of course, but the bar was a lone outpost on the edge of the neighborhood. The decor hadn't changed for decades: dusty statuettes of Jack Benny and Jimmy Durante behind the bar, a mournful deer's head high above it, yellowed stills of Rocky Graziano, Joe DiMaggio, and Louis Armstrong along the back wall. A string of Christmas lights along the top shelf lent the only bright note. You could get Rolling Rock or Schaeffer on tap for a buck and a half and even a good shot of Jameson's only cost three bucks. The prices were not the draw for Jack—he rarely drank more than a couple of beers—but Monsalvo's drew no lawyers, no yuppies, and no cops, himself excepted. He could unwind there, as much as he could do so anywhere.

The evening had grown cool and he was glad to take his seat at the bar, to feel the presence of his fellow customers, like horses at a trough, content in the warmth given off by each other's flanks.

Pat the bartender, a prematurely leather-faced young man, slapped a cardboard coaster down. "What'll it be, Mr. Jack?"

"Just give me a Schaeffer. I'll be right back—I'm goin' to the can."

"Don't look in there," Pat said sadly.

"Why not?"

"It's Monsalvo. After forty-seven years, he suddenly decided to make an 'improvement.' You'll see."

Jack pushed open the swinging door of the men's room, with its appalling, mossy urinals, decaying black-and-white tiled floor, mottled mirror. He was shocked and pleased to see a gleaming electric hand dryer affixed to the graffiti-scribbled wall. A plaque next to it offered a list of instructions:

1. Press Button.

2. Place Hands Beneath Air Blower.

3. Rub Hands Briskly Together.

Below that, someone had already written an addendum: "4. Wipe Hands On Pants."

Jack grinned; must've been a fellow toiler for the city.

Back at the bar, he eavesdropped on an old-timer's conversation.

"More than thirty years I knew the man," said the humpbacked little guy, wearing a cap that might have looked sporty several decades before. "Every day he was out there on his route, delivering through rain, through sleet, through all that crap. Every day he came back to the PO and yakked about the high life he was gonna live down in Florida soon as he retired. Finally, last month, he gets the gold watch and flies down to his condo by the beach. Three days later we get a call from his wife: the poor bastid dropped dead of a heart attack."

Jack picked up his drink and moved to an empty seat down the bar. He couldn't even go out for a drink without hearing about bodies.

"How ya doon?" said a curly-haired young guy at the next stool. He nodded at the tag stitched to his uniform shirt. "Name's Rich. I'm a plumber's assistant. No jokes, please. Whaddaya do?"

"I work for the city," Jack replied.

"Oh, yeah? What department?"

"In Brooklyn. You see the Mets game last night?"

"Tell him what you do, Jacko," called a voice from down the bar. "He's a homicide detective."

A customer three seats down abruptly pushed back his stool, slapped some money on the bar, and strode out the door.

"Thanks a lot," Pat said to the loudmouth down the bar. "You're gonna empty out the fuckin' place."

"Homicide," repeated the plumber's assistant, clearly impressed. "Hey, listen, you ever watch *NYPD Blue*? You think that shit is real, or what?"

"Excuse me one sec."

Jack got up and walked past the end of the bar into a phone booth. Inside, he pushed the door shut to block out the noise. He closed his eyes and leaned forward to feel the cool glass against his forehead. Was this what a confessional would be like?

All of a sudden, he wanted to call his ex-wife. He thought of her body, of the first time he'd ever touched her. Modest, she'd worn loose-fitting clothes the first couple of times they went out. One night he drove her home from a movie, kissed her in the front seat, slipped his hand up inside her blouse. He'd been so surprised by the fullness of her breasts. He pictured her in the bath, tits rising up out of the water, slippery pink islands. She had a wonderful body and they'd always enjoyed each other that way. In the beginning, anyhow.

He remembered the bad times and the urge to call ebbed away. He left the booth, tossed some money on the bar, and walked out into the night.

He drove slowly down a side street, scanning the houses to the left. He was only half a mile from the Gowanus Canal, but even in the dark it was clear he was in a much different neighborhood. People lived here, and the houses were well kept, if not fancy like the brownstones of nearby Brooklyn Heights. The only thing separating Boerum Hill from the tide of gentrification sweeping the rest of downtown Brooklyn was the low-income housing project around the next corner. Every year Brooklyn South Homicide made at least one visit to the Gowanus Houses.

He pulled up in front of a vaguely familiar red row house. His son had moved onto the block two years earlier, but Jack had only been to the house once, to pick Ben up and take him to a local restaurant for an hour of awkward non-conversation. Light filled a third-floor window, but he didn't know if that was the boy's apartment. *The boy,* that was how he still thought of him, though Ben was now—he made a quick calculation—twenty-three years old. He'd been eight when the divorce went through.

An iron fence separated the house from the sidewalk, and Jack was glad that a bright light shone over the stoop. There were no bars on the windows, though—not very wise in this neighborhood. Up in the window, a shadow moved past the curtain so quickly he couldn't tell if it was male or female. Did Ben have a girlfriend? He didn't even know.

His son had worked since college as an assistant to a commercial photographer, but the last time Jack saw him, Ben announced he was trying to become an independent filmmaker. "Experimental documentaries," whatever that meant. (Jack didn't understand the things the boy was interested in. His ex-wife had encouraged the kid to go to a fancy college up in New Hampshire, and Jack had paid for it. Sometimes he felt like a sucker.) The conversation had dried up and he'd driven his son home; Ben didn't ask him in. The memory still rankled. Like Mr. Gardner's son, the kid never called, unless there was an emergency or some communication his mother wanted to pass along. Jack gripped the wheel.

What are you doing here, anyhow? Running a stakeout on your own son?

Up on the third floor, the light went out.

26

three

Ben Leightner turned on his stereo and played the first half of the first song of three different CDs. He turned the stereo off.

He picked up a filmmaker's magazine and flipped through it, unable, for once, to fantasize himself into its pages. The new Orson Welles? The new Scorsese? Tonight he couldn't even imagine himself the new Ken Burns.

He glanced at his phone, which sat mute on his editing desk, a door laid on two sawhorses. He ran through a mental list of his friends — which didn't take long — wondering who he might call. One had a new girlfriend and never went out these days. Another had recently taken a job writing for a cable-TV cartoon and couldn't seem to talk about anything else . . . He gave up on his list and sat staring at the phone, willing it to ring. The room was so quiet he could hear the clock plunking away the seconds. *I got a phone that doesn't ring* — it would make a good line for a blues song, some old Mississippi Delta singer rocking on his porch. Blind Lemon Pledge.

He got up, wandered into the kitchen, opened the refrigerator, shut it. He returned to the living room, flopped down on his futon couch, clicked on the TV. For a few minutes he watched a sitcom, the star a young guy his age who sat on his couch in his apartment and was visited by an endless parade of friends and pretty girls and relatives and coworkers. He clicked the set off. Every TV show was about people who always had other people to talk to. You never saw a show about a guy who lived alone and read a lot.

He looked at the phone again, that dead piece of plastic. Dropping all ironic detachment, he sent two deep, silent questions out into the ether. *Why am I different?* And *What's wrong with me?*

He sat limp on the couch for another minute and then finally — disgusted with himself — he got up and turned off the lights. He'd just been avoiding work, was all; he'd feel better once he started. He popped a tape in the VCR, clicked the remote, and the TV sprang to life. On screen, the late-day sun caught the reds and oranges and earth tones of Red Hook's brick warehouses and bathed them in a special honeyed light.

The Hook was screwed up, but Ben loved it.

Earlier that afternoon, he'd packed up a couple of cameras and set out for the waterfront. With the weight of the camera bag and tripod pressing on his shoulders, he felt as if he were going to *work*, like his grandfather striding down to the docks with his longshoreman's hook.

He walked across Smith Street, where black and Latino kids hung out in front of the bodegas; beyond Court Street, where yuppies pushed baby strollers into video stores and cappuccino cafes; on past the swanky brownstones of Cobble Hill. He didn't see many people outside there, though he could glance into the windows of their brownstones to see them sitting in their living rooms, under expensive Tiffany lamps.

The edge of the neighborhood was marked by a deep gash, a channel cut into the earth for the Gowanus Expressway. He crossed a bridge over the highway into Red Hook.

The direct route would have been southwest, but that would have taken him through a giant low-income housing project. The Red Hook Houses stretched for block after block in the center of the neighborhood. He would have loved to film there, but a young white guy wandering around with a camera would undoubtedly raise suspicion. In his mental map of the neighborhood, the Red Hook Houses were an uncharted area, like the edge of an ocean populated by fantastical sea monsters. With drive-by shootings and drug deals gone bad, several people got killed there every year. (Which meant that his father, the Big Homicide Detective, had probably been inside. Ben considered asking if he could tag along sometime, but it had been months since they'd spoken.)

Instead of entering the projects, he turned west toward the waterfront, along a deserted side street called Seabring. He loved the exotic, vaguely Shakespearean names of the streets. Imlay, Verona, and Beard. King and Delavan. Visitation. Pioneer. An old dockworker had told him that the neighborhood itself was named for an Indian chief, but he researched the matter and found that early Dutch settlers had named it Roode Hoek for the color of the soil and the shape of the land curving out into New York Bay.

Once upon a time, the waterfront had been one of the busiest ports in America. Now it was almost a ghost town. Just across the harbor rose the crazy bustling Erector set of Manhattan's southern skyline, but the Hook was so quiet that the wind was a presence; it whispered over the cobblestones and flowed around the deserted warehouses; it sifted through primitive, fernlike ailanthus trees. In the distance you might hear the faint fairground tinkling of a Mr. Frostee ice-cream truck, or the ringing of a buoy out in the harbor. Breathe deep and your lungs filled with salty ocean air.

In the Brooklyn Historical Society, a turn-of-the-century mansion paneled with dark, ornately carved wood, he'd sat in front of a computer calling up grainy old photos of the Hook as it had been a hundred years before: humble row houses; ships docked at mist-shrouded piers; horses straining to pull coal wagons; bleak-eyed immigrants staring defiantly at the camera. A world of brick and water and hard manual labor.

He planned to make a film exploring what had happened to the neighborhood. Interviewing old-timers or digging through library files, he liked to think that in his own way he was a detective, like his father. Though Jack Leightner had grown up in the Hook, he never brought his son there — the man seemed to have bad memories of the place and never spoke of his early life.

The Hook was a place of mysteries, not the least of which was his own father's past.

He stopped in a bodega for some coffee. A chubby little girl next to the counter stared at him — because he was white? Because he was so tall and thin? Because of his acne-scarred face? — but she brightened when he pulled out a Polaroid, took her picture, and handed her the snap.

He walked on past block-long factories, old buildings with rusty shutters more beautiful than any painting in the Museum of Modern Art. The late sun cast shadows through chain-link fences onto vacant yards, or lots filled with sleeping old delivery trucks. There was still some shipping along the waterfront; down at the Brooklyn Marine Terminal a few huge loading cranes reared up over the horizon like dinosaurs. The tin-covered windows of an abandoned warehouse caught the sun and filled with gold, a broken El Dorado. Though Ben was alone here, he never felt lonely.

Near the water, he walked down a narrow cobbled street of little houses, aluminum-sided, working-class. Had his father grown up in one of them? This one with the wild roses growing up the side, or that one with a small American flag flapping listlessly in the breeze?

He pulled out a video camera, set up the tripod, and filmed some wind-chewed leaves shimmying in the branches of an old sycamore tree, its trunk covered with flaking patches (like bad skin). He concentrated so hard on framing the shot that he forgot the world outside the viewfinder. When he looked up, a Latino kid about ten years old was sitting on the curb several yards away. The kid wore a Knicks jersey that hung down over his knees; his hair looked like his mother had trimmed it around a bowl. The boy shifted a jawbreaker from cheek to cheek and squinted up.

"Yo, mistuh. Why you wanna be filming a *tree*? Ain't nothin' up there."

Ben ignored him.

"Yo, mistuh," the kid said. "Why don't you take *my* picture?"

Ben grinned. "All right." He turned the camera and peered through the viewfinder as the kid transformed himself into an awkward little marionette. "Relax," he said. "I have to focus. I'll say 'cheese' when I'm ready." The kid let out a big breath and his shoulders slumped. He scratched his head. Ben filmed him while he was waiting.

Now he sat on his couch, reviewing some footage he'd grabbed at the end of the day, a zoom shot down a side street toward the Red Hook Houses. Just a few seconds of tape because a group of sullen homeboys had sauntered down the block in his direction and — panicking — he'd stuffed the camera back into the bag.

If his father had been with him, he wouldn't have had to worry. But then, there was never a cop around when you needed one.

four

The next morning, Jack arrived at work half an hour late. He'd slept badly, woken every few hours by roiling dreams. Toward dawn he finally sank into a deep sleep which swept him past the clock's alarm.

The Homicide Task Force was based in a modest building on Brooklyn's southern edge, on Mermaid Avenue, two blocks from the Coney Island boardwalk. Unlike most precinct houses, the building was new and clean, with fresh white paint and smart green trim. (No graffiti, no handprints on the cinderblock walls, no stale reek of human desperation.)

Jack parked in the gated lot in the back, then jogged in past two uniforms lounging behind the front desk like fish sellers awaiting the morning's catch.

"So don't say hello," called Mary Gaffney, a tall, pretty cop with red hair pulled back in a tight bun.

Without missing a beat, Jack spun around and kissed the back of her hand. He enjoyed flirting with the woman but she was married, with a two-year-old daughter.

He climbed the back stairs and then unlocked a couple of security doors to reach the Homicide squad room. It could have been an insurance company office with its central row of double desks, its wheeled aquamarine desk chairs. The wanted posters on the front door were a giveaway, though, as were the computers lining the back wall — no self-respecting private company would have put up with such outdated machines. The walls were thick with the usual clutter of bulletins and photos, charts and signs. Two computer-printed banners ran across one wall. *He who is not pursued escapes. Socrates.* And one which always gave Jack a chill: *If a man is burdened with the blood of another, let him be a fugitive unto death. Let no one help him. Proverbs 28:17.*

He signed in to the command log, annoyed that he'd missed the usual confab with the departing shift; he liked to know what had happened in the borough overnight.

"Nice of you to drop in," said Carl Santiago, one of the four other detectives on his shift. They were all casually attired: khaki pants, short sleeves, bright ties. The members of the task force didn't go for the designer suits and expensive watches favored by some of the precinct detectives. They didn't need the flash — they'd been selected as the most mature, stable, and seasoned of cops. The unofficial squad motto summed it up: "The Best of the Best."

Jack made his way back to the supply room. Another reason to be on time: the coffeepot on one of the gray metal shelves was empty save for a congealing puddle of tar.

Detective Sergeant Tanney, the squad supervisor, poked his head in the room. "Can I see you a minute, Leightner?"

He followed the sergeant into his office, hoping he wouldn't be rebuked for his lateness. When he'd started out, he looked up to the middle-aged detectives on the force. Now that he was middle-aged himself, the power kept moving into younger hands. Tanney, in his mid-thirties, had fine, very curly red hair, a neatly trimmed mustache, a face that was almost pretty. He seemed slightly insecure, like Ryan O'Neal trying to be believable in a tough-guy role.

Tanney was new as the team leader—he'd been transferred three months earlier from Brooklyn North and the verdict in the squad room was still out regarding his trustworthiness and allegiances.

On the wall above the sergeant's desk, an erasable chart kept tabs on which cars were assigned to which detectives. Clusters of red pins covered a Brooklyn map, one pin for each homicide of the year. On the wall to the right hung a clipboard for each of the seventeen precincts in Brooklyn South—Tanney pulled down one marked "76 Squad." "You caught that John Doe along the Gowanus yesterday, right?"

"Yeah. Why?"

"His name is Tomas Berrios."

"What, did we miss his wallet?"

"Don't feel bad—his wife ID'd him. He didn't show up for work yesterday, so his boss called to find out if he was sick. The wife didn't know anything about it—she'd sent Berrios off to work with a bag lunch. By three A.M. she was getting frantic so she called the Seven-six. One of their uniforms drove her down to the morgue first thing this morning."

Jack was relieved on two counts. One, the sergeant hadn't embarrassed him by calling him on the rug for the lateness. More important, he didn't have to be the one to notify the victim's family of the death. "Does he have a sheet?"

"Just a couple of minor things. Possession, marijuana, three years old. And a disorderly conduct, five years ago. He got in a scuffle with some guys outside a bar after last call. Did you guys get any witnesses?"

"There's a barge captain who does a run along the canal every day, but we haven't talked to him yet. Does the wife have any idea who did it?"

"She wasn't in any condition for an interview. Why don't you and your partner pay her a visit?"

Yet another reason to be on time: as the last detective in, Jack had drawn the squad's worst car, a Chevy Lumina with a cranky disposition. He pulled out of the lot into a Brooklyn street bustle: at the intersection, clumps of black and Hispanic kids were hanging out, eating chips and popsicles, riding bikes and popping wheelies. Between a Chinese take-out joint and a liquor store, three plump women stood in front of a Dumpster, enjoying a shrill shouting match.

It would have been faster to head toward Neptune Avenue, but he drove a block south to Surf Avenue to catch some ocean air. The weather was damp and gray; ahead the flared tower of Coney's Parachute Jump disappeared up into fog. A little farther on, the abandoned Thunderbolt roller coaster writhed in the mist, the convulsed skeleton of a snake. Even this early in the day, Coney Island smelled like fried grease.

Several blocks ahead, a cheerleader stood on a corner. As Jack neared, she turned into a crack whore with sunken cheeks and bad skin. Glancing to the right, he caught a glimpse of the boardwalk — it disappeared into a solid white mist, the edge of the world.

Several years before, his colleague Carl Santiago had asked if he wanted to go along on a visit to the detective's son. The kid was in the Navy, on a cruiser docked on Manhattan's West Side. Carl beamed with pride as his boy gave a tour of the ship, including a look inside the nuclear-missile bay. They walked between the gleaming rockets as if through a forest of white trees; Jack could reach out and touch their cool trunks. Solemnly Carl's son warned them that if a fire alarm sounded, they would have only thirty seconds to escape — after that, the entire chamber would be sprayed with a mist so dense a man would drown breathing it in.

By the time he reached the Shore Parkway, the morning fog had burned off and he was treated to a spectacular view across the water to Staten Island. As he rounded a bend the Verrazano-Narrows Bridge, that beautiful soaring span, came into view and raised his spirits.

The 76th Precinct house sat on the edge of Carroll Gardens, a stone's throw from the Brooklyn-Queens Expressway and the border of Red Hook. Jack parked in one of the diagonal spaces out front. Good smells wafted toward him from the Italian bakery on one corner and the pizzeria on the other.

The detectives' squad room was a grubby fluorescent-lit office with a barred holding pen against one wall. The wheezing air conditioner in the window, assisted by several fans, ruffled papers on the desks and walls. The whir of the fans added to the clamor of phones ringing, scanners crackling, detectives wisecracking to each other across the room. Their massive gray desks were enlivened by personal touches: pictures of kids, a scruffy little house plant, a plastic troll with long orange hair.

Gary Daskivitch sat behind a desk in the middle of it all, typing on an old IBM Selectric. Every case brought a big folder of paperwork and Daskivitch was digging into his required field reports, the DD-Fives: Notification and Response of Crime Scene Unit, Interview of the First Officer, License Plates at the Scene . . . While he pecked away with one finger, he maneuvered a cold slice of pizza into his mouth.

Jack grimaced.

"What?" Daskivitch said. "I found it in the lounge — must've been left over from the night watch."

Jack snorted. "That pizza looks DCDS." Deceased, Confirmed Dead at Scene. "Did you hear we got an ID on our vic?"

Daskivitch nodded. "The wife is home. And I located the barge guy—he lives in Sunset Park."

Jack crossed to the lounge in back, crowded with a card table, two cots, an ancient TV, and a vinyl couch (two green cushions, one red). He poured himself a cup of coffee and glanced at some papers taped to the cinderblock wall: a sheet listing detectives' pay grades—inspirational reading—and a handwritten sign saying, Please Put Your Cigarette Butts in Ashtray. This is Not Your House.

He sauntered out into the squad room. "Let's roll."

Like Jack's son, Tomas Berrios had lived near the Gowanus Houses in Boerum Hill on a side street halfway between working class and gentrified.

The iron gate clanged shut behind the detectives as they crossed the concrete yard and climbed the stoop to a brick row house. At ten A.M., the sun was already high in the sky. Daskivitch wiped his forehead; the big man was a heavy perspirer. Next door, salsa music blared out of a third-story window. Its frenetic rhythm got on Jack's nerves; it sounded like a wind-up toy wound too tight.

He rang the middle buzzer.

After a moment, the intercom crackled with a sharp woman's voice, Spanish accent. "Are you the funeral home?"

"No, ma'am. We're with the police department."

A pause. "She already speak to the police this morning."

Jack turned to his partner and sighed. He hated this part of the job. "We just need to talk to you for a minute."

He wasn't sure if she heard, but then the door swung open to reveal a squat Hispanic woman, wider than she was tall.

Her chest was pushed up like a fighting cock. She dried her hands on the hem of a quilted housecoat, looked suspiciously up at the two men, then turned and led them to a narrow staircase. She pulled her way up with both hands on the banister, pausing in mid-climb to announce, "I'm the mother-in-law."

She led them inside her living room and showed them to an enormous pink couch.

"I know what you people think," she said. "You think a young Hispanish man must be involved with some kind of trouble."

Jack didn't know whether "you people" meant whites or cops. Probably both. He looked olive-skinned and vaguely Semitic and people were often confused about his background — Spanish? Italian? — but there was no doubt about Daskivitch. He was so big, intimidating, and Midwestern-football-player white. So *police.*

"It's not true," the mother-in-law continued. "He doesn't have no problems with the law. Look how he takes care of his family." She gestured around the living room.

The apartment reminded Jack of his own parents' home. A castle of the working poor, each piece of furniture purchased after much saving, the design elaborate to cover shoddy craftsmanship. Smoked mirrors, chrome, fake leopard skin. Studio pictures of the kids on top of the gigantic old Buick of a TV.

He took out his steno pad. "It's a beautiful apartment, Mrs. . . . ?"

"Espinal."

"Ma'am, we just want to find out who did this to your son-in-law. Do you think we could talk to your daughter? What's her name?"

"Recina. You can't talk to her right now. This morning the

doctor he gave her something to make her sleep." Mrs. Espinal sank into an armchair, a deflated ball of feathers. "She was hurting herself, digging into her arms with her nails after she saw him."

"Do you have any idea why someone might have done this to your son-in-law?" Daskivitch asked.

"He was a superior young man. Never a problem, everybody on the block like him. My daughter, this morning, she said . . ." A sob escaped. "She said he was tied with ropes."

Shouts and laughter came from the hallway leading to the back of the apartment. A little boy ran into the front room. At the sight of the two strangers, he skidded to a halt on feet covered with Spiderman socks.

"Stop shouting, Mando, Mami's sleeping," said a small voice from the hall. A tiny girl appeared.

"Armand," said Mrs. Espinal firmly. "Go with your sister into the kitchen—you can have a pudding."

The boy walked backward, staring at the detectives as he pulled his sister down the hall.

"They don't know yet what happen," Mrs. Espinal said. She sighed bitterly. "Just the other day, for the Fourth of July, Tommy went down to Canal Street to buy some fireworks. I told him, no, the children are too young, something bad might happen . . ."

Jack pictured the young father down on Canal Street, buying illegal fireworks out of the back of someone's car, carrying the bag proudly home to his kids, handing them each a sparkler. When he first looked at a body it was usually just flesh, a puzzle. It was in the interviews later that the victims came alive in his mind.

"Do you know if he owed anybody money?"

"Look at this chair," she said. "Look at this couch. All paid for. He has a good job, no reason to owe nobody."

"Mrs. Espinal, I'm sorry to have to ask this question, but some time back your son-in-law was arrested on a marijuana charge. Do you have any idea if he's been using drugs?"

Mrs. Espinal pushed angrily out of her chair. "That was a long time ago, a mistake. When he was just a boy. Now he's good, like I tell you."

Jack raised his hands. "All right. Where did he work?'

She settled back. "In Manhattan. In a big building on the Upper East Side, very fancy. The Bentley."

"What did he do?"

"He was a porter. Like a doorman, only he was in the back. He wasn't allowed to be with the people so much, because he speak like a Dominican."

Jack jotted notes. He looked up. "Did you get along with him?"

Mrs. Espinal considered this shrewdly. "I am his mother-in-law. We live in the same house. Sometimes, we have a little argument. One or two times, he call me some names . . . But we never fight about how he treat my daughter or the kids. He was a good father, a good husband."

Mrs. Espinal's confession made Jack feel better about the interview. Even innocent people lied routinely to the police — at the least, they spun, tweaked, rearranged, and shaded the facts to come up with a safer truth, a more flattering or forgiving one. If she claimed that everything was perfect in the Berrios household, he would have taken her whole statement with a grain of salt.

She seemed to honestly believe that her son-in-law had no enemies, but one thing was sure: Tomas Berrios had managed to piss *somebody* off. This was no random killing, no drunken bar fight flaring into unpremeditated homicide. Whoever killed Berrios had taken the trouble to rough him up, stab him in the most efficient manner possible, attempt to methodically dispose of the body.

• • •

A group of four young men, early or mid-twenties, approached the house. Subdued, serious. One of them, a pale-faced kid, had a disproportionately large head topped with a yellow Afro. He held a bouquet of flowers.

As Jack and his partner stepped off the stoop, the group held their ground with a studied indifference to show that they were not intimidated by the presence of two obvious cops.

"How ya doin'?" Jack said as he pushed out through the gate.

The kids looked off into the distance. They seemed pretty harmless for homeboys.

"You guys friends of Tomas, huh?"

Three of the kids examined their complicated basketball shoes, but the one with yellow hair answered. "Did you find out who did it?"

His comrades groaned in disgust. "Yo," said a handsome, sharp-faced kid with jet-black hair. "Shut the fuck up. You don't gotta talk to no cops."

"We're just here to help," Jack said. "Cool your jets."

Despite the seriousness of the situation, the youths made a big show of holding their sides and guffawing. " 'Cool your jets,' " repeated the sharp-faced kid. "Man, you must've been watching *The Mod Squad*."

Daskivitch stepped forward. "He means 'chill out,' you little punk."

The kid backed against the fence.

Jack moved his head subtly to the side, signaling Daskivitch to back off. The kids were lippy, but not hinky — they didn't act as if they had anything particular to hide.

"What's your name?" he said calmly to the kid with the yellow Afro.

"His name's BigHead," said the wiseass kid. "You're the detective, maybe you can figure out why."

"Cut it out, Ramon!" the kid with the yellow Afro said. "My name's Hector."

"Dask, why don't you talk to these gentlemen here?" Jack said. "Hector and I are gonna take a stroll."

"Leave him alone, mister," said one of the other kids. "He's a retard."

"*You* the retard!" said Hector, glaring back.

"C'mon," Jack said, tugging the kid away from the others. They walked off down the street, Hector looking back over his shoulder as they went.

"When's the last time you saw Tomas?"

Hector squinted. "Last night. I mean two nights ago. We was riding."

"Who was?"

"Me, Tommy, Nicio. Felix. Ramon. Them over there." The kid nodded back toward his friends.

"Riding what?"

"Our bikes. Tommy's the boss."

"Motorcycles?"

"Naw, man. Bicycles."

Jack pondered this information. He'd heard of bicycle crews acting as couriers for drug dealers. This kid didn't seem to have the smarts for that action, but the others?

"Where did you go?"

"Around. Out Fourth Avenue. We was going past Bay Ridge and Coney. To Floyd Bennis."

"Floyd Bennett Field?" There was a Coast Guard base out there. All of a sudden, Jack had a vision of a drug connection—this thing might turn into something big and ugly and blow up in his face. "Did you meet anybody there?" If the answer was somebody from the Guard, he was screwed.

"Naw. We just stopped to take a piss."

"Any special reason why you went there?"

"Naw. We go all over. Don't matter where. We just ride."

"Do you meet people?"

"I told you, mister. We ride. Tommy likes to go to the bridge." Hector blinked. "Liked." His friend had only been dead for a day.

"Listen, Hector. Whatever you tell me, it's just between you and me. Nobody's going to get in trouble. We're just trying to find out who did this to Tommy, okay?"

Hector nodded.

"Was he carrying any drugs when you went on these rides?"

"No . . ." Hector chewed his lip. "Not really."

"Not really?"

"It's fucked up to talk to cops."

Jack lowered his voice. "Don't worry about what your friends tell you. This is important."

"I have to go back."

"Nobody's going to get in trouble. Just tell me what happened."

"He"—Hector turned to look down the street—"he had some *chiba*. Just enough for a couple of joints. That's all, mister. I swear."

So much for a drug-free Tomas Berrios. Nobody got whacked over a couple of joints, but at least this was a start. "Who did he buy it from, Hector?"

The kid squirmed. "I don't know, mister. He never told me nothin' about that."

Jack sighed. "You said Tommy liked to go to the bridge. What bridge?"

"Verrazano."

"Why?"

Hector shrugged. "He likes to sit in the park next to the bridge. To chill. We talk."

"Did you talk to him there the other night?"

"Yeah. Everybody was bustin' on me 'cause I was late. But he didn't care. He was all hyped up."

"About what?"

"My bike's too small. He said, 'Tomorrow, I'm gonna buy you a new mountain bike. Replace that piece of shit.' "

Jack's eyes narrowed. "Where would he get the money for a new bike?"

Hector shrugged again. "I don't know. He had a good job. He was making, like eight or nine dollars a hour."

Jack rubbed his hand over his mouth. This kid was no rocket scientist—you didn't go around buying people new mountain bikes on less than three hundred take-home per week. "He was talking about 'tomorrow,' huh? What did he say was gonna happen 'tomorrow'?"

Hector shrugged again. "I don't know."

"Did he say anything else?"

"Yeah."

Jack leaned closer.

"He said don't let him forget he was s'posed to buy some Woolite for Mrs. Espinal."

five

As the detectives drove out Fourth Avenue toward Sunset Park, the midday sun flared on the asphalt. Bodegas flew past, auto-lube garages, auto-supply stores. Places to buy fuzzy dice or Playboy air fresheners. On the radio, the dispatcher chattered away, the woman's voice always in the background of the detectives' lives.

Tomas Berrios had cycled out this same way less than forty-eight hours earlier. Five young men, pumping along the avenue at night, calling out to each other, laughing, joking — the image grew in Jack's mind. He tried to draw it out, expand it. Where were they headed? Who did Tomas Berrios expect to meet? Put enough of these images together, and he'd create a mental movie of the vic's last days.

Near the Park, they passed a bus depot named after Jackie Gleason.

"Look at that," he said, grinning. "You gotta love this borough."

Daskivitch shifted his weight in the seat. "So what's your take? I still think it looks like a Mob hit."

"Mafia sounds glamorous, but I think this kid probably just got in over his head with some bad local player. Took the drugs, owed the money."

Stopped at a light, he glanced to the west down a San Francisco–steep hill: past the end of the street, the grand orange Staten Island ferry plowed the slate-blue water of Upper New York Bay. In the intersection ahead, a stout middle-aged woman with permed hair shuffled across at a stoic, deliberate Brooklyn pace. Jack reached into the pocket of his sports coat and pulled out a couple of tablets.

"You got candy?"

"Just some antacids."

"You all right?"

"Would you shut up with that? I'm fine."

Daskivitch shrugged.

On the north side of the Park, many of the storefronts were covered in Asian lettering. Times changed. Back in Jack's father's day, the neighborhood had been known as Little Finland, home to thousands of Scandinavians skilled in the building trades. That was before the Gowanus Expressway forced out many of the old Finnish homeowners, before the same highway ripped the heart out of Red Hook and the old man.

When Jack's parents first got married, they lived in a nice little house in the center of the Hook. Back in the 1940s, when city planner Robert Moses dreamed up the expressway, its path ran directly through the house. The city had condemned and demolished the property, along with hundreds of other homes.

The highway continued on through Sunset Park. Though residents there had pleaded with Moses to place the route along Second Avenue, a marginal industrial strip, the planner ignored them, calling their thriving neighborhood a slum. He ran the elevated highway right above Third Avenue, the vital center of the place, a boulevard of little mom-and-pop stores, of newsstands and family restaurants. Half the buildings along the route were torn down. The new highway was so wide that it cast the avenue below into darkness. The surviving businesses didn't survive long, with the thunder of trucks and cars overhead and the gloom below. After the central arteries of Sunset Park and Red Hook were destroyed, the blight spread through the smaller streets.

The Gowanus Expressway was followed by the Belt Parkway, the Brooklyn Battery Tunnel, and the Brooklyn-Queens Expressway, massive construction projects that further isolated the Hook from the rest of Brooklyn. More bad news arrived in the 1960s. In the old days, stevedores like Jack's father lifted everything out of the ships by hand. But shipping technology advanced—cranes were able to hoist giant metal containers directly out of the holds. Red Hook caught on to the change too late and most of the shipping moved to yards in New Jersey, where it was easier to load the containers directly onto trains.

Once, after his father's funeral, Jack asked his mother why the old man had been so tough. "He was always kind of hard," she explained. "But he turned *mean* after Robert Moses tore down our home."

Raymond Ortslee lived on a quiet street near the eastern edge of the Park. On the corner a red and yellow plastic sign read Muchachos Grocery. Across the way stretched a row of little houses with diamond-shaped windows cut in their front doors. White filigreed iron fences surrounded the tiny yards. Jack parked between a dented van and a re-painted Mustang.

The barge captain's building sat ten yards back from the sidewalk, across a dismal yard. A dog barked somewhere in the back as Jack and his partner entered the cracked driveway. The apartment house was boxy and covered in faded mustard-yellow paint; one section of the façade was slightly darker, where some shingles had been replaced. An exterior staircase crawled up to the third story, where faded aquamarine curtains hung in the windows.

As Jack led the way up the staircase, he saw one of the curtains move slightly. The doorbell rang inside with a harsh metallic clatter.

The detectives waited on the landing. Daskivitch stepped forward and rang the bell again.

"He's in there," Jack said quietly. "Right behind that curtain."

Daskivitch rattled the knob. Suddenly the door swung open and they were looking into the barrel of an ancient rifle. Behind the weapon stood a small man, wild-eyed behind heavy spectacles. The barge captain's hair was gray and bristly but it had been Brylcreamed back — he looked like a wet otter.

Jack and his partner traded a wary look. Without a word, they moved to opposite sides of the landing: if the guy opened fire, he wouldn't take them both out.

"I didn't see nothin'," the man said desperately. "I'll swear to it in court. You guys don't have nothing to worry about."

"Point the gun down, Mr. Ortslee," Daskivitch said firmly.

The man continued to point the rifle, but he pulled off his eyeglasses. "I'll say I wasn't wearing these. Look, I'm blind as a bat without 'em. I'll say my eyes were bothering me and I took 'em off. Please, I'll do anything you guys want."

"We're detectives," Jack said. "NYPD."

The man blinked and put his glasses back on. He peered out from the doorway, ready to dive back inside. "I'm not fallin' for that," he said. "I know damn well who you guys are."

Moving slowly and deliberately, Jack took out his shield. Then he reached into his wallet and pulled out a card.

"Here," he said. "Call this number and ask for Sergeant Tanney."

The man blinked down at the card. He stared out of the dark doorway. The door closed. They could hear him locking it on the other side.

"Jesus," Daskivitch said, "did you see that fucking gun?"

Jack wiped sweat from his forehead. "It was prewar."

"It was pre-*Civil* War. It's a whaddayacallit, a fowling piece."

"A blunderbuss."

"That's right. What the Pilgrims used to shoot turkeys."

Both men grinned at their fortune to be standing there alive and in one piece.

After a moment, the door opened again.

"I'm sorry, officers," the man said. "The gun is registered. Perfectly legal. I've got the papers."

They sat in Ortslee's living room, low-ceilinged like an attic. Despite the bright day outside and the big windows facing the street, the room was dingy and dim, paneled with cheap, dark veneer. It smelled of mothballs and sweat and mildewed carpet. The furniture was splintered rattan that looked like it belonged on a patio.

"Was it you who called to tip us off, Mr. Ortslee?" Jack said.

"I don't wanna get involved in this."

"You already are. Did you make the call?"

Ortslee struggled with himself, then gave a dismal nod.

"What did you see?"

"It was far away. I couldn't see nothin'."

"This is a very serious matter," Jack said patiently. "We'll keep anything you tell us entirely confidential."

"I was far off. Probably seventy-five yards."

"And?"

"There was two of them. Throwing something over the fence. That's all I know." Ortslee rose. "I gotta get ready for work now." He scuttled out of the room.

The detectives followed. They caught up with him in his bedroom. A big suitcase lay open on the bed, half filled with jumbled clothes.

"Don't fuck with us," Daskivitch said.

"I really didn't see nothin'," Ortslee replied. His hands shook as he lifted a stack of shirts out of a dresser drawer.

"If you want, we can discuss this down at the precinct house," Daskivitch said. "We could charge you with obstruction of justice. One way or another, you're gonna tell us what you saw on that canal."

"I know how this works," Ortslee said. "I watch *NYPD Blue* every week." His eyes darted to Jack. "You play the good cop and he plays the bad cop. Well, I'm not gonna fall for it."

Jack chuckled.

"That damn *NYPD Blue*," Daskivitch said, shaking his head. "And I was so looking forward to my bad cop routine."

"I can't stay here," Ortslee said. "They're gonna figure out how to find me. And if they already killed one guy, why would they stop there?"

"Relax," Jack said. "If you couldn't see them, they couldn't see you, right? Tell us what happened."

"How'd it go?" asked Daskivitch's boss, Sergeant Riordan. The man slouched on the edge of his desk in the Seven-six squad room, rubbing his jaw as if he had a toothache. The pain of command.

"Jack called it," Daskivitch said. "The barge is motoring

along, the captain's up on deck checking a pressure gauge for the plutonium or whatever-the-hell-poison he's hauling, and he glances up and sees this thing come flipping over the fence."

"A 'thing'?" Riordan asked.

"Yeah—it was our vic. First the bargeman thought someone was dumping trash along the canal—which seems to be the big sport over there—but then these two white guys come climbing over the fence after it. He couldn't see too well on account of the trees and shrubs and crap, but then the perps see *him* and they wig and scramble back over the fence."

"What kind of a look did he get? Could he ID 'em?"

"Doubtful. He says he was seventy-five yards away."

"You want to bring him in and show him some pictures?"

"He swears he never saw their faces."

"He's just a little hermit who watches too much TV," Jack said. "I ordered him to stay put in case we need him again. Gary gave him the number here in case he suddenly remembers something, but he seems pretty useless."

"What's next?" Riordan said.

Jack picked up a glass paperweight from his partner's desk and hefted it in his palm. "I've got a couple of snitches to see."

"You want company?" Daskivitch asked.

Riordan looked up at the clock. "You guys are gonna be heading into OT soon."

Daskivitch looked dejected. "You want me to punch out?"

The rest of New York City was ecstatic that the murder rate had dropped to a fraction of its peak ten years before, but the detective squads had suffered budget cuts. Business, as it were, was off.

Riordan sighed. "Go with Leightner. God knows, you might actually learn something."

six

They sat in Jack's car, just up Atlantic Avenue from a little grimy bunker of a bar called the Luray Inn, the kind of dive where a customer might try to unload coat pockets full of boosted cigarettes or supermarket steaks. Jack shifted, but the back of his shirt stuck to the seat — they couldn't keep the air conditioner running because they might have to wait for hours. Daskivitch, mercifully, had given up drumming on the steering wheel and they sat in a companionable silence. Jack was optimistic: they'd started with an anonymous dump job, but in just over twenty-four hours they had an ID and a possible drug connection.

On the sidewalk next to the bar, two tiny Arab kids were goofing around. Two old mattresses rested against a brick wall, and one of the kids pressed the other between them until he yelped. When he escaped, they switched roles. It didn't take a lot to entertain little kids.

On this side of the street, a customer emerged from a Salvation Army thrift store. Through the plate-glass window Jack watched a friendly cashier make small talk as she rang up a sale. A young couple came out of the store, the pony-tailed girl wearing a backless cotton blouse, the boy in a tie-dyed T-shirt.

"Can you believe this?" Daskivitch said. "That sixties bullshit is coming back again."

The fact was, Jack had missed a lot of the legendary sixties the first time around. The Groovy Decade had passed Red Hook by: while Greenwich Village kids just a few miles across the river were turning on to pot and Bob Dylan, the Hook remained solidly conservative, a place for working men and out-of-work veterans. There was drink, yes, and there was crime, but he never knew a hippie or a head until he got on a troop transport and flew four thousand miles away from Brooklyn. By the time he came back, even cops had long sideburns.

Motion near the end of the block.

"Here they come," he told Daskivitch. "The woman's called Janelle. The guy goes by T."

The man was grizzled and homely, a little black guy trying to walk like a big black guy; the woman white, one hand cocked back to hold a cigarette, swinging tight, a nervous metronome. She followed behind, taking mincing steps like someone wearing high heels for the first time, though she wore sneakers.

"Why's he called T?"

"He likes to drink tea? Thinks he's Mister T? Who the hell knows?"

Janelle wore vinyl toreador pants and a low-cut orange top. Her body said thirty, her smoke-and-liquor-ravaged face sixty. She stopped to take off a shoe and shake it out.

They were a couple — Jack knew they'd been together for ages. He wondered what it must be like for them walking into the Luray, the black guys inside thinking, *What's this brother doing with that white skank?* the Caucasian customers asking the opposite question. There was a bravery there worthy of at least some small admiration.

"Wait up, T!" she called out, voice like a garbage compactor.

Jack chuckled. "She turns tricks now and then, if you can believe that. Mostly, they just wander around working lame street cons. She tells people she needs a train ticket to go visit her kid in the hospital. Or he does a brown-bag drop." It wasn't a brilliant scam — the perp put an empty bottle in a bag and then walked around a corner and got somebody to bump into him. He dropped the bag, the bottle broke. He told them it was expensive booze; tried to shake them down for five or ten bucks.

"Cute. Can you trust their info?"

Jack shrugged. "Sometimes. They're boozers."

As the couple came near, he leaned out the window. "How's it going, T?"

The man spun around to scope out the avenue, checking for friends or foes. "All right. How're you, Detective?"

"I can't complain."

The man leaned in, but pulled back when he saw Daskivitch. "Who's he?"

"My partner. It's okay."

The woman came up behind her mate and perched her cigarette hand on her hip.

"You're looking good today," Jack told her. She rolled her eyes, but couldn't suppress a grin. "Listen, I need some help. Do you two know a guy in the neighborhood, name of Tomas Berrios?"

"Shit" said T, disgusted. "He got killed yesterday and we don't know nothing about it."

"How did you know he was killed, then?"

T snorted. "If I didn't know what was going on around here, you wouldn't come looking for me."

"You're absolutely right. So can you help me?"

54

T pinched the sides of his mouth. "I could use a little help, myself."

Jack reached into his wallet and pulled out a twenty, which immediately disappeared into the man's back pocket.

"He hangs out with a bunch of kids. They got bicycles." T stopped and scanned the avenue again.

"I gave you twenty bucks for that?"

"What else you wanna know?"

"You know anybody might have a thing against him?"

T shook his head.

"How about drugs? Was he buying?"

T squinted. "Could be."

"Like what? Blow? Crack? Pills?"

The man shrugged. Jack reached into his wallet and pulled out another twenty, held it up out of reach.

"Uh, yeah. Blow, I think."

"Who does he buy from?"

T shrugged again.

"Forget it," Jack said. "Forty is plenty."

T pinched the sides of his mouth again. "I dunno, Detective . . ." He seemed to make a decision, closed down. Maybe forty bucks wasn't worth crossing a murderous dealer.

Jack watched Janelle behind him as she imagined sitting down in the Luray, setting a fresh pack of smokes on the bar, ordering that first cold drink.

She pushed T out of the way, leaned into the window, and mumbled into Jack's ear.

She grabbed the twenty and her man and they were gone.

The detectives sat in the car near Tomas Berrios's house, watching a building down at the far end of the block for the subtle undertow of street action that would mark a drug set.

Jack picked up the radio and made a call to BCI, the Bureau of Criminal Information. After he gave the color of the day, the ever-changing code that identified him as a real cop, a clerk ran the address through the computer to see if it had been the site of any prior arrests. It hadn't.

A lookout stood out on the sidewalk in front of the building. A scrawny kid, Hispanic. In the past forty-five minutes, only a couple of customers had approached him. They'd sidle up and murmur, he'd take a quick look around, then turn to the intercom by the door. He gave them the nod and they disappeared inside for a couple of minutes.

Daskivitch shifted in his seat. "Jeannie and I rented *Titanic* after work last night. I think we were the last holdouts on the planet, but she's been bugging me, so I finally caved."

"How was it?"

"You didn't see it either, huh? It's a real treat—you get to see hundreds of dead people."

"Don't tell me how it ends."

It was after work for most of the population and there was a lot of traffic down the block, day-jobbers heading home from the subway. Even so, Jack knew that if he and Daskivitch tried to approach the building, they'd be raised in a second—the lookout would zip inside to warn the player in his burrow. Then they'd have to go get a warrant.

"If we want our guy to talk, we need to surprise him," he said. He pushed the door open and stepped out of the car.

Five minutes later he returned, carrying a paper bag from the corner deli.

"What's that?" Daskvitch said.

"Secret weapon." He pulled out an overstuffed sandwich and removed the plastic wrap. "Double the egg salad, that's the trick."

"What, you're gonna bribe the guy with a frikkin' sandwich?"

Jack grinned. "Watch and learn, Grasshopper." He took off his sports coat and tie and set them on the back seat. He drew his gun from his shoulder holster, then removed the harness and added it to the pile. Daskivitch looked on, mystified, as he pulled out his badge and dropped it and the gun into the bag.

The late-day sun caught only the tops of the buildings, but it was still hot down in the street. Twenty yards ahead of Jack, the lookout leaned against a parked car, listening to a Walkman. The job must get dull, standing alone out there for hours at a stretch. But the guy was alert; his shaved head swiveled from side to side like a nervous bird's. He was maybe nineteen, wearing a T-shirt and those dumb baggy bell-bottoms the kids were into this year.

Two teenage girls strolled up the block. "So he acksed me did I want to go ovah to his house Saturday," one of the girls said as they passed Jack. "He said his muthah was gonna be out." Her big gold earrings jangled as she shook her head in disbelief.

Jack squeezed the sandwich until the filling oozed out the sides and down his wrist. And that's how he closed the gap, a guy walking down the street completely immersed in trying to eat a sandwich without spilling egg salad on his pants.

He walked past the lookout, dropped the sandwich, and yanked his badge out of the bag.

"Police!" he said, whipping around. He shoved the badge in his back pocket, grabbed the shocked lookout, shoved him into the doorway, and twisted his arm behind his back. Then he leaned out and waved down the street.

"Yo, get the fuck off me," the kid muttered. "I ain't do nothin'."

"We've been watching you for days. You're going to jail right now."

"You don't got shit. Ain't no law against standing on no sidewalk."

"Oh, yeah? We have a video of you." An empty threat, but if the kid had been stupid enough to hand over any drugs out in the open, he might fall for it.

"Bullshit," the kid said, but he lacked enthusiasm.

"Tell you what." Jack leaned forward and spoke calmly into the kid's ear. "You get me buzzed in and I'll let you walk. I never saw you."

Daskivitch jogged up, breathless, a big bear trying to look little. The kid's eyes widened as he saw more law closing in.

"How many people upstairs?"

"Fuck you."

"Listen," Jack said patiently, "you might be up for a couple of years, but I'm offering you a get-out-of-jail-free. Now, how many?"

"I'm gonna get beat."

"You'll get worse than that in the House of Detention, a little guy like you."

The kid stared mournfully down at his new Nike sneakers, considering this impeccable logic. "Just two," he muttered.

"Okay," Jack said. "That's good. Now all you have to do is buzz up and tell them you need to use the john."

"*Come on*, man."

"*Let's go*," Jack said, losing patience. It was only a matter of seconds before some concerned young citizen came along, saw what was happening, and gave a warning call upstairs.

The kid scrunched up his face. Then he reached out and pressed the buzzer for 4D. The intercom squawked.

"Yo," the kid said. "It's me. I gotta take a piss."

The lock clicked open.

Jack turned to Daskivitch. "Hold on to our little friend until we get up."

The door was heavy steel, with a little wire-hatched window in the middle. Jack peered in; the hallway was empty.

He pushed through, followed by Daskivitch, who practically carried the lookout under one arm. The door thunked closed behind them. Jack reached into the bag and pulled out his gun. He noted irritably that there were no napkins in the bag—and for once he was out of hand wipes. He smeared his shooting hand against a wall to get rid of some egg salad. In twenty-four years with the NYPD, he'd only fired the gun twice—once into the air when he was an overzealous beat cop chasing a purse snatcher, once into the leg of a serial rapist diving out a back window—but the weight of it was comforting in his hand.

The stairwell was airless and humid and painted a sickly green that he couldn't imagine someone actually choosing. By the time he reached the fourth floor, his shirt was soaked with sweat, and not just because of the heat.

The hall light was off.

The lookout squirmed.

"Don't let him go until I get through the door," Jack whispered to his partner. "And keep him quiet."

Daskivitch nodded and held a big meaty hand over the scared lookout's mouth.

Jack made his way along to 4D. Sweat beaded his face and he licked the salty liquid off his upper lip. He tried the door: locked. He gave a quick rap and mumbled, "It's me."

The door swung open to the panicked face of a chubby little Hispanic male, mid-twenties.

"What the . . . ?" The guy spun around and shouted to someone inside the apartment. The door started to swing shut.

"Police!" Jack shouted. He stuck his foot in the door and slammed all his weight against it. The door gave way and he barreled through, pushing the kid back into the room. He swung him around and twisted one of his meaty arms behind his back. Over the kid's shoulder, he saw a fat gray-haired woman sitting on a white leather sofa. She wore orange sweatpants, but she didn't look like exercise had ever been on the agenda. She stared openmouthed.

Daskivitch ran in, gun up, breathing hard.

Jack guided the kid over next to the woman and pushed him down into what little space was left on the sofa. Daskivitch stationed himself by the door, blocking an end run. Jack glanced around: big new TV, two VCRs, a giant boombox, a couple of cell phones on a coffee table. It looked as if someone just had won a shopping spree in an electronics store — the boxes were still stacked in a corner. The room was decorated with several large velvet tapestries: Jesus on the cross; a crouching leopard; Julio Iglesias grinning painfully, as if he needed to visit the can. Below the leopard was an altar flanked by gaudy prayer candles, dedicated to some saint Jack didn't recognize.

The kid may have been dealing coke, but he certainly didn't look like a user. He was stuffed into his baggy shorts and tank top like a sausage.

"Okay," Jack said amiably. "Let's have a little talk."

"Fuck you, man! Who you think you are, all busting in my apartment with a gun and shit when I'm not doing nothing but watch TV, scare my moms —"

"Who are these people, Mellow?" The woman adjusted a pair of glitter-framed eyeglasses.

"They must've got the wrong apartment," the son said. "You okay, Mami?"

For a second, Jack's heart sank. What if he'd screwed up, if T and Janelle had sent him on a wild-goose chase? But then, solid citizens didn't need a downstairs lookout.

The woman moved to hoist herself up.

"Ma'am," Jack said, "I'm gonna ask you to stay on the sofa with your son." He turned to the kid. "You mind if we take a look around?"

"Look all you want," the kid said magnanimously. "We don't got nothing to hide."

Jack and Daskivitch traded surprised looks. Ninety-nine times out of a hundred, a kid like this would demand to see a warrant. It was obvious that he wasn't a big-time dealer, but even so he shouldn't be *inviting* a search. "Take a look around," Jack told his partner.

He lowered himself into a pillowy armchair and watched Mellow and his mother while Daskivitch disappeared down the hall.

The kid picked up a remote and turned up the volume on the big-screen TV. "You like the soaps, cop? Why don't you stay and watch with us?" He leaned forward and took a potato chip from an economy-size bag on a coffee table and crunched it deliberately while staring at Jack.

"Mellow?" Jack said. "They call you that 'cause you're such a laid-back guy?"

The mother snorted. "He used to like marshmallows when he was a baby." Evidently she had too. She reached forward and grabbed a couple of chips.

Jack stared at them for a minute. They sat there coolly munching chips with two detectives in the apartment, yet somehow their composure seemed thin. The kid glanced around the apartment, scratched the side of his nose.

Something was definitely hinky.

"You find anything?" Jack called out.

Daskivitch came back into the room. "Zippo."

"You try the kitchen?"

"Not yet." Daskivitch crossed the living room and disappeared again.

Jack stared at the couple on the couch. They stared smugly back.

Too smug. It was the look of smart street dealers when a squad car pulled up. No savvy dealer would have stash on his person when he could be searched at any moment. Jack had found the little envelopes hidden in many places nearby, though: in the middle of a public trash can, inside the base of a lamppost, in a magnetic key case stuck under a parked car, even in a potato-chip bag . . .

"Mind if I have a chip?" he asked.

The mother went pale and struggled to rise out of the sofa.

Jack leaned forward and grabbed her outstretched wrist. With his left hand, he dumped the bag upside down onto the glass tabletop. He shoved aside a heap of chips and grinned at a handful of tiny wax-paper packets. The mother must have shoved them in the bag when her son called the warning.

"Dask!" he called.

His partner trotted back.

"Lookee here," Jack said. "Do me a favor and escort this wonderful example of a mother out of the room and take a statement."

The woman whimpered as Daskivitch led her down the hall. Lovely, Jack thought. Family values. He'd been a cop too long to be surprised.

He stared at Mallow. *Don't say anything for a moment; let him sweat.* The kid didn't look like a big bad murdering drug dealer, but he was certainly a lying weasel. Maybe he *had* gotten into a fight with Berrios; maybe he had a big friend

62

willing to work the victim over. In the heat of the moment, Berrios gets stabbed . . .

Mallow scowled. "My mother didn't know nothing about this."

"Why don't we fingerprint the packets, then?"

"Fuck you," Mallow said. He didn't have anything else to offer.

Jack pulled his chair forward until his knees were touching the kid's. "You think you're in trouble now? Try murder one."

Mallow's eyes went big. "What the hell you talking about!"

"You know one of your neighbors, name of Tomas Berrios?"

"I heard about it. That shit is *wack*."

"Did you know him?"

"No. I mean, I saw him around, but — "

"Did he buy from you?"

"No."

"Play straight with me. Maybe I can at least keep your mother out of jail."

Mallow pressed his fingertips against his temples. "Fuck. I don't . . . okay, I knew him. He bought from me a couple of times. Just some reefer."

"Any coke?"

"Never."

"I heard different."

"Man, he was a pussy. All he ever wanted was *chiba*. That's all."

"How much did he owe you?"

Mallow shook his head. "I don't give credit. I don't have the muscle to collect. What am I gonna do, send my moms over to their house?" He rubbed his palms against his thighs. "Listen, man — I deal a little smoke, maybe a few grams of blow. That's it. Don't try to pin some *murder* thing on me, all right?"

"Where were you Sunday morning? Say, from eight A.M. to noon?"

"I was on Staten Island all weekend, man. I went to see my daughter."

"Are you lying to me, Mallow?"

"No, sir. I swear it on my moms."

"Yeah, she's real trusty."

"My ex-wife's whole family was there, mister. Her moms, her sisters, her cousin . . . It was a birthday party for my daughter."

Shit. Jack would call to check, but the alibi sounded solid. He sighed. "I'll tell you what I'm gonna do. I'm not gonna take you in right now. You or your mother." The truth was that a narcotics bust probably wouldn't have held up in court, considering the way he and his partner had gained access to the apartment, but Mallow and Co. couldn't be sure of that. "But I want you out on the street every god-damn second, listening for any word about who might have killed Tomas Berrios. Here's my card—you call me if you hear anything. Leave a message if I'm not in." Jack leaned in until he was inches from Mallow's face. "And if I ever hear that you're still dealing, or that you had anything to do with the Berrios murder, *anything*, I'm gonna personally come back here and make sure you *and* your mami go away for a hundred years. You follow me?"

Mallow shook his head, dazed at his good fortune.

"Right now, I'm gonna need phone numbers for every-body who was at your daughter's birthday."

Daskivitch whistled in disbelief as they settled back into the car. "A day like this, it really does a lot for your faith in humanity."

Jack sighed. The day hadn't done much for his faith in

cracking the case either. But he turned to his partner and grinned. "Egg salad and chips."

Daskivitch shook his head and started the engine.

"You wanna get some dinner?" Jack said.

"I gotta get home. The wife's expecting me."

"How long you been married?"

Daskivitch scratched the side of his big square head. "Actually, it was just a few months after we worked that case in the Gowanus Houses."

"Things going good?"

"Yeah. I like it a lot. I'd hate to be single again, I'll tell you that." He winced. "Uh, sorry. You're divorced, right?"

Jack nodded.

"So, you seeing anybody, or what?"

Jack sighed. "I get out now and then."

seven

Sheila Dixon turned after she opened the door. "I'm just finishing up something on the computer. There's wine — help yourself."

Jack watched her small figure stride down the hall toward the back of her Brooklyn Heights apartment. It was after ten P.M. He'd dropped Daskivitch off at the Seven-six, eaten some eggplant parmigiana at an Italian place near the station house . . . He'd felt foolish calling Sheila so spur of the moment, but she didn't seem to mind.

He took off his coat and slung it over the back of a rocking chair. In the hallway, a row of sinister wooden masks stretched toward the bedroom. Between the front door and the hall hung an abstract painting, a sprawling, messy thing. Bookshelves covered the far wall. History, art history, books with French titles. Sheila taught at Columbia University. They'd met a couple of days after the murder of a local dry cleaner, when Jack was canvassing some of the victim's regular clients. Sheila had sat on this couch drinking a glass of wine, looking through the sliding glass door, which gave out onto a wooden deck with a spectacular view of the Manhattan skyline. She offered him a glass and — since it was near the end of an evening shift — he accepted.

He sauntered into the cramped kitchen. As usual, an open bottle of expensive wine stood on the counter. He peered down into a case in the corner; nearly empty. He didn't think Sheila was an alcoholic, but she definitely drank a lot. Maybe the quality of the wine made her feel better about drinking so much of it, about drinking it alone. He poured himself a glass, then peeked into her refrigerator. Other than a container of lactose-free milk and a couple of take-out cartons, it held only row after row of condiments. Curry paste. Hoisin sauce. Olive paste . . . In the five or six times he'd been here, he'd never seen her cook — she was too busy with her work. Maybe she put the condiments on the take-out food.

He wandered back into the living room, his mind never idle. If this was a homicide scene, who would have killed her? Disgruntled student, maybe, academic career ruined by a failing grade? Too *Columbo*. Most likely it would just be an interrupted B and E. Up over the deck, through the sliding door. Maybe the perp would leave some prints on a take-out food container, a mid-job snack. Jack would guess his nationality by the type of condiment left out on the counter.

"What are you thinking about?" Sheila asked, putting a hand on his shoulder.

He spun around, guilty over his morbid preoccupations. "Hm? Just enjoying the scenery."

"That moron next door put a floodlight out on his deck. It really interferes with the view."

Sheila sipped her wine. Petite Caucasian female, mid-thirties, short brown hair, fairly sexy figure, lipstick-model lips.

"This wine's pretty good," Jack said.

"Not really. It's not very complex. I should have taken it back after I opened the first bottle." She came around the sofa and perched on the far end. "To what do I owe this unexpected visit?"

"I don't know. You need a reason?"

She lit a cigarette and took a deep drag. "I guess not. The inscrutable Detective Leightner."

"Actually, I'm feeling pretty scrutable tonight."

She considered him without so much as a grin.

"That was a joke," he said. "Did you teach today?"

She pulled a shred of nicotine off her tongue and grimaced. "Don't ask. I don't know why they keep admitting these brain-dead kids."

Jack didn't come around often: her relentless negativity was hard to take. If he said the weather was nice, she'd point to a bad forecast; if he complimented her apartment, she'd complain about the lack of space. A couple of times he'd tried to tactfully point out this pattern, but Sheila had been surprised and defensive. She was always talking about spirituality, about being *centered* and *grounded,* but her cool exterior seemed brittle to him, the cap on an angry inner life. In short, she was a pain in the ass, but the next time he was feeling too single, he'd probably overlook that again and come back for more.

"What are you working on back there?"

She brightened, as he knew she would. The one thing that always improved her disposition was talk about her research. Sheila had her problems, but he liked listening to someone with such a vivid life of the mind. He wondered if he wouldn't have enjoyed college himself, given the chance.

She allowed herself to relax back into the sofa. "I'm writing about a book from the seventies called *The Denial of Death.*"

"Oh, yeah? What's it about?"

"Well" — she took a sip of her wine — "it's a psychoanalytic — actually post-Freudian — work. The premise is that much of human civilization, from religion to war to art, has been developed by people to defend themselves against their fear of death." She stopped as he rose from the sofa. "Am I boring you?"

"Not at all," he said. "Hey, death's my middle name, right?"

She didn't crack a smile.

"I'm just getting some more wine," he said. He went into the kitchen, returned with the bottle, and topped off their glasses.

"Maybe we should talk about something more interesting," she said. Meaning, he gathered, that he wasn't supposed to be able to handle an intellectual conversation. But wasn't he a professional thinker too? He'd taken his own courses: Estimating Time of Death, Forensic Entomology, Death by Asphyxia and Narcotic-related Deaths, Interrogation Techniques . . .

"Why don't you tell me about *your* work," she said.

"Like what?"

"Like, I don't know — do you think you have a different attitude toward your own death than most people? Do you believe in an afterlife? You never talk about what you do."

"I don't know," he said. He'd started to feel relaxed — now he recognized a clamping-off he always felt when asked such questions by someone who wasn't a cop or a doctor or a forensics expert.

"You don't know *what*? Surely you must have thought about these things. I mean, you have this job where you deal with *dead people* all the time."

He stood up, crossed to the sliding door, and looked out at the glowing skyscrapers across the river.

"Well?" she said. "Tell me something."

He tugged on the knot of his tie. "You really have to be there."

"Where?"

"You have . . . I don't know. You have to have seen it."

"That's silly. I don't have to go to the pyramids to learn about Egypt."

He turned sharply. "Nobody's talking about pyramids. I'm talking about . . . I don't know — "

"*What?* Like this is supposed to be some macho thing that a woman can't understand?"

"How about a little baby girl with half of her head blown off? You want to talk about that?"

Sheila winced.

Somehow there always seemed to be a tension between them and he didn't know whose fault it was. "Look, I'm sorry," he said. "I just don't feel like talking about work after a long day. Okay?" She didn't respond.

An awkward silence.

"Am I keeping you up?" he finally asked.

Sheila didn't answer. She had to drink a certain amount before she'd admit she wanted sex too. Before then, he had to pretend that wasn't the reason for his visits. He leaned over to kiss her. She let him, but didn't respond.

Christ, he told himself. Get up. Leave. What are you doing here?

The first few times, they'd kissed like hungry teenagers because they didn't know what to say to each other. Now they went straight into the main event.

Jack slid below the sheets and started to kiss the inside of Sheila's thighs. He worked his way forward, deeper. Her muscles stiffened — not with anticipation, but distaste.

"Come here," she said, pulling him up. And then she moved down his body, took him in her mouth, and began to suck him with a detached earnestness, offering the act to avoid exposing herself. He lay back and tried to relax. Outside the bedroom window, the leaves of a tall tree shimmered silver in the street light.

After his divorce he'd been free to get laid as much as he could, with whomever he wanted. After years of bachelorhood, now he realized that the best sex he'd ever had was with his wife. She'd known that sometimes the greatest gift you could give someone in bed was to trust them enough to let yourself go. Was that all behind him now? Lord knew, most of life's other milestones were: high school graduation, the army, marriage, having a kid. What was left?

He couldn't unwind enough to come. He pulled back, rolled Sheila over, and pushed into her from behind, taking pleasure, when he had wanted to give it.

After, she went right to sleep, but he tossed and turned. He wasn't used to sharing a bed anymore; he hadn't had a real relationship since the divorce. The woman next to him was a stranger. He gently disengaged from her arm and rolled onto his side. Pictured Tomas Berrios, lying on his side down by the canal.

Halfway through the night, he finally dropped into an uneasy sleep.

He was walking along, being pulled . . . he held a leash tugged by a huge, wolflike dog. He looked to his left — his brother Peter was walking by his side. They weren't talking, but the silence seemed okay. Then the dog lunged at his brother, and Jack was sprayed in a vicious red gout of blood.

eight

At the height of the morning rush hour, Ben Leightner's neighbors hurried toward the Bergen Street subway station and their jobs. They paid little attention to the visible world — they pondered what to buy for dinner, or why their spouse had refused them sex the night before, or how to make the boss appreciate their work. They hurried down the sidewalks looking inside, instead of out.

Ben walked slowly, surveying the world.

Once he'd seen an incredible, perfect rainbow arcing from the clock tower of the Williamsburg Savings Bank to the caged roof of the Brooklyn House of Detention. Nobody else noticed it because nobody looked up. A woman saw him standing on the corner, staring at the bright arc. She stopped, someone else did — soon they were a group of strangers, smiling up in awe.

A few people *did* look. On his block an old Puerto Rican grandmother leaned out of her third-story window all day, her massive bosom resting on her forearms, her forearms resting on a pillow. She wore a pink nightgown and had her hair pulled back in a tight bun. She watched everything that went on — the street was her private movie.

Best of all was a little kid who lived a couple doors down.

Ben often paused to watch him playing by the curb, The boy spent hours just moving sticks and pebbles around the base of an old sycamore tree. It made Ben remember what it was like to be five or six: you could look at a rough, cracked square of sidewalk and imagine you saw canyons, valleys, rivers. Grains of sand were people, pebbles were cows.

There were others on the street who passed much of their time alone.

By nine A.M., he was deep in Red Hook.

He stopped to film a little fenced-in garden with overgrown rosebushes leaning over a sky-blue statue of the Virgin Mary. He concentrated so hard on framing the shot that he didn't hear the front door of the house open.

"Why you wanna take a picture of my yard?"

A round little old guy dressed in a blue Adidas running suit stood on the porch. He'd owned the suit so long it had gone in and out and back in style again—some young hipster would probably pay a fortune for it now. He squinted up at the morning sun, then down at Ben.

"Whatcha wanna take pictures around here for?"

"I like your statue."

The man grinned widely. "You like it? It's the real thing: I got it in It'ly."

"It's great." He was not the kind of person who could just walk into a bar and strike up a conversation. Especially not to pick up women—he didn't have much luck with that. But this was one of the good things about his work: people liked talking to him.

"Whaddaya taking the movies for?"

"I like the neighborhood."

"Bahh." The man waved a hand past his nose. "This neigh-

borhood's crap—excuse my French. You shoulda seen it in the old days. We had movie theaters, grocery stores, bars all up and down the street."

Ben realized that in his travels around Red Hook he hadn't seen a single theater or supermarket and only a couple of bars.

"Really?"

"Oh, sure. We had the shipyards goin' and all the workers and their families. Hundreds of sailors walkin' around. You could go out on a Friday night and drink in seven different places without goin' more than a coupla blocks."

"Have you lived here a long time?"

"My whole life."

Ben froze, struck by a sudden thought. So far he had only a vague plan for a broad documentary about Red Hook. But what if he personalized it, made it more about his father—and maybe even his grandfather? The notion made him nervous, but excited.

Shy now, he took a step forward. "Did you ever know somebody named Jack Leightner?"

The man chewed his lower lip. "Leightner, yeah, I remember."

"Did you know him well?"

"Jack? Nah, he was just one a the neighborhood brats. But his brother—that kid was an amazing ball player. Shortstop. I used to go over to the diamond over there on Bay Street sometimes and watch them play. I'd bring 'em sodas." The man shook his head fondly. "I worked down by the water at the White Rock plant. You know White Rock?"

"Isn't that a soda company?"

"You bet. But the plant closed. The whole neighborhood has gone to hell." The man shrugged. "Whaddaya gonna do?"

"Do you remember anything in particular about Jack Leightner?"

The man flapped a hand, a little crabby now. "I told ya. I didn't really know him. He was just one a the kids that used to run around here." He brightened. "Hey, listen — you wanna take a picture, take one of me and my wife. Don't go away." He disappeared inside the house.

Ben checked to make sure he had enough tape left in the camera.

A minute later, the man came out on the porch leading his wife, a plump little orange-haired lady in a faded housecoat.

"This guy's makin' a movie about the neighborhood," the man said. He turned to Ben. "This gonna be on TV, or somethin'?"

"Who knows?" Ben said. "Maybe someday. Is it okay if I film you?" he asked the woman.

"I guess it'd be all right," she said. "Wait, let me take this off." She removed the housecoat to reveal a Let's Go Mets T-shirt.

"You ready?" the man asked. He put his arm around his wife.

Ben nodded.

Instantly they transformed themselves into the stiff little plastic couple on top of a wedding cake.

nine

Jack found Daskivitch hunched down behind his desk in the Seven-six squad room. Closer inspection revealed that the detective was using some Crazy Glue to repair the thick rubber sole of his shoe.

"You wanna be careful with that stuff," Jack said. "Might be kind of embarrassing to have to walk around all day with your hand stuck to a shoe."

"Thanks, bunk," Daskivitch mumbled, frowning at his handiwork. "Any calls from our friend Mallow and his mom?"

"Nope." Jack beelined for the lounge and the coffee maker.

"I phoned the vic's wife again," Daskivitch called out. "Her mother-in-law said she's still sedated."

Jack reemerged gulping down a cup of coffee. "We're gonna have to talk to her soon."

"The funeral's Thursday morning."

"That's good. I'm off tomorrow and Wednesday, but I think we should check that out. For now, how about one of us runs some interviews at the vic's job while the other guy follows up on Plates at the Scene." That report made it possible to track down owners of cars parked by the canal on the day of the murder, in hopes they might have witnessed something.

"Where you wanna begin?"

"I'll start with a shave. You have a razor I can use?"

Daskivitch looked up from his shoe. "Hey, you look like shit."

"Thanks. I had a hard time sleeping."

The young detective dropped the glue applicator on a copy of the *Post* and stared up at his partner. "Wait a minute — those are the same clothes you wore to work yesterday. You little slut. I bet you were out all night doing the flat tango."

Jack grinned despite himself. "Give it a rest." Sheila had promised him that her alarm clock was reliable, but it wasn't, and only his own internal clock woke him in the morning, too late to stop off at home.

"Anybody special?" Daskivitch asked.

Jack sighed. "Not really. She makes me want to shoot myself in the head."

"Use at least a thirty-eight," Daskivitch said. They'd both seen what happened when a would-be suicide didn't use enough firepower. He brightened. "Hey, why don't I hook you up? My wife has some nice-lookin' friends."

Jack winced. "Please — don't bother."

"You don't wanna grow old alone, do ya?"

Jack didn't answer. Should he be touched by the young detective's concern or offended by the familiarity? "I haven't had a blind date since I was twenty," he finally said.

"How'd that one go?"

"I married her. You know how that turned out."

A pause.

"Let me just ask Jeannie if she knows anybody," Daskivitch said. "Theoretically speaking. All right?"

Jack sighed. "Don't go to any trouble."

Daskivitch grinned. "No trouble at all."

The Bentley was a big building, probably built in the sixties, all green glass and chrome. It was several blocks east of the Gold Coasts of Park and Fifth avenues, yet ritzy enough to have two doormen. One of them swung open the door as Jack approached, but there was no deference in the gesture. Anyone except a bum who came to the main entrance would have to be treated as a potential guest, but the man had clearly looked Jack over—his off-the-rack gray slacks, inexpensive blue blazer—and made a quick judgment.

Jack didn't get into Manhattan much, except for an occasional visit to One Police Plaza, the monolithic NYPD headquarters down by the base of the Brooklyn Bridge. Like his father, he was a Brooklynite to the bone—the old man had only been above Times Square a couple of times in his life. Maybe he had a point—who needed to go somewhere just to be looked down on, even by doormen?

An elevator chimed open in the lobby, followed by a scrabbling of paws on the marble floor. A little dog with a face made entirely of wrinkles strained at a leash, which led to an elderly woman in the type of high-collared suit that Jack associated with presidents' wives. Her mouth was pulled back in a permanent Nancy Reagan face-lift half-grin.

The doorman, a white-haired man with the guarded face of a solitary drinker, transformed himself into a genial butler. "Good afternoon, Mrs. Lambert," he called to the lady, who swept by without a glance. The younger doorman rushed up to hold the door for her, then bustled out into the street to flag a cab.

The elder doorman's sour look returned. "Can I help you?"

Jack cleared his throat. He was a senior detective with the New York Police Department — why did he feel like the ten-year-old from the wrong side of the tracks who didn't even have other poor kids over to visit, because they might see the old man in the kitchen with his big bushy eyebrows and perpetual gloomy squint, sucking the marrow out of a soup bone, eating cloves of garlic like a Russian peasant?

He flashed his shield. "I'm with the NYPD. I'll need to speak with the super."

Normally, when confronted with a shield, people either got defensive or effusive, as if to demonstrate that they had nothing to hide, but this man kept his cool. He turned to a podium, picked up a phone, and pressed a button on a computerized switchboard.

"He's out of his office right now," the doorman said. "May I ask what this is in regard to?"

Jack ignored the question; there was no reason the doorman needed to know. "I'll wait."

Giant bowllike lamps of frosted glass hung from ceiling chains and shone over the lobby's marble floor. In front of a huge mantelpiece, several silk-upholstered armchairs were posed around a coffee table topped with a grand arrangement of fresh flowers. It was like a hushed museum display of a living room. Jack pulled off his jacket, draped it over one of the chairs, and sat. He snuck a look at a mirror to run a hand over his hair.

"I'll have someone take you down to the office," the doorman said abruptly.

"All right." *Just because you've got some gold braid on your hat, that doesn't make you a general.*

The doorman pressed another button on his console. An unmarked door near the back of the lobby opened and out trotted a young guy in blue work pants and a blue shirt with a tag stitched over the pocket. Mike. His hair was slicked back and his short sleeves revealed the biceps of a body-builder.

"The officer is here to see Mr. Guzman," the doorman said. "Take him to the back, would you?"

Mike reached out his hand for a friendly shake. "Ay, 'ow you doon?"

Jack was grateful for the Brooklyn accent.

He might have fallen through a rabbit hole. After the opulent lobby, they walked down a flight of stairs into what looked like a lower passageway of a Navy ship, like the one that had taken him to the Philippines in 1966. The same glopped-on industrial gray paint coated the walls. He followed the porter around a corner.

A model-handsome young man leaned against the wall next to a service elevator. A garment bag lay folded over at his feet.

"Is someone helping you?" Mike asked.

"I'm the waiter for the Robbins'."

"They having a dinner tonight?"

"Yeah."

"You've been here before, right?"

The waiter unfolded a stick of gum and nodded. "Yeah, unfortunately. The guy's got about twenty zillion dollars, but he never tips."

"Tell me about it," Mike agreed.

The elevator door opened. The metal walls were scarred and dull. The operator was a doleful little man with a pinched, birdlike face. He confronted the waiter.

"Was that you pressing the goddamn button? Once is enough. You gonna drive me crazy in here."

"Sorry, buddy," the waiter said halfheartedly.

"This guy's going up to the Robbins'," Mike nodded toward the waiter. "And this gentleman"—he nodded toward Jack—"needs to go down to see Mr. Guzman."

"I'm running late because of an audition," the waiter said to Jack. "Would you mind if I go up first?"

"No problem." Jack wanted to get a feel for Tomas Berrios's working life. Another image to add to his mental store: a young man in a little metal cage, riding up and down with no view and no fresh air. A man would have to have precious little ambition to put up with such a dull job. Or he'd be frustrated as hell—which might be what drew Berrios into trouble.

They rode up in silence. The operator brought the elevator to a smooth stop and the doors opened onto a landing in the gray stairwell. Through a half-open door, Jack could see directly into a large kitchen, which appeared to be empty, save for a cooking smell so good it made his mouth water.

For all the security at the front of the building, access to the apartments seemed easy once you were in the service area.

"Hello?" called the waiter as he strolled into the apartment. He moved out of sight as he said, "Sorry I'm late. I had to wait forever for the service elevator."

The operator shook his head. "Fuckin' college kids." On the way down, he looked quizzically at Jack.

"He's a cop," Mike explained. He turned to Jack. "You here 'cause of Tommy? Man, I can't believe it. I worked with the guy for years."

"Do you have any idea who might have done this?"

"Me?" Mike sighed. "Far as I can tell, the guy didn't have an enemy in the world. At least he never said anything would make me think different." He shook his head. "Jesus, he had a wife, little kids. I'll tell ya, soon as I can get enough savings together I'm getting the hell out of this city."

Jack turned to the operator.

"Tommy was a good kid. I hope you find the bastard that did this and string him up by the balls."

In the basement, Jack followed Mike down a fluorescent-lit hallway past a couple of wheeled luggage racks.

"You can wait in here," the porter said, gesturing to a tiny office. "I'll find the boss."

Invoices and memos covered the battered metal desk; a bulletin board was thick with union notices and memos from the management company. On a poorly photocopied list of tenants, Jack recognized the name of a movie actor, a state assemblyman, and a TV news anchor. Outside the barred, grimy window, a ramp led up a service alley.

He wondered if Daskivitch was having any luck finding witnesses. So far the case was going nowhere. Since Tomas Berrios rented his apartment, he had no mortage. A little computer work revealed two credit cards, but the combined debt came to only $478.07. Berrios didn't own a car and had no outstanding medical bills. There was no obvious reason why he'd need money.

After Jack's conversation with Hector the BigHead, he and Daskivitch had canvassed the neighbors. Tomas was a little loud sometimes when he was out on the stoop with his buddies, but he had never caused any real problems on the block. He came home from work, played with his kids, went to the store for his wife and mother-in-law. Jack called Eddie Reilly, the neighborhood's Community Patrol officer and a good cop—he didn't sit in a squad car all day, but actually got out and walked the streets, talked to people on stoops and outside of bodegas. If Berrios had been into any dirty business, Reilly would likely have known, but the CPOP officer had nothing really bad to say.

Berrios had not been an angel—after all, he did have a sheet—but he didn't seem to have any major known enemies. Still, someone had been angry enough to beat him around the head and truss him up like an animal. And it was easy enough to pull a trigger, but you had to really want to hurt someone to use a knife.

"Sorry to keep you waiting," the super said briskly, dropping a section of heating duct and a tin snips on the desk. A compact man, he dropped into his office chair, then wheeled across the concrete floor to brush his chalky hands together over a wastebasket. His short, curly hair was dusted with the same chalk. His lips were pressed together and he had a tense jaw—a worrier. Dark circles marked his eyes, as if he hadn't slept in a week.

"How you doing?" Jack said. "I'm Detective Jack Leightner, with the NYPD." He stood up and leaned across the desk, offering his hand. The super reached out to shake it. As Jack grasped the man's callused hand, he turned his own hand clockwise. It was a simple interrogator's test: if Guzman let his hand be easily turned, it indicated he might make a compliant interviewee. If he resisted, he might be difficult. The result was inconclusive.

"Everybody here feels terrible about what happened to Tommy," the super said. "We're taking up a collection from the staff and tenants for his family." He searched through a stack of papers on top of his desk, and then began opening the drawers. "I'm sorry. It's very busy. I need to find a purchase order."

"What did Tomas do here?" Jack asked.

The super rummaged. "He was a porter."

"Which means what, exactly?"

"He collects—collected—trash from every landing and

put it out back, he helped maintain the building. He lent a hand to the tenants if they wanted something moved or fixed in their apartments. Mostly, he ran the service elevator."

"He had access to the apartments?"

"Access?" The super stopped his search. "Only if someone asked for him."

"Someone?"

"A tenant. Or maybe a housekeeper or maid, if they needed help with something. Listen, no offense, but why do you want to know this? He was killed in Brooklyn, right?"

"I'll be honest with you, Mr. Guzman. We have no idea who did this to Tomas, so we need to talk to everybody who knew him. Is there anybody here he was particularly friendly with?"

"Friendly? I don't know what you mean — we're all friendly on the staff."

The super rubbed his nose and Jack wondered if this might be a "tell" — an involuntary sign that the super was hiding something.

"What about the tenants?"

Mr. Guzman sat up straight. "We don't get involved with the tenants, mister. We have our place back here, they're up there — we don't get involved in any troubles. Okay?"

An interview was like a medical checkup: you prodded and poked until you met an odd reaction. Jack had touched a sore spot. He shifted gears. "How does someone get a job here, to be a porter?"

"We're careful who we hire. Very careful. If we get someone through an agency, it has to be a bonded agency. If they come through the union, they have to have references, someone to vouch for them."

"And Tomas?"

"He got the job because his uncle worked here for many years. If Ray said somebody was okay, he was okay. With

Tomas, I never had a serious problem. He would never do nothing to give his uncle a bad name."

"Where I can find this Ray?"

"You'd need a psychic. He passed away eight months ago."

"Of what?"

"Cancer of the lungs."

No foul play there. Jack stood up. "Thanks very much for your time. If you think of anything else, here's my card. You can reach me at this number anytime—if I'm not in, they'll page me. One more thing: I'm going to need a list of all the tenants and staff."

The super threw his hands up in the air. "This happened in Brooklyn, mister. In Brooklyn! We have some very important tenants here and the management company won't want me to give out their names. Why do you need this?"

Jack sighed. "I can go straight to the company and get the list, but that would be a waste of my time. One of your employees has been killed—do you understand? That's important too."

To Jack's astonishment, the super sank back in his chair and began to cry. He waited while the man searched through his desk, found a tissue, and turned away to wipe his eyes. After a moment, Mr. Guzman turned back and wadded up the tissue. He threw it at the wastebasket and both men watched as it hit the rim and fell in.

"Three points," Jack said. "Outside shot."

"I'm sorry, mister," the super said. "I'm just trying to do my job. I'm under a lotta pressure here."

Running an exclusive building with wealthy, demanding tenants would be tough, Jack thought, but a superintendent subject to crying over the stress wouldn't last long. "More pressure than usual?"

Mr. Guzman nodded. "The management company is telling me I have too many people on the staff. They want me to let somebody go. The union says they can help me, but I think in the long run the company is gonna win. I'm trying to deal with this problem, and then this happens with Tomas." He stood up and pulled the list of tenants off the wall and handed it over. "Take this, mister. Don't go to the company. I haven't told them about Tomas—if they find out we got a police investigation here, that's all I need. I'll help you with whatever you want."

Jack sat down. "Did the employees know that someone was about to be laid off?"

Mr. Guzman shook his head. "I was waiting to make sure this had to happen—I didn't tell anybody."

Jack pulled out a cigarette. "Let me ask you this: if you had to let someone go, would Tomas have been on your list? Was he a good worker?"

"He never gave me no troubles. Except for that stupid hair under his lip."

"Was that a problem?"

"I wanted him to shave it. But he did a good job. I can't say he liked it all the time. Running a service elevator is not a job for a young man. Anyhow, the staff liked him."

"How about the tenants?"

The super rubbed the side of his nose again. "Sure. He was a friendly guy."

Mike came through the door. "Mrs. Steinberg says she's having a problem with the exhaust fan over her stove."

"Did you check it out?"

Mike rolled his eyes. "I said I would, but you know how she is. Said she needs *you* to do it. Right away."

The super turned to Jack. "Are we finished?"

"I guess so," Jack said. "For now."

ten

Something was burning.

As Jack stepped through the front door of the house, he smelled smoke. He couldn't see any, but something was definitely wrong. He hurried up to the first landing, but the smell got weaker. He jogged down the other way, into the basement hall. The smoke was visible there, a pall over the dim bare bulb.

"Mr. Gardner!"

"In here," came a faint reply.

Jack rushed down the hall and swung open the furnace-room door to find Mr. Gardner dropping a handful of papers into a metal trash can; flames lapped up.

"What's the matter?" the old man said, his eyes big through his thick glasses.

"What's the matter! Jesus, I thought the whole house was on fire."

"I'm just gettin' rid of some old things."

Jack peered into the barrel. He was shocked to discover that the papers were photographs — before his eyes, Mrs. Gardner's kindly face browned, curled, and flared into ash.

He remembered the paramedics carrying her out of the house on a stretcher; remembered her husband sitting in the near-empty funeral home chapel, his head sunk onto his chest as if all the air had been let out of him. Jack had been especially depressed to see that all three of the bouquets by the casket were identical, as if bought at the same cheap florist.

He reached out to stop Mr. Gardner as the man lifted a pile of his late wife's clothes out of a plastic bag.

"It's okay," Mr. Gardner said, pulling away and dropping the clothes into the flames. "I have a fire extinguisher ready, just in case. I'm sorry about the smoke."

Jack pried open a window. Fresh air rushed in, dissipating the bitter fog.

He turned back to his landlord, who dropped another sheaf of photos in the can. Jack stood and watched, appalled. After a moment, he shook his head, and left the room.

He went out into the backyard, sat in Mr. Gardner's ancient lawn chair. Smoke curled out of the basement window, sifted through the magenta rosebushes, wafted like incense up into the early evening sky. Was Mrs. Gardner up there somewhere, a kind angel in an apron and a faded housedress? The image pleased Jack, but he didn't believe it. The real afterlife was memory, a temporary immortality in the hearts of those left behind.

He watched the dusk settle down over the trees; let his mind drift. Often he'd look out his kitchen window to see Mr. Gardner sitting in this same spot. Aside from daily shopping expeditions and puttering in his workshop or the yard, the old man didn't have much to do all day. He rarely read. He sat quietly in the backyard, thinking. Remembering. The yard was conducive to that, a green oasis, its calm disturbed only by the chittering of birds and an occasional child's shout or car horn rising over the rooftops.

Smoke poured out of the basement window. It seemed wrong, but Jack reconsidered. Maybe Mr. Gardner was seeking a sort of release, a freedom from memory. And who was he to judge the man for that?

eleven

The Iglesia de Dios Pentecostal was a long, low bunker, lit by weak fluorescent lights that cast a pallor on the congregation. A preacher in a sherbet-green polyester suit led the funeral service. His voice distorted the little loudspeakers flanking the stage. Mrs. Espinal sat in the front row, holding her grandchildren on her lap while next to her a young woman, presumably Tomas Berrios's wife, clasped the sides of her head and rocked with grief. The casket, resting on the stage in a cloud of flowers, was closed.

In the back row, Daskivitch straightened his tie and leaned close to Jack. "Last funeral I went to was for Johnny Briggs, this guy I worked with in Narcotics. He got shot undercover, while he was doing a buy."

"Was he wearing a vest?"

"It wouldn't've mattered. They shot him in the head."

"Eeesh."

"I'm glad to be out of Narco," his partner continued. "But not as glad as my wife. Undercover was a bitch. Half the time you worry you're gonna get popped by some scuzzball doper. The other half you're hoping you don't catch one from some gung-ho off-duty Transit rookie."

Everyone around them rose and joined hands. The pastor

said something in Spanish and they sang a hymn. Jack — a Jew in church — looked around to see if anyone noticed he wasn't singing. When the hymn was over, the pastor said something else. The members of the congregation turned to one another, exchanged strong hugs, then rose and began to file up the aisle toward the casket.

"Where you going?" Daskivitch said as Jack stood up.

"Just paying my respects."

He clasped his hands over his belt and waited as the line plodded forward. He'd seen so many dead people, so many funerals. Cops. Drug lords, innocent bystanders, guilty wife beaters. Abandoned kids, elderly parents, trial witnesses, hit-and-runs. People killed by guns, by baseball bats, by lye, by suffocation, by rat poison, even a World War I bayonet.

A little butterball of a woman stood in line in front of him. Farther up, he recognized Hector's big head.

The woman turned with a friendly gold-capped smile and asked Jack a question. She stopped when she saw his puzzled expression. *"Habla español?"*

He raised his hands apologetically. *"Un poquito, solamente."*

The woman shrugged and turned around.

He was glad the casket was closed. His father had wanted an open casket, Lord knows why. It was against Jewish tradition, but the old man never cared about that. Maybe he wanted to force the world to acknowledge him one last time. When he died of a stroke (due to high blood pressure — which surprised no one), he left only debts. Jack had debts of his own, so the funeral had been arranged on the cheap. The embalmer had done horrible work; the corpse looked like a budget taxidermy job. Sitting in the front row of the funeral parlor, contemplating the walk up to the casket, Jack had expected to be seized by grief or rage, to shout or sob, but when the moment came, he'd felt nothing, been a walking pillar of stone.

The line shuffled forward. The smell of the garish, waxy flowers assaulted Jack's nostrils; he breathed shallowly through his mouth. As he approached the casket, he pictured Tomas Berrios lying inside the wooden box in his best Sunday suit, pictured the knife wound in his side and wondered if the funeral director had bothered to cover it up. And suddenly, out of nowhere, water welled up behind his eyelids and started to seep out. He pressed his eyes closed with his fingers, but it didn't help. He stifled a sob, hoping his partner didn't notice anything amiss, stepped out of the line and headed for a side door in the chapel.

Along a dim hallway, he found a bathroom. He went in, locked the door, and sat down on a radiator by the back wall. He blew his nose loudly. What was wrong with him? He prided himself on staying calm in any situation, but he'd lost control twice within just a few days. He took out a cigarette, noting with disgust that his hands shook as he raised the match.

Maybe he was overworked. Before this Berrios case, he'd worked almost double time for two straight weeks to crack a nasty revenge murder in Bensonhurst. Maybe he just needed a little rest. When was the last time he'd taken a real vacation? He could hardly remember. He took a deep drag from the cigarette; the nicotine soothed him. Yes, he decided, that was it: he just needed some R and R. Even a veteran could get stressed out by too many days in a row on such a job.

Daskivitch found him outside the chapel, waiting on the sidewalk.

"Where the hell'd you go?"

"The smell of those damned crappy flowers was getting

to me," Jack said, scratching the side of his mouth. "I needed some fresh air."

Daskivitch shrugged; he seemed to accept the explanation. The detectives watched the congregation spill from the doorway into the bright morning sun. Nobody seemed hinky, although one of Tomas's friends, a handsome kid with a sharp face, made a particular effort to scowl as he walked past.

The detectives waited until everyone filed out. The last to leave were Mrs. Espinal and the grandchildren and Tomas Berrios's wife.

Jack stepped forward. "Excuse me, ladies, I want to say how very sorry I am about what's happened."

"This is my daughter Recina," said Mrs. Espinal.

The wife stared through him, her cheeks sticky with tears. A pretty round-faced girl, a little on the chunky side.

"I'm Detective Leightner, ma'am. This is my partner, Detective Daskivitch. I know you probably don't want to talk now, but if you can think of any reason why this might have happened . . . ?"

"He never hurt nobody," Recina Berrios said.

"I'm sure he didn't. All the neighbors have been saying what a good man he was."

"I can't understand it. Why would someone do this?"

"Was he acting any differently before . . . ?"

Recina considered the question. The way she looked around, Jack knew immediately that she had something to tell.

"Mrs. Berrios?"

"Mami," she said to her mother. "Would you take the kids back to the house? I'll be there in a minute."

"Please don't keep her for a long time, Detective," Mrs. Espinal said. "We got a lot of people coming over."

They watched as the grandmother took the children by the hand and walked off. The tiny girl kept turning to look back over her shoulder.

Recina Berrios bit her lower lip. "I know my husband. He would never do nothing to hurt his family. But he *was* talking different."

"What did he say?"

"That things were gonna get better for us. That soon we'd have a bigger place. Maybe even get my mother her own apartment."

"How? How could he afford that?"

Recina sighed. "He wouldn't tell me. He said to trust him. I didn't say nothing because I didn't want a fight. But I wish . . . I wish I didn't let him out of the house until he told me."

"Is there anything else, ma'am?" Daskivitch said.

Recina stared down at the sidewalk for a moment. Then she reached into her purse. "This morning, I found this in the pocket of the shirt he wore his last day at work." She pulled out a piece of newspaper and handed it to Jack.

It was a scrap of an article, part of a gossip column. Something about Madonna.

"The other side," Recina said. "It's his writing."

Jack turned the paper over. On it, Tomas Berrios had written something in pencil.

Nine a.m. 7 Coffey.

"Do you know what this means?" Jack asked.

Recina shook her head.

"Let me have a look," Daskivitch said. He considered the paper for a moment, then looked up. "So? Maybe he was supposed to get breakfast for the guys at work. His spelling's not so great, but —"

"No," Jack said. "Coffey is an address. It's a street in Red Hook."

twelve

As Daskivitch drove toward the Hook, Jack sank lower into his seat. Though he had grown up there, he only returned on police business. And rarely. As best he could, he avoided cases in the neighborhood (but subtly, like an illiterate covering his handicap).

Daskivitch drove over the Brooklyn-Queens Expressway and into the Hook. The faces now were unfamiliar to Jack — some Puerto Rican kids laughing and swinging their knapsacks at each other next to a bus stop, two old men sitting in folding chairs outside a fix-a-flat shop — but the streets flurried with ghosts.

"I guess you Homicide guys used to be pretty busy around here," Daskivitch said as they drove by the Red Hook Houses, block after block of identical brick buildings. Groups of black teenagers in designer athletic clothes huddled on the corners, staring sullenly at the detectives as they passed.

"Yeah. Back in the eighties, when crack was peaking, they used to have two or three shootings in there a week. It was open season. It's calmed down a lot." In 1992, a popular elementary-school principal had been accidentally killed in the crossfire of a drug shooting in the projects. Afterward, they'd been targeted by massive police sweeps.

"I still wouldn't go strolling inside at night."

"I used to live there," Jack said.

Daskivitch nearly ran a red light. He turned to Jack in astonishment. "You're shitting me, right?"

Jack shook his head. "I was born in the Houses. Lived there till I was twelve."

"Were you the only white kid?"

"It used to be different. Fifty years ago, the Houses were filled with dockworkers. We had Italians, Irish, Poles. And Russians, like my old man."

Back in the sixties, he'd run with all kinds of kids. Sons of Norwegian pipefitters who worked down at Todd's Shipyards. Puerto Ricans. Blacks. His father shouted at him many times for hanging out with "those people," but that never kept him from his friends. There was Chino Nieves, whose boyhood claim to immortality was that, in the middle of a stickball game, he hit a Spaldeen fourteen stories up onto a projects roof. And Kiki Rosado, who would limp home a decade later after four tours in Nam with the 101st Airborne, covered with medals, paralyzed on his left side, deaf in one ear.

"Back then," he said, "there was none of this garbage along the streets. The grass in those courtyards was *green* — you could get a five-dollar ticket just for walking on it. Nobody was allowed to hang out in the hallways."

"And now you've got people murdering each other in there."

"Well, this was before crack." Before crack, before the docks died out, before a lot of things.

A few blocks to the south stretched a large playing field. During the Great Depression, the area had been a wasteland of rough jerry-rigged shacks known as Hooverville. Shortly after his father arrived in America, when the magical prospect of unlimited work was spoiled by the Crash, the old man ended up living in one of those shacks. He dreamed of someday owning his own home. The expressway smashed right through the dream.

Daskivitch stepped on the gas. At the corner of Bay Street, Jack peered out the window.

"Just up this block there's a giant city pool. There's a wall around it, but we used to boost each other over at night in the summer, a bunch of guys and girls. We'd bring cold six-packs, smoke some reefer."

"*You* smoked pot!"

"Hey, I wasn't always such a fossil. We had some hot times in that pool."

"Skinny-dipping?"

"Almost. Things were more uptight back then. We kept our underwear on." He laughed and shook his head. "To this day I have never seen anything sexier than Maria Gonzalez climbing out of that water with her nipples poking through her bra." And, he might have added, her wet panties barely concealing her lovely bush. The Crystals singing "Da Doo Ron Ron" in the background, or Little Peggy March, "I Will Follow Him." He'd been fifteen, walking around trying to conceal a perpetual hard-on. Jesus, life had been simple. All he had to worry about was staying out of his father's way and trying to get laid.

Some of the older guys'd had jobs down at the A-Con company, where they dissassembled trucks to ship them over to Vietnam. The end of the war put them all out of work—yet another blow to the neighborhood. By that point the Hook was punch-drunk. The place had gone so far downhill that you could buy a whole block of houses for a hundred grand.

Jack looked out in sorrow and disgust. A former patrol

partner had described Red Hook as an area were you didn't have to look hard to find a place to piss out in the open. It was a desert, a no-man's-land.

His chest tightened. He hadn't had an asthma attack since he was a kid, but every time he came back to the Hook he wondered if he might. The flashbacks were intense, an overpowering jumble: his father's belt buckle snapping across his back; the first time he'd fallen in love; the smooth, reassuring touch of his mother's hand on the back of his neck; that first great shock of the cold pool water on a summer day. Going back to Red Hook was love shot through with pain, like visiting his mother in the hospital during her last illness, watching her too-patient face turn gaunt and strained. He'd been helpless then and he was helpless now.

The midday sun glared down, threw almost no shadow, baked the block-long, windowless factories and deserted streets. Beyond the projects, the Hook looked like part of some backwater Texas town. Light glinted so harshly off the chrome trim of the few parked cars that his Ray-Bans seemed useless. Down at the end of a block, a stooped man in brown work clothes emerged from behind a stack of wooden pallets like a pilgrim appearing in the desert, and for a second Jack could almost believe it was his father.

On a sidewalk, in the shade of a construction Dumpster, a big white dog lay on its side, panting. The passing image tugged at Jack's memory. A dream? Something to do with a dog—he couldn't remember.

Daskivitch cut through his reverie. "Hey, spaceman—this is Coffey Street. Which way do I go?"

Number 7 was a garage marked R. H. Auto Body, sandwiched between a little aluminum-sided house and a big boarded-up warehouse. Barbed wire spiraled above the sliding door to keep thieves from going in over the roof. The door was half open, but Jack couldn't see anybody in the dim interior. He and his partner got out of the car and slowly crossed the cobblestone street.

Something clanked in the depths of the garage. Jack waved his partner over to the other side of the doorway.

"Anybody there?"

The clanking stopped.

A small Hispanic man in mechanic's overalls ducked under the door and came out onto the sidewalk, blinking in the light. He was stooped over, as if he were balancing an invisible heavy trunk on his back. He wiped his hands on a rag so saturated with oil and grease that Jack didn't see the point.

"Are you the owner of the garage?"

"Owner? *Por favor, no hablo inglés.*"

"I'll deal with this," Daskivitch said. He spoke with the man in fluent Spanish. (Extra points for the rookie.) "He says the boss is out. Says they weren't here on Sunday."

Jack took a photo out of his pocket, courtesy of Mrs. Espinal. It showed Tomas Berrios, in a sky-blue tuxedo, smiling stiffly at the camera. "Ask him if he's seen this man."

Daskivitch held up the photo and spoke. Jack watched carefully to see if there was anything odd about the mechanic's reaction.

Nothing. The man shrugged and shook his head. He looked truthful, as far as Jack could tell.

"Can I help you?"

The detectives turned to a big, paunchy man striding up the sidewalk. Sweat circles marked the underarms of his beige polyester polo shirt. His aviator sunglasses looked out of place on his round, doughy face.

Jack pulled out his badge. "We're detectives with the NYPD. And you are . . . ?"

"Charles Greenlee. I'm the manager here." He turned to the mechanic. "Did you finish the SUV? *Finito?*"

The mechanic shook his head.

Greenlee groaned. "Get in there," he ordered. "Finish it. *Rápido.*" He turned back to the detectives and shrugged apologetically. "The customer is supposed to pick up any minute. What can I do for you?"

Jack held up the photo. "Do you know this man?"

The manager removed his sunglasses and considered the picture. Jack noticed that his eyes were red and wondered if he was some sort of user. He looked up and smiled pleasantly. "Nope. Never seen him." Suddenly he sneezed. He took out a handkerchief and rubbed his nose. "Sorry, I got hay fever. Most people just get it in the spring or the fall, but . . ." He shrugged.

"Were you here last Sunday morning?"

"Nobody was here. We were closed. We're always closed Sundays."

"The garage was locked?"

"It better have been. Leo here is usually the last one out on Saturday nights. It would have been locked unless he screwed up. Which wouldn't be surprising. No, wait—I opened up on Monday morning and everything was fine."

"Would you mind if we stepped in to look around?"

"I don't see why not. We run an honest shop. Would you mind if I asked what this is all about?"

"We're conducting an investigation," Jack said. "Homicide."

"Whoa," the manager said. "I thought maybe you guys were looking for chop shops or something. What does this have to do with *homicide*?"

"I'm not at liberty to discuss that," Jack replied. "Can we come in?"

Greenlee suddenly sneezed. "Whoo—pollen, ragweed, I don't know what it is. Uh—maybe I should call the owner."

"Who would that be?"

"It's a company. Maybe I should get permission from them."

"You can do that, but if they say no, we'll just have to come back with a warrant. It's up to you."

The manager threw up his hands. "Hey, listen, we've got nothing to hide here. Go ahead. I was just doing my job."

Jack and his partner stepped under the garage door. The SUV was up on a lift and Leo stood beneath it, hammering away at the chassis. A *Playboy* centerfold of a big-breasted blonde in farmer's overalls was tacked to the wall, over a workbench. Idly, Jack wondered at that: in this politically correct era, what did female customers make of the display? But then, Red Hook had always been behind the times.

The shop seemed clean and well run, with all of the tools hanging neatly. Any one of them could have battered Tomas Berrios's face, but only lab tests could tell. Jack glanced down, looking for bloodstains, but the concrete was only soaked with oil.

A phone rang in the back corner. "Excuse me a second," Greenlee said, and trotted toward the back.

"Whaddaya think?" Daskivitch said.

Jack frowned. "I don't know. Why would Berrios come to an auto body shop if he didn't own a car? Could he have been looking for a job?" He glanced over at the manager, deep in a phone conversation. "Do these guys seem hinky to you?"

"Not really."

Jack nodded. Both men seemed okay to him too.

Greenlee hung up and hurried back, wiping his nose again. "Sorry about that."

"What's the name of the company that owns the place?" Jack said.

"P and L Enterprises."

Jack wrote that down in his steno book. He took another look around.

"Is there anything else I can do for you?" Greenlee asked. He tucked his handkerchief in his coat pocket.

"Not right now. Thanks for your help."

They ducked out under the door. Jack lit a cigarette.

"What do we do now?" Daskivitch said.

Jack walked over to the little house next door and rang the buzzer. A moment later, an unshaven old man popped his head out the door. His frizzy hair was wet and he wore an ancient plaid bathrobe.

"Yes?"

Jack held up his badge. "We're police officers."

The usual "I didn't do anything but I'm nervous anyhow" flashed across the man's face. "Yes?" he repeated.

"The garage there — are they usually closed on Sundays?"

The man nodded. "Always."

"Were you here last Sunday?"

"No, sir. I was in Arlington, Virginia. Visiting my grandson."

"Does anybody else live here?"

"Nope. Just me."

"Who's on the other side, that warehouse?"

"Nobody, That's been shut up for years."

Jack sighed. "Sorry to bother you."

Relieved, the man pulled his head back in.

Jack looked across the street. Another long, windowless factory wall took up most of the block.

"Let's roll," Daskivitch said.

Jack didn't argue. They climbed into the car and took off, turning onto Van Brunt Street.

"What do you think?" Daskivitch said.

Jack shrugged. "I think we've put in a lot of hours with damn little results. This isn't exactly a priority job — the press and Downtown don't give a damn. I hate to leave a case open, but this doesn't look very promising."

"You want to call it quits?"

Actually, that sounded okay to Jack. You had to be gung-ho to be a good detective. Maybe he was getting tired, jaded. He thought of Berrios's wife and the two little kids. "Let's give it a little more time."

Daskivitch pulled to the curb in front of a bodega. "Hey, I'll spring for a couple of coffees."

"Last of the big-time spenders." His partner started to get out, but Jack stopped him. "It's okay. I'll get it."

Inside, the bodega was cramped and not terribly clean, but the coffee brewing behind the counter smelled good. Café Bustelo, said the handwritten sign.

"Dos cafés," Jack told the woman behind the counter. He knew that much Spanish.

While she poured, an old-timer shuffled up to the counter holding a six-pack of diet soda. He looked vaguely familiar.

The man stared at Jack. "I know you."

"I don't think so."

"Yeah, sure I do. I used to live in the Houses. Don't you remember me? Mr. Keller."

"On the second floor? With the little dog?"

"That's me. You were Petey Leightner's brother, right? I used to watch him play ball. He woulda made the majors." The old man shook his head. "That was such a terrible thing . . . Hey, where you going?"

Jack turned and pushed his way out of the store, ignoring the calls of the woman behind the counter.

"Let's go," he said, tight-lipped, settling into the seat beside his partner.

"Where's my coffee?"

Jack looked down at his hands and discovered they were empty. "They were out."

"What, are you kidding? A bodega that runs out of coffee! This *is* a fucked-up neighborhood."

thirteen

"How come you're not at work?" Jack said.

"The studio didn't have a shoot scheduled for today," his son replied.

Jack picked up his menu. He worked on shootings; his son did shoots.

Their waitress came by. "Would you like a cup of coffee?"

"I'm good," he said. He looked across at his son. "You want anything? A soda, anything?"

Ben shook his head glumly.

The waitress pulled a dupe pad from her apron. "Are you gentlemen ready to order?"

"I think we need a minute," Jack said. He wondered if he shouldn't have suggested a swankier place than this Greek coffee shop. No—he hadn't seen the kid for a while, but it was better to keep things light, not make a big production out of it.

His son looked thin and pale; as usual, he compromised his tall frame by hunching his shoulders, sticking out his neck, storklike. The boy was dressed in jeans and a faded plaid shirt that looked too hot for the day. His curly hair was getting long and he had a little tuft of hair under his bottom lip. Jack flashed to the body by the canal, blinked.

The boy was a good four inches taller than his father, but that was America for you: the kid eats better than his old man. At Ben's age, Jack had carried a lot more muscle, but he'd earned it in the Army and couldn't wish such an experience on his son — being ordered around all day and bored to tears most of the time. (Of course, he wouldn't have been bored if he'd been stationed in Nam.)

The kid always seemed shy. Jack was tempted to blame his ex-wife for that — she was the one who had done most of the child-raising. Then again, he was the one who had left his son without much of a dad. Who knew? Maybe it was just the boy's personality. Though Jack loved his son, he had to admit — guilty thought — that sometimes there was something *unlikable* about the boy. He was so drawn into himself, so wrapped up in his own air of unhappiness . . .

Ben had a big angry-looking pimple emerging below his mouth. He propped his chin on his fist, as if casually resting it there, but it was clear that he was trying to hide the blemish. The human weakness of the gesture opened Jack's heart.

After a minute, the waitress returned. "You know what you want?"

"I think I'll get the veggie burger," Ben said.

Jack set his menu down. "Why don't you get a real burger?"

"I don't eat meat."

"Since when?"

Ben scowled. Message delivered: *You would know if you'd taken more of an interest in my life.*

The waitress looked on patiently.

"At least get the Deluxe," Jack said. "It comes with fries."

"I don't eat fries."

"Why not?"

"Because. They're bad for my skin." The boy blushed.

Jack turned to the waitress. "I'll have the meat loaf."

Even the simplest talk led in the wrong directions. He looked around the coffee shop. Nautical theme: a deep-sea diver's helmet, a big plastic lobster and crab trapped in a fishnet, a giant swordfish shellacked and mounted on a board. He considered asking his son if he had a girlfriend, but decided the question might seem too intimate.

"How come *you're* not working today?" Ben asked.

"I am. Even a busy cop gets to eat lunch."

"Anything exciting?"

"The usual. Still scraping 'em up off the sidewalks." He'd never believed in bringing his work home. Even if he wanted to, there was no way to communicate the crazy things he saw to someone who didn't know the job, and it wasn't appropriate to talk about them with a little kid. Of course, Ben wasn't a kid anymore, but what the hell. He wanted to get to know his son—the last thing he needed to talk about was work.

They shifted in their seats, looked around the coffee shop until the silence grew awkward. Finally, the waitress appeared with their food.

"How's your mom?" Jack asked. He knew Ben didn't like to discuss the subject, but felt that he ought to ask. And he wanted to know.

"She's fine."

Fine. Jack drummed his fingers on the table. It was ridiculous: he knew twenty ways to get the most hardened street punk to talk, but he couldn't get more than three words out of his son. Pretty soon they'd be discussing the weather.

"How's Ted?" he asked. His ex-wife's boyfriend. Or something—"boyfriend" didn't sound right when applied to a middle-aged man. She'd been seeing the guy for a couple of years. He owned a blueprint-duplicating business in Bay Ridge. Or something — the details weren't clear.

"He's fine," Ben said.

Ben wondered why his father had suggested this lunch after he hadn't bothered to come around for half a year.

Their visits were always few and far between. Sometimes they got together for the holidays. Neither was very religious, so they didn't really celebrate Hanukkah. That didn't bother Ben so much, but he always felt like he should be doing something family-oriented on Christmas Eve. (Christmas was a hard time of year for Jews: he spent a month every year bombarded by commercials, carols, and crèches, advertisements for a party to which he wasn't invited.) A couple of years back — out of loneliness? A sense of familial obligation? — he'd called his dad; they spent a glum evening watching a cheesy Hollywood movie and then eating dinner at a Chinese restaurant haunted by an odd crew of Jews, Muslims, and *Taxi Driver*-type loners.

And now, after all this time, his father took him out to a cheesy coffee shop. He spread some mustard on his veggie burger and glanced across the booth. His dad still drove him nuts the way he ate: he cut his meat into little pieces, then ate it — then ate all of his potatoes, then all of his vegetables. It got to a point where Ben wanted to scream. *Just eat it together, for chrissakes! It all ends up in the same place!*

Before they ate, his dad always had to go to wash his hands. He was an odd guy. The few times Ben had seen his apartment out in Midwood, it was so neat he almost couldn't believe they were related. In the medicine cabinet, his father had everything perfectly laid out. On the ledge over the toilet, same deal: deodorant, razor, shave cream, all stretched out in a well-spaced row. If Ben put a cup down on the kitchen counter, he'd look back a few minutes later and it would be drying in the dish rack. Order, order, order. And this was a guy who dealt with murder and mayhem all the time at work.

The old man was dressed in gray slacks, a white shirt, a navy polyester sports coat, and a red and blue striped tie, probably also polyester. Ben remembered a few times when he was a kid and got dragged by his parents to a cop's retirement dinner or some other NYPD affair. A few of the younger cops seemed mildly aware of modern fashions, but the older guys, all crew-cut, looked as if they'd ordered their clothes from a 1950s Sears catalogue. It seemed his father still had an account there.

His dad lit a cigarette. That was another thing: he didn't understand how the man could smoke. You'd think that after looking at dead people all day, you wouldn't want to rush your own funeral.

His father looked pale, shaken up somehow. He was just fifty, but today he seemed older. Ben wondered if something was bothering him at work, but when he asked, his dad gave the stock answer he'd heard a thousand times since he was a kid: "The usual," the man said. "Still scraping 'em up off the sidewalks." He was a pro at not giving anything away about himself. The strong, silent type. That might be good enough for John Wayne, but what about the Duke's kids?

A couple of booths down, two little boys sat having lunch with their father. They swung their legs back and forth, dunked fries in ketchup, giggled. Having a great old time with Pop.

When Ben was little, the other kids envied him. What could be neater than having a dad who was a real, live po-liceman? One time he wanted to bring his father's gun to show and tell. Naturally, his father said no, so Ben asked for his nightstick. No. He finally settled for the hat. At least the other kids were impressed.

Later, when he was in high school, having a cop for a dad took on a whole new meaning. He got a lot of flack, heard a lot of pig jokes. In college, the word "fascist" came up a lot.

But basically, his dad being a cop just meant that he wasn't around a lot when Ben was growing up.

He considered telling his father about his plan for the Red Hook documentary. Maybe the old man would open up more about his past if the issue was put in a historical context. He was just working his way around to raising the subject when his dad asked about his mom. That made Ben's neck itch. Sure, whatever happened between them must have been complicated, but his mom was the one who'd suffered. As for her boyfriend, his dad didn't need to know. Ben could hear an edge in his voice whenever he asked about Ted. It made him think about the gun he knew his father carried inside his sports coat.

The moment to bring up Red Hook seemed to have passed. They finished their meal in silence. Ben's chest constricted at the thought that they might have completely run out of conversation. He didn't know why it was so hard to talk to his father, couldn't explain to himself his mysterious dread.

Jack took a sip of coffee. "You making any movies now?"

His son stirred a cup of herbal tea. Almost imperceptibly, he nodded.

"Where do you get the actors?"

"I don't use actors."

"You don't? How can you make a movie without actors?"

"I *told* you. They're documentaries."

"Oh." Jack stubbed out his cigarette in the ashtray. There was a lot of money to be made in Hollywood, but documentaries didn't sound like the way to do it. What the hell, let the kid figure it out on his own; he was single, with no responsibilities.

He took out another cigarette, tapped the end on the table, lit it.

His son frowned and waved the smoke away.

Jack flashed on a moment when Ben would have been three or four.

The kid had reached up and knocked a pack of cigarettes off the dining room table, spilling them out on the rug like pickup sticks. Jack shouted, and suddenly he heard his own father's bitter voice coming out of his mouth, felt his father's stern wrath clenched in his own hands. He pictured his belt slipping out of the loops, imagined slashing at his son's little back — and it terrified him. He hadn't only withdrawn from his wife. Being a father meant getting angry sometimes, being willing to say no, to exercise discipline. But if he backed off, he could spare the boy the abuse he himself had lived through as a child. And so he'd pulled away.

Sometimes you did wrong just trying to do right.

"I thought you gave that up," Ben said.

He shrugged. "With my job, it's hard not to smoke." Usually, he smoked to calm his nerves. Sometimes, he needed the cigarettes to block out the smell of a decomposing victim.

His son fingered the tuft of hair under his lip.

"Nice soul patch," Jack said casually.

"How do you know what it's called?"

"I know a lot of things," Jack said, enjoying the shocked look on his son's face. He knew soul patches. He knew do-rags, nipple rings, ear cuffs, tattoos, and many of the other things young people wore in order to proclaim, *I exist.* He knew about them because they made convenient markers for identifying the youngsters after they died.

For the first time, his son looked interested.

Under the table, Jack's beeper went off. He unhooked it and read the message.

"Sorry, son. Gotta get back to work. I can drop you home on the way . . ."

"That's okay. I can walk."

Grudgingly, Jack stood up. If they'd only had a few more minutes, they might have worked past the small talk.

At least the kid seemed relatively healthy, no major crises. Jack wanted to hug him, but the kid would probably balk.

"Take care." He reached across the booth and they shook hands, like strangers concluding a business meeting.

He went to the cash register and paid, then went back to a corner outside the bathrooms where he could take out his cell phone in private. While the phone rang, he watched his son walk out of the coffee shop, awkward, gangly.

His heart ached.

fourteen

The vic was a little kid.

The cops hated that.

Officers with kids of their own hated standing here at night inside this bright-lit Laundromat, listening to the child's young mother as she sat sobbing in a molded orange plastic chair. Even if they were childless, they hated it because — unlike the drug dealers, wife beaters, drunk drivers, and other skels who comprised the greater part of the victim pool — this kid was an innocent. And they hated the fact that the shooting robbed them of their most potent weapon against the death they faced every day: their ability to joke. Dark humor could be discovered in the grisliest of adult crime scenes, but not even the most hardened wisecracker could find anything funny about a dead kid.

Several uniforms stood out in front of the Laundromat, making sure that the onlookers, residents of the housing project across the street, stayed behind the cordon. Normally the homeboys in the crowd would have been busy eye-fucking the police, but even they were subdued by the sight of the small corpse visible through the window.

Jack stood just inside the door, taking in the crime scene. After almost a week on the Berrios case he was still free to pursue it, but he'd been put back in the task force catching rotation, and this was his new case.

On a normal evening, the scene inside would have been loud, like a men's club, with groups of detectives standing around chatting amiably above the corpse, but the grave murmur of voices tonight was broken only by the occasional squawk of a walkie and the loud *tichit!* and FLASH of the Crime Scene photographer's camera. The room bustled with men in varied attire: uniformed patrol cops, detectives in suits, undercovers in jeans and sweatshirts, the ME's boys in pale blue scrubs. In the middle of the narrow fluorescent-bright room, a Crime Scene detective knelt to set numbered yellow stands next to bullet casings on the floor. Another detective stooped over a measuring tape, calling off the casings' distances from the small body, which lay under one of the Laundromat's folding tables.

In a back corner, the kid's mother sat clutching a pile of clean socks to her chest as if it were a doll; she was sinking into deep shock. Jack recognized Marty Lutz from the Seven-oh, a bullnecked, crew-cut detective, gently trying to extract a statement.

Anselmo Alvarez stood watch over the corpse. The Crime Scene chief shook his head gravely as Jack approached. Below the table, little basketball sneakers stuck out from under a white sheet. A red pool seeped out from the side onto the blue linoleum. Alvarez pulled back the sheet: the vic was approximately seven years old, male, black. A bullet wound gaped purple in his gaunt little chest. White soap grains dusted his close-cropped hair.

The detectives looked down in silence. What could you say?

Lutz flipped his steno pad closed and left the mother to her grief. He came over.

"Ay, Leightner, how's it goin'?"

"What's the story?"

Lutz ran a hand over his flat hair. "From what we've been able to put together, this all started because of a broken dryer in the basement of the projects over there. A black male resident comes over here to finish his laundry. The place is full, so he takes somebody else's clothes out of a machine." Lutz pointed to where a Crime Scene detective wearing an air-filter mask was brushing print powder over the front of a dryer. "A white male comes in, 'Hey, why're you taking my clothes out when they're still wet?' They talk some shit. The white guy leaves, but five minutes later he comes back with a *nine* and pops off a few rounds. The kid was in the way."

The case sounded like a grounder: there'd been several witnesses to the shooting, and two of them even knew where the perp lived.

Lutz glanced around. "The Crime Scene guys are going nuts because there's a round unaccounted for, but they'll find it." The number of bullets had to match the number of casings.

One of the uniforms at the door came over and tapped Lutz on the shoulder. "Excuse me, sir. You've got a call."

The detective trotted off.

A minute later, he returned, smiling grimly. "We got the bastard. Another criminal genius—he went straight to his mother's apartment, in his own fucking building. Some uniforms picked him up."

Lutz stepped away to spread the good news. A muted cheer went up in the room. Alvarez bent over the little corpse.

Jack drifted out of the Laundromat. He stopped to talk to one of the uniforms. "I'm Jack Leightner with Brooklyn South Homicide. Do me a favor: if Detective Lutz comes looking for me, tell him I'll meet him down at the Seven-oh in a little while."

Below the concrete seawall, waves sloshed gently against the shore. It was cooler here because of the wind off the water. Out on the dark bay, the Statue of Liberty raised her torch and, beyond that, tiny orange lights twinkled on the Staten Island and Jersey shores. The Garden Pier was a tiny park, a patch of concrete down at the end of Conover Street, just beyond a city auto pound and a vast abandoned warehouse. In the dark, Jack could just make out the huge faded white letters on the side: Red Hook Stores.

He sat on a wooden bench inhaling the briny air. Tonight the Hook didn't tighten his chest. Tonight it was home. Out on the water, distant buoys rang gently, soothing. Far to the south, the light-beaded cables of the Verrazano Bridge swooped across to Staten Island. The park was a good place to clear your head of bad pictures.

Even if there wasn't a heaven, he thought, God ought to make one for the little kids.

When he himself was growing up, he'd spent a lot of time down here. There were no official parks back then. You clambered out onto the rocky coastline, or snuck out onto one of the company docks.

The White Rock soda factory was just around the bend. The workers were all locals, and when the bosses weren't looking they'd hand out free cases to family and friends. Every household on these streets had as much soda as they could drink. Jack and his buddies tied rope around the cases and lowered them into the bay to cool.

Soda wasn't the only thing that magically made its way from the waterfront into the streets. In the days when the docks were crazy-busy, before security cameras and computerized inventories, crates disappeared so regularly from shipments it was like a neighborhood toll. There was a trade in evaporated goods. Why take the bus to the stores downtown when you could buy a toaster or a bottle of booze from the back of someone's car for a fraction of the price? One legendary time, part of a clothing shipment disappeared off a dock—suddenly it seemed like every man in the neighborhood had happened to buy the same brown suit.

Out on the bay, the Staten Island ferry slid past like a glowing apartment building. A couple of seagulls appeared overhead, pieces of paper tugged by the wind; they planed off, cawing, and disappeared into the night.

The good old days. It was easy to see them through rosy glasses of nostalgia, but Jack knew better. Yes, there was sometimes trouble in the projects now, but when he was a kid crime had flourished like barnacles on the piers, the Mob working hand in hand with the longshoremen's union to loot and pillage the incoming shipments, to control who worked and who didn't, who fed their families and who starved. When he was a boy, the top mobster had been Albert Anastasia of Murder Inc., also known as "Big Al" and "The Mad Hatter." Neighborhood kids used to scare each other whispering about his chief enforcer, the notorious pipe-wielding Totto Mack, nicknamed "Totto" for Salvatore and "Mack" because he was almost as big as one of the trucks shouldering down to the docks.

In 1957, Anastasia was whacked by Larry and Joey Gallo while he sat in a barber's chair in Manhattan's Park Sheraton Hotel. After that, Jack saw members of the Gallo gang standing around on Hook corners in their dark wool coats, porkpie hats, pointy black shoes. "If I ever see you talking to those bums," his father told him, "you'll never leave this house again."

Some things got better. Just a few yards away from where

117

Jack sat now, a giant concrete pipe had once opened out onto the bay. Back then, before anybody called themselves an environmentalist, the neighborhood's raw sewage funneled directly into the water. On a hot summer day that didn't stop kids from jumping in.

His brother Petey, two years younger, liked to joke around a lot. Acting as if he'd been shot by Al Capone (Red Hook's most famous criminal son), he'd hold his side and fall into the water . . .

Nobody could figure out why Jack and his brother were so different. Jack didn't like to swim — he wasn't very good at it — but Petey had been a champ. He'd won a trophy for it over at the Bay Street pool. Not to mention his prowess at baseball. Adults in the neighborhood used to stop him on the street all the time, tell him how much they enjoyed watching his games. The kid was blessed. A natural athlete, handsome, always grinning. Even the old man rarely raised his hand against him. Everybody loved Petey.

Jack sighed and rubbed the heels of his hands against his eyes, pushing away the memories of his brother. Over thirty-five years he'd become very adept at that.

He stood up and looked at his watch. Detective Lutz was probably wondering where the hell he was.

Which was only a couple of blocks away from 7 Coffey Street.

After almost a week's work, he had no idea why Tomas Berrios had been killed, or even where. He had a corpse, and a possible witness in the barge captain, but not a shadow of a suspect. If he wrote the case off now, nobody but the guy's family would particularly care, though Sergeant Tanney wouldn't be thrilled to see another Unsolved added to the year's stats.

Blocks away, a dog barked. It was eerie how sound traveled in the neighborhood, each shout or car horn as distinct as an object in the desert.

Jack took one more deep breath of the ocean air. He'd go check in with Lutz, punch out, and then ... What? He was not far from Sheila's apartment, but surely it was better to be alone than to put up with her bitterness. Bad sex wasn't necessarily better than no sex at all.

Here he was, half a century old — shouldn't he have figured life out a little better by now?

One afternoon, after Ben was born, he and his wife had taken the baby on a walk through Prospect Park. They crossed a stone bridge over a lily-pad-covered lake. It was autumn and brilliant red and yellow leaves were falling on the water, perfect as a calendar picture. He looked at his young wife and little Ben burbling away in the stroller and it struck him that they were a family. After all the doubts and worries of the pregnancy, suddenly he was completely happy and sure that he'd made the right choices.

Now he was going to go home and drink a beer and watch TV by himself.

How had he screwed it all up?

"Where d'you go?" Lutz asked when they met back at the Seven-oh.

"I had to make some calls. How's the case?"

"Couldn't be better."

"You got good witnesses?"

"Are you kidding? I should start a glee club — I've never seen so many *yo*s willing to sing in my life. For once they had a chance to stick it to a white guy. You wanna talk to the perp?"

"No, thanks. I'm gonna call it a night."

119

• • •

On the way back to Midwood, his beeper went off. He pulled over in front of a deli and checked the number: Gary Daskivitch.

The young detective picked up on the first ring. "That you, Jack?" He sounded excited — it must be a good break.

"What's up?"

"You doing anything tomorrow night?"

"No, I'm off. Why?"

"I talked to Jeannie."

"Who?"

"My wife. Remember what we were talking about? She's got someone for you, and she's free tomorrow."

Jack scratched his ear. "Tomorrow? What are you talking about?"

"I talked you up to Jeannie; Jeannie talked you up to her friend. Bing — she wants to go out with you."

"Listen, kid — I appreciate the effort . . ." He was about to tell the younger detective to mind his own business, that he was a grown man and perfectly capable of getting his own dates — but he realized that wasn't true. Aside from Sheila, who didn't quite count, he hadn't been on a "date" for many months.

He watched a teenage couple smooching on the corner outside the deli, kissing as if they were each other's only source of air.

"Gary," he said. "The truth is, I'm just too old for this stuff."

"Too old! Jack, listen — I've seen this woman. If you say no, you're making a big mistake."

fifteen

Since he'd just taken his turn in the rotation, Jack was able to spend the next day in the squad room catching up with paperwork and worrying about how he'd somehow agreed to a blind date.

It was Saturday. When he was young he'd looked forward to the weekends. Now they were just busy shifts for the Homicide Squad, an excuse for mutts and businessmen alike to pop each other in bars, run each other off the roads, stagger home and put a premature end to their marriages.

After work, he took a shower, then wasted ten minutes trying on one shirt after another. Too formal; too casual; unflattering color. Jesus, a *blind date*.

He looked at his watch. Five twenty-five. He wasn't meeting the woman — Michelle Wilber was her name — until seven. He changed shirts again.

He drove, as instructed, to the western edge of Prospect Park. A row of ornate Victorian mansions faced a line of grand old Brooklyn sycamores, which bowed in the breeze like dancers at a ball.

Fifteen minutes early.

He parked and stood in front of a bronze monument dedicated to the Marquis de Lafayette. A little boy had climbed up the base of the statue and was earnestly trying to break off the tip of the marquis's sword. If Jack thought the kid had any chance of succeeding he would have ordered him to stop, but he was already conscious enough about looking like a cop. He'd tried to dress casually, but as he scanned the crowds drifting in and out of the park, he noticed that he was the only man wearing a sports jacket.

Along the edge of the park, clusters of black working-class families enjoyed elaborate barbecues — they wore baggy shorts, basketball jerseys, bright T-shirts. The air thumped with competing boomboxes. At the entrance, a mostly white contingent from Park Slope funneled in for the concert — they wore straw summer hats, linen pants, and fancy sandals; carried expensive picnic hampers. They walked as if they believed themselves terribly important.

As the few single women approached, he searched for Michelle's identifying red shoulder bag. *Is that her?* he wondered. *I would be glad if this was her . . . I hope that's not her . . .*

He glanced at his watch again, seized by an urge to bolt, go home and crack a beer, maybe watch a little TV with Mr. Gardner.

A uniform emerged from a squad car to shift the wooden barrier blocking the entrance to the park. Jack remembered a case he'd once worked inside there. The victim was a stockbroker who lived in a nearby brownstone. Because a few ritual *santería* objects had been found under a nearby tree, a rumor soon spread that the broker had been the victim of a voodoo cult. (Later, it turned out he'd simply been jumped by a couple of kids who wanted his deluxe mountain bike.) The press had gone crazy, and not just because of the voodoo angle: any time a Wall Streeter was killed, it hit the papers big.

Jack turned to watch a little boy run shouting after a

radio-controlled toy car as it scooted along the sidewalk. When he turned back, a woman with a red bag was walking toward him.

She wore jeans and a white buttoned blouse and she had slightly frizzy long black hair and long legs and a nice body and she looked far more at ease than he felt and much better than he'd expected. He'd been picturing someone homely, somebody who couldn't get a date on her own—which was, of course, unfair, coming from him—and he'd steeled himself for an evening of small talk and faked interest. She was—as he'd made Daskivitch find out—in her early forties.

He imagined his partner winking, giving him a wicked I-don't-hear-you-complaining-now grin.

"Jack Leightner?" she said.

"How did you know?" His self-description over the phone—"medium height, brown hair . . ."—had been so vague it could fit half the men in the city.

"I got Jeannie to make her husband describe you," she admitted with an embarrassed grin. "I wasn't going to go out with just *any* guy, you know."

"I hope I'm not a letdown, then."

She grinned wider. "Not at all."

They strolled into the park and found the bandshell and bought some dinner at a food stall. At another stall they found some delicious fresh-brewed Brooklyn beer. They made small talk about the park, and the weather, and how he'd met Daskivitch, and how she knew Jeannie, and she didn't rush to grill him about what it was like to be a homicide detective, for which he was grateful.

There was the usual awkward moment when she asked if he had any brothers and sisters. "No," he said, which was true, technically.

He narrowed his eyes and sipped his beer.

When they got around to discussing his job, Michelle didn't ask the usual first questions. (Does it gross you out seeing dead bodies? Have you ever shot anybody? Do you watch *NYPD Blue*?)

They were sitting on a grassy hill overlooking the stage. On their laps they balanced Styrofoam plates heaped with fried chicken and collard greens and candied yams. The audience wandered in, a crazy-quilt assortment of New Yorkers: a group of Rastas with big knit caps; a tall Japanese woman in a miniskirt, perched on Rollerblades; two Indian men in khaki shorts and polo shirts . . . A trio of uniformed cops leaned over a metal crowd barrier, relaxed as hell, enjoying their plum assignment. Down on the stage, roadies scurried around adjusting microphones and drum stands, which glinted under the bright floodlights.

Michelle turned and asked, simply, "Does your job make you sad?"

He was about to tell her that you got used to it, that detectives were professionals and they didn't get emotionally involved, that you had to look at the bodies objectively, scientifically — but he stopped himself.

"Sometimes."

Overhead, up in the trees, cicadas whirred like 1950s movie spaceships.

"Do you like your work?" she asked. "I mean, *can* you like it?"

"Sure," he said. "It's a people job."

She laughed, then covered her mouth. "I'm sorry. It's just that, they're *dead* people."

"That's just the beginning. We have to deal with the crime scene, where there's all sorts of people I work with: other detectives, the technicians, the medical people . . . After that, it's about a network of people. You figure out who lives around the victims: their friends, their enemies, their loved ones . . . You talk to them—that's a big part of it."

"It sounds fascinating."

"Every now and then. Mostly, it's a lot of boring details."

Down below, the seating area was filled rapidly. "Do you want to find some seats?" she asked.

"Not really. I like it here, with the trees and all." He pulled back a piece of crispy chicken skin. "What about *your* job?"

She tucked her hair behind her ear. "I work for a company that rents out equipment for parties."

"Equipment?"

"Glasses, plates, chairs . . . that sort of thing. It's not very exciting, compared to your job. Although . . ."

"What?"

She grinned. "We had a client last month, this Wall Street guy, a multimillionaire who was throwing himself a fortieth-birthday party. It was great for us: he ordered everything top of the line, the finest plates, silverware, linens . . . The party must have cost hundreds of thousands of dollars. But the guy was a nightmare to deal with, rude, arrogant, really unpleasant. The party was in a ballroom, with two hundred stockbrokers in black tie and their wives in designer dresses. At the end of the dinner, he wanted a line of waiters to march in carrying flaming desserts."

"What happened?"

"Well, they lit the desserts and the waiters all tromped in—and it set off the sprinkler system all over the room."

Jack grinned. Like all cops, he relished a good story and he admired Michelle's economy. If his ex-wife had told it, she would have described each plate, each piece of silverware, the color of the napkins—it would have taken three hours to get to the climax. "Sounds like your job's kind of exciting, after all."

· · ·

He got up and threw their plates into a heaping garbage can.

Michelle rubbed her hands together. "As long as you're up, would you mind getting some napkins?"

"Here." Jack reached into his jacket pocket and pulled out a couple of hand-wipe packets.

"Do you always carry those around?"

Jack nodded sheepishly. "It's not that I'm a neat freak, or anything . . . The job can get kind of messy."

She wrinkled her nose. "Yikes."

"Let's talk about something else."

Michelle twisted a silver ring on her little finger. "Jeannie tells me you were married."

"Boy, she really gave you the full report, huh?" Jack picked up a twig and bent it, testing to see when it would snap. "I got divorced fifteen years ago."

"And you never remarried?"

"Nope."

"Why not?"

He shrugged. "I guess I've been busy with work." He looked at Michelle. "Have you been married?"

"Yes. My husband died."

"I'm sorry." Jack pulled out a pack of cigarettes.

"Don't be sorry," she said. "I knew he was ill when I married him. He had emphysema."

Jack winced. "You don't probably don't want one of these, then?"

Michelle shook her head.

He put the cigarettes back in his pocket. "You knew he was dying when you married him?"

"I didn't know it would happen so soon."

He considered this, wondering what kind of woman would make such a brave — or foolhardy — move.

"Why did you get divorced?" she said. "If you don't mind my asking . . ."

Where to begin? The early days when he and Louise made love every night or morning; the nights when he began to notice that she wasn't quite returning his kisses; her complaints about his overwork, his lack of involvement with their child; the arguments about money; the times she pushed him away; the mornings he noticed they no longer made love in the mornings; the nights when he lay next to her unable to sleep, rigid with anger, desire, frustration, hurt. He'd blamed her, called her cold, but some deep nights he lay awake wondering what was wrong with *him*, why he couldn't seem to be the husband or father he should have been . . .

"It's kind of complicated," he said. He opened his towelette and wiped his hands. "I guess we just grew apart."

The treeline grew dark, but the sky flared with the last evening light. The band filed out onto the stage. They plucked a few strings, adjusted some levels — and suddenly they took off like a horse bolting from a gate, one guy sawing away at a fiddle, another squeezing the hell out of an accordion, a guy up on a riser slapping a piano, the ponytailed drummer hunched over his kit, flying . . .

"What *is* this?" Jack shouted over the music.

"It's called *zydeco*," Michelle shouted back. "From New Orleans."

"What's that guy scratching?"

"It's a washboard. He's got thimbles on his fingertips."

The seating area turned into a sea of standing, bobbing people. Jack glanced over his shoulder: all around them, under the trees, couples danced.

"Do you dance?" Michelle shouted.

"Not really," he said, but that didn't stop her from pulling him to his feet. He twirled her away, pulled her back, spun her around. Grinned like a fool.

Later, after the music was over, she found her shoes on the grass and he picked up his sports jacket and folded it over his arm. They slipped into a horde of people streaming toward the exit.

He was stunned by the novelty of being out on a Saturday night, of walking through a crowd with someone at his side, keeping an eye out to make sure she was close.

She sat in her car. He stood outside, leaning over with one arm against the roof. "I had a really good time tonight."

She smiled. "Me too."

"I have to admit, I wasn't really expecting to." He caught her expression and hastened to add, "Nothing personal, you know. It's just . . . the whole *blind date* thing . . ."

She nodded.

He looked down at his watch. "It's getting late. Uh, thanks for coming out."

"Thanks for dinner." She slipped her key into the ignition.

Jack straightened up and put his hand on the back of his neck. "Listen, do you think you might like to get together again? I could have a barbecue at my place, invite Gary and his wife over . . ."

"That sounds fun."

"Okay," he said. "All right. Maybe, uh . . . Tuesday night?"

She started her car. "Call me."

He bent down and leaned in through the window for a kiss that lasted just a moment longer than he'd expected.

She started the car and pulled away from the curb. He stood, grinning, and watched her drive away.

sixteen

As Jack approached the entrance of the Bentley again, a group of teenagers streamed past him into the building, jostling and shouting. It was three-thirty; they must have just gotten out of school. The boys wore blazers with a crest over the pocket and the girls wore plaid skirts. They were awkward with the afflictions of adolescence: braces, acne, bodies expanding in odd proportions. Some of the girls had a precocious fashion sense, with expensive shoes and sexy makeup that looked sad on their little faces, but they still seemed *soft*. The neighborhood was a bubble: they wouldn't have to worry about getting jumped on these streets, or wonder if their parents could keep up with the rent, or face the humiliation of going to school in shabby clothes, as he had. One day soon, they'd inherit the world.

If he could feel intimidated by this glitzy building, and its snotty doorman—and he was a middle-aged man with a respectable job and all of the authority of the New York Police Department behind him—what must it have been like for a young Dominican guy coming here every day from an overcrowded little Brooklyn row house? If he could feel resentful of the privileged young kids, what had Tomas Berrios felt when he knew that his own kids would have to go to some overcrowded

Brooklyn public school, a place where even elementary-school kids had to worry about boxcutters and Mac-9s?

It might cause a young man some unhappiness.

Jack usually enjoyed trying to verbally intimidate and out-wit the bad guys, but he didn't relish bringing that pressure to bear on a working stiff, especially when the man was already as hard-pressed as Arturo Guzman. While shower-ing that morning, he'd rerun his interview with the super in his head, remembered small evasions, possible tells.

The super sat now with his hands gripping his knees, looking down at the floor.

Jack leaned forward. "I'll say it again. When I left here the last time, you weren't being a hundred percent with me. Now we can have this discussion in a little room down at the Seventy-sixth Precinct in Brooklyn and you can lose a day of work, or you can help me out right here."

"What do *I* know?" the super said miserably. "What can I tell you?"

"Well, that's the question, isn't it?"

"If I knew something, some *thing* Tomas had done, or some trouble he was in, I would tell you."

"All right. Maybe it's not some big thing. Maybe it doesn't seem very important. But I know you're holding back." The key was to give the super a way to spill that would allow him to believe he was doing the right and necessary thing. Even murderers could be encouraged to talk if you helped them rationalize their confessions: *You didn't mean to kill him, right? He jumped forward, and you happened to be holding a gun, was that it?*

"I don't know nothing," repeated Mr. Guzman.

Disliking himself for doing so, Jack pressed on. "I don't want to, but I could go to your management company and say that you're refusing to cooperate with a police investigation . . ."

"It's not important," the super said in a small voice.

"*What's* not important?"

"You asked me if he was especial friends with anyone here."

"That's right. And?"

"There is somebody."

Marie Burhala's hands trembled, but when she saw that Jack had noticed, she tucked them under her thighs. The Romanian maid was a small young woman with a long braid of shimmering chestnut hair. A purple birthmark ran along one cheek, but somehow that flaw only accented her shy beauty. Jack had not given her any notice to prepare for the interview — she wore flip-flops, gray sweatpants, a purple T-shirt. Her gaze kept darting from him to the super, who sat glumly in the corner.

Jack hoped she'd provide a good lead, but he wasn't ready to jump to the conclusion that her nerves were any indication of involvement in the Tomas Berrios case. If he was from a former Communist-bloc country and had been brought down to a grim basement room and confronted with a police detective, he supposed he'd be nervous too.

"You work as a maid here?" he asked.

"Yes. For Mr. Heiser." Her Romanian accent was thick, but she seemed to speak English pretty well.

"What floor?"

"Fourteenth," the super said.

Jack gave him a sharp look. "Thank you, but let's let Ms. Burhala answer."

"The fourteenth floor," she said, reaching back to tug on her braid.

"How long have you worked for Mr. Heiser?"

"Almost one year," she said, sending a scared look to the super.

"How long have you been in this country?"

"Almost one year and a half."

"How much does Mr. Heiser pay you?"

She mumbled something.

"I couldn't hear you."

"Two hundred dollars every week."

"For how many days a week?"

"Every day except Sunday."

Jack did a quick computation. If she worked fifty or sixty hours a week, which seemed likely, considering that she lived in, she was making maybe four dollars an hour. Less than minimum wage. Why would she do that? He saw his advantage.

"You married?"

She shook her head, a pained expression on her pretty face.

"Green card?"

She crumpled. "Please. I do very good work for Mr. Heiser. I never make any problem." She started to cry. "I can't go back. I have to make money for my family. Please, mister. *Please*."

Jack leaned back, satisfied with himself. He didn't need a vacation; his recent lapses were just a fluke. He was still one of the best detectives around, sharp as a freakin' tack.

He leaned forward. "Listen, Marie, I don't work for the Immigration Service. I'm not here to check up on your papers. I'll tell you what: if you help me with some other questions, I'm going to pretend I never asked about the green card. You understand me?"

She stared at him in disbelief. He handed her his handkerchief and she wiped her eyes.

"Do you understand?" he repeated. She nodded carefully.

"Did you know Tomas Berrios?"

She turned toward the super, as if hoping that he might be able to explain the sudden shift in the conversation.

"Look at me," Jack said. "Did you know him?"

She nodded, mesmerized.

"Were you friends with Mr. Berrios?"

She nodded again.

"Would you say that you were good friends with him?"

She turned toward the super. "Just look at me," Jack said. "Would you say that you were more than good friends?"

"I . . . he had a wife, children."

"I know that. Tell me the truth: did you have a sexual relationship with Mr. Berrios?"

"No!" she cried. "Never. I'm not . . . it wasn't like that."

Jack sat back in his chair and ran a hand over his mouth. He was getting somewhere. He wasn't sure where, but progress was being made.

"What did you do?" he asked softly.

"He was very nice. We would talk, that's all. On my mother, I swear it."

"Where would you talk?"

She glanced guiltily at the super. "Tomas would come in sometimes."

"To Mr. Heiser's apartment?"

She nodded. "If no one was at home. Sometimes I would give him something to eat. Sometimes . . ." She stopped as if concealing some shameful secret.

"Yes?" Jack said eagerly. "Sometimes *what*?"

Marie Burhala turned away from the super. "Sometimes we watched *The Jerry Springer Show* on the TV."

Jack stifled an impulse to laugh.

Now he had another image to add to his mental movie: Tomas Berrios entering a fourteenth-floor apartment through the back door. He considered his next question. If the porter and the maid had been having an affair, if she'd been angry because he wouldn't leave his wife . . . He doubted that this small, shy woman could have stabbed Berrios to death, and even if she had, that didn't explain the two men dumping the body in Brooklyn. He wondered if Romanians were like Albanians, nursing vicious family feuds.

"Do you have any family in New York?" he asked. "Any brothers?"

"No. No one. I have only a sister. She lives with my mother in Brasov. In my country."

"Do you have many friends here?"

She shook her head sadly.

Mr. Guzman shifted in his chair. "It's true, mister. She never goes out. Even on Sunday, she only shops around here. It's no good for a young person, to live like this."

"How old are you, Marie?"

"I am nineteen."

Jesus. A nineteen-year-old kid, practically on her own in a foreign country, working for some rich stranger. She'd have to be pretty plucky. He felt sorry for her, trapped in such a job when she should be out having fun with other young people. He felt sorry, but he'd come for information.

"Did you ever have an argument with Tomas? A fight, maybe?"

She shook her head firmly. "Never. He was my friend."

"How did he get in the apartment?"

Marie looked confused. "I let him in."

"Personally? You were always there to let him in?"

She thought about that. "Sometimes . . . sometimes if I was busy in the house, I left open the back door."

"Did he ever come in when you weren't home?"

She looked puzzled. "How would I know?"

Good point. He tried another angle.

"Did Mr. Heiser ever see Tomas in the apartment with you?"

The young woman tugged her braid.

"Marie?"

She winced. "Mr. Heiser was coming home early one day, and Tomas was in the living room with me. We were watching the TV."

"When was this?"

"It was . . . I think perhaps three weeks."

"Did Mr. Heiser say something to Tomas?"

"He is not easy man to get along with. He —"

"Did he say something?"

"He told Tomas it was not *app . . . app . . .*"

" 'Appropriate?' "

"Yes. He told Tomas that he must never enter the apartment unless he is working, that he should know his place."

"Did Mr. Heiser sound angry? Was he heated up about Tomas being there?"

"No, not heated up. He was . . . *cold*. Like is not worth his time to explain such things."

"What did Tomas do?"

" 'Do?' What can he do?"

"Did he say anything?"

"Mr., he is a servant here. He cannot say something. He went out."

"Was he angry? Did he say anything to you later?"

"He said he does not like it when Mr. Heiser speak to him like a child. Then he — how you say?" She raised her shoulders.

"He shrugged?"

"Yes. Shrugged. After all, Mr. Heiser is not only tenant who speaks to staff like children."

"Did Tomas mention it again?"

"No — only to say he was sorry he cannot visit me."

Jack stood up. "I think that'll do it for now. Thank you for your cooperation."

seventeen

The next afternoon, as Jack drove along broad, tree-lined Ocean Parkway, where Orthodox Jewish parents walked their neatly dressed kids home from school, he turned on the radio. An oldies station was playing the Drifters. The horns swelled and Ben E. King swelled with them: *This magic moment* . . . The afternoon light glowed, cool air flowed in the open window, and somehow the corny sentiment seemed to point to something real. Of course, he acknowledged with a grin, that might have something to do with the calls he'd made last night to Daskivitch and his wife, and to Michelle, inviting them to his barbecue. Now he had a night to remember, and one to look forward to.

At task force headquarters, he jogged in, made a Groucho face at Mary Gaffney as he passed the front desk.

"Someone's in a good mood today," she said.

He grinned, tapped an imaginary cigar, and trotted upstairs. He spent several hours plodding through paperwork, then took a break to go downstairs and chat with the desk cops.

He had just come back up and was headed for the supply room and a cup of coffee when Vince Grasso, one of the other detectives on the squad, looked up from his desk.

"Jackie L.—you got a phone call a couple minutes ago."

"From who?"

"Gary Daskivitch over at the Seven-six."

"Is he there now?"

"Nah. He left a message, though. Said it was urgent."

Grasso looked down, gave his big walrus mustache a tug. "Hold on a sec, my desk is such a fucking mess . . . I wrote it down somewhere . . . Here." He held up a pink message slip. "He wants you to meet him right away at this address."

Jack gripped the steering wheel so hard his fingernails dug into his palms. He sped along the Shore Parkway, which afforded spectacular views of the sunset over the bay and the Verrazano Bridge. He ignored the scenery. The parkway turned into the Gowanus Expressway, marching on monster stilts over Third Avenue, into Sunset Park.

The yard was full of squad cars, unmarked cruisers, and Crime Scene vehicles. An unseen dog howled as Jack climbed the exterior staircase to the third story, where faded aquamarine curtains hung in the windows.

The screen door had been sliced open and the lock was popped. Jack badged the uniform out front, entered the little vestibule, walked on into the low-ceilinged living room. The room was airless and humid—the windows were all closed. It still smelled of mothballs and mildewed rug, but over those scents pressed the sweet metallic odor of blood. A Crime Scene detective crouched by a red streak on the musty shag carpet to clip a sample, which he dropped into a plastic envelope. A photographer stood in the corner next to a big old TV, shooting down at the top of it, where a square of the surface was free of dust. "Looks like a VCR's missing here."

In the corner, another tech dusted a china cabinet filled

with a series of presidential plates. The doors were open and the shelves inside in disarray. Jack picked up two broken halves of a plate and put them together to form Richard Nixon's jowly face. (What a strange and terrible thing: to be admired and respected as the president of the United States, then fall so low and be reviled.)

He glanced up at the ceiling and his heart froze: the stucco held a spray of little red dots he recognized as castoff, the splatter pattern made when a perp yanked a weapon back in preparation for another blow. Or stab.

He followed a trail of bloodstains across the carpet toward the back of the apartment. Halfway across the room, a partial shoeprint marred the edge of a sticky pool of blood.

"Did you guys get this?" he asked the nearest Crime Scene tech.

"You bet. I'll bring in a saw to take up that carpet and get it to the lab."

Jack took a deep breath, then continued on toward the kitchen.

He stood in the entry; the first thing he noticed was a wide blood smear on the inside of the back door. He moved in past the kitchen table, to a point where he could see the bottom of the stain, which led down to the corpse of Raymond Ortslee. The barge captain knelt against the bottom of the door, as if he had toppled forward while searching for a mouse hole — or praying. He wore only boxer shorts and a T-shirt with yellow sweat stains under the armpits; he'd probably been home alone at the time of the attack. The side of his right wrist bore two deep red slashes: defensive wounds he'd sustained while raising an arm in a useless attempt to protect his body from a knife. Red streaks ran down the bottom half of the door; they marked where his grasping fingers had fallen short of the knob.

Jack flashed on a *World Book* picture he'd been fascinated by as a kid: it showed the ashen mold of an ancient Roman trapped in the volcanic eruption at Pompeii, his body curled in a fetal position as he raised feeble hands against the death raining down from above.

Gary Daskivitch knelt next to the body, his necktie flung over one shoulder to keep it clear of the blood. As Jack moved close, his partner glanced up, then wordlessly pulled back the T-shirt to reveal another nasty stab mouth under the man's protruding ribs.

Jack went clammy. He forced himself to draw several deep breaths, then took out a handkerchief and wiped off the sweat beading his forehead.

Daskivitch looked up. "You all right?"

"How did you know he was here?" Jack said grimly. There was no routine reason why a Seven-six detective would be immediately informed of a murder in the Seven-two.

"The Crime Scene guys found my card on the body. It was in his fucking shoe."

Jack turned away from the body. The techs had left their sooty print dust on the door, the rusting stove, the cabinets . . .

Daskivitch tugged nervously at his tie. "That Berrios murder was no amateur job. These people figured out how to track this guy down."

"Speaking of which —"

"I know. We need to check with whoever's in charge of the canal to see if they got any strange calls. I think it's the DOT."

A big droopy-eyed black man in a sharp double-breasted suit came through the door. Ed Colby, from the Seventy-second Precinct. Jack had met the detective before, when they were both working Robbery.

"Nice of you to drop in," the detective said. His left eye twitched, an involuntary tic. The other cops at the Seven-two had taken to calling him Detective Winks.

"This your case?" Jack asked.

"Yes, it is. You rookies screwing up my crime scene?"

"We'll get out of your way."

Colby hitched up his pants. "Way I see it, the vic's in bed, the perp comes in through the front door there, starts searching around. Vic wakes up, comes out, confronts the perp in the living room." Colby pointed to the front of the house; his eye twitched. "Perp assaults him there—that's probably where he gets the defense wounds, vic goes for the back door and the fire escape, doesn't make it. The drawers in the bedroom are open; some stuff looks like it's missing in there." He pointed to the living room. "I think we got a B and E gone bad."

"Robbery, huh?" Jack rubbed the back of his neck and exchanged a look with Daskivitch.

"Yeah. We found his pants upstairs. The pockets are turned out, wallet's gone . . . what? What do you guys know?"

"Let's get some air," Daskivitch told the detective. "I'll fill you in."

Jack stayed in the kitchen, staring down at the barge captain's abused body. A wave of nausea swept over him. He leaned against a counter and pressed a hand to his stomach. He squeezed his eyes shut, willing the queasiness to disappear.

Be professional, he told himself. Look at the whole picture. Find the evidence. He took another look at Ortslee curled up by the door and then—he couldn't help it—he knelt down and lifted the little man up.

Daskivitch walked through the door. "Did I leave my—?" He stopped in shock. "Jesus Christ—what are you doing!"

Jack looked down at the frail body in his arms. "I don't know," he said weakly.

Daskivitch turned to see if anyone was behind him. "Jack, you gotta put him down."

Groggy, he complied.

"*Fuck,*" Daskivitch muttered. He wet some paper towels and wiped the blood off Jack's hands. "Come on," he said, and tugged Jack's arm to lead him out the back door onto the fire escape.

Jack sank down in the corner. The iron rails pressed into his back. He breathed deep of the night air, trying to free his nostrils of the scent of blood. Above the door, some sort of strange flying beetle was zittering around a bare light bulb. Down below, across a shadowy asphalt lot, a couple of cops leaned against a squad car, shooting the shit and laughing.

Daskivitch paced back and forth, rubbing his chin. "Jesus, guy, what the hell were you thinking?"

Jack didn't answer.

Daskivitch crouched down. "What is it with this one, Jack? Why is this case different for you?"

Jack considered the question as if he were staring at a foreign object. "I don't know."

"You don't know, or you won't say?"

Jack sat silent for a moment, then raised his head. "We killed the barge guy, Gary. *I* killed him."

"What!"

"I laughed at him. I ordered him to stay put."

Daskivitch turned to look down into the lot. "Maybe . . . maybe Colby was right. Maybe this was just a bad B and E. A fluke, you know? A coincidence."

Jack snorted. "How many burglars go around carrying knives?"

"Maybe he found it in the kitchen."

"Come on, Gary. It was the same goddamn perp."

Daskivitch sighed and scratched the back of his head. "Maybe we screwed up. But it's like my first partner on patrol taught me. You learn from it, then let it go. Right?"

Above the door, the beetle kept smacking its head against the light. Jack smiled bitterly. "Let it go. Sure."

"You gonna be okay?"

Jack shrugged.

His partner stood up. "All right. You better not go back in there. Why don't you head down this back way? I'll go inside and tell Colby you got an emergency call."

eighteen

Jack jolted awake in the middle of the night. His heart was palpitating, constricted, and he was panting. He didn't know if he was having his first asthma attack since boyhood, or his first heart attack. He pushed himself up to a sitting position and clutched the sheets, willing his breath to slow.

After a few minutes it did, and the bands across his chest eased.

Shaken, he got out of bed and drank a glass of water. Had he been having a nightmare? He couldn't remember.

He did remember Raymond Ortslee, crouched down by his back door, begging for help. Begging *him* for help.

He turned on the TV and tried to focus on an infomercial for an abdominal exerciser. Then he turned off the TV and lay staring up into the dark.

Daskivitch called in the early afternoon.

"Hey, bunk. Jeannie wanted me to ask what we can bring over."

Jack didn't answer.

"We're still on for this evening, aren't we?"

He looked out his kitchen window. Down in the sunny backyard, his landlord was repairing the leg of a garden table.

"Jack?"

"I don't know," he answered. "I'm not sure I'm up for a party, after what happened the other day."

"You mean Ortslee?"

"That shouldn't have happened."

Daskivitch was silent for a moment. "Well," he said. "There's nothing we can do about it now, right?"

"Yeah, there is. We can catch the bastards who did this."

"I'm with you. But today . . . come on. You need to forget about it for just a few hours. You don't want to bum Michelle out, do you?"

Outside, Mr. Gardner flipped the table over and rocked it to make sure it was steady. He was always puttering around in the yard, pruning the roses or building a barbecue out of spare bricks or painting all of the lawn furniture a light purple that made it look like some kind of modern art. Looking down on him from above, Jack noticed that his white hair had a sea-green tinge in the back. The old man hitched up his pants and stood still for a moment, as if listening to some distant sound.

Suddenly his cat scrabbled up over the chain-link fence and Mr. Gardner snapped out of his daydream. The cat raised its head and let out a tortured yowl. It was in heat, Jack realized. So much for self-sufficiency.

"All right," he said, finally. "Just bring a six-pack or something."

He had less than three hours to clean up and shop before his guests arrived.

He mopped his kitchen floor, cleaned the toilet, polished the bathroom mirror. By the time he got around to scouring the kitchen sink, he was starting to feel better about the evening ahead. When he heard Mr. Gardner clumping up the basement stairs, he impulsively stuck his head out into the hall.

"Hey, listen, Mr. G.—I'm having a couple of friends over for dinner this evening. Why don't you come down and join us?"

The old man hitched up his pants. "Oh, no. Thanks, but I wouldn't wanna be a bother."

"No, really. You can help me with the barbecuing."

That did the trick. Mr. Gardner smiled shyly. "I don't wanna be in the way."

"Come on down in a couple of hours."

Avenue M was the commercial strip that time forgot. There were no supermarkets or chain stores, just family businesses on the ground floor of two-story brick buildings. Outside the markets, old brown and yellow signs in 1950s script: Norwegian Schmaltz Herring Only $1.49 Lb; Homemade Rugalech, Challah, Babkas. Chinese Cuisine—Glatt Kosher. Other signs were in Hebrew, so Jack could only guess what they said. Lotto banners swayed like party decorations in front of newsstands where *Playboy* would never be sold. The avenue still had men's hat stores, for chrissakes.

Outside Goldie's Deli, he listened to the cheery, tinny melody of a five-cent mechanical pony being ridden by a little Hasidic boy. Along the sidewalks came a parade of ancient pensioners, slow-moving, dignified trolls.

He hadn't eaten anything all day. He stopped in to Goldie's for a quick bite, ordered some fries from the Puerto

Rican guy behind the counter. On his right sat a tiny, ancient, bent-over woman in a red designer suit. She launched into her own order. "How much for the french-fried onions? Does the sandwich come with slaw?"

He looked closer at this sparrow's big jewelry and saw that it was fake. Her collar was stained. Despite her natty outfit, she wasn't being stingy about the onion rings: she couldn't afford them.

Mr. Gardner in his empty apartment, this little lady making an afternoon out of her deli lunch—they gave him a chill. He'd seen shootings, decapitations, car crashes, all sorts of quick, violent ways to die. What scared him more was the thought of growing old and infirm alone.

When his sandwich arrived, the woman turned to him and said with a sweet smile, "You're young. I could never eat what you're eating. Enjoy. It's *good* to be young."

They got up to leave at the same time. He stood behind her patiently as she tottered toward the door, moving as if on tiny wheels.

On the way home, guilty thoughts of Raymond Ortslee kept drifting into his head, but he did his best to brush them aside. This was an evening to relax. To get away from work. *Let it go.*

He and Michelle exchanged shy smiles. She wore a short skirt and a blue and white striped T-shirt that showed off her figure. Over her shoulder, Daskivitch winked. Jeannie stuck out her hand. They'd all come together in Daskivitch's car.

He would have expected his partner's wife to be a tall blonde with teased hair and big boobs, but Jeannie was a surprise, a small lively redhead. She said she worked as a fund-raiser for breast cancer research. Jack's respect for his partner went up another notch.

Daskivitch wore Bermuda shorts and a nice polo shirt, but with his athletic socks and hi-top Converse sneakers, he still looked like a giant kid.

Jack led everyone into the backyard. Round slate flagstones made a walkway across the small lawn to Mr. Gardner's new barbecue, where the old man stood squirting lighter fluid on the charcoal. A pair of tongs rested on a side table, which he had constructed by resting a marble slab on two porcelain toilet tanks. Dusky roses trailed up the chainlink fence at the back of the yard.

Jack made the introductions.

"Oh, hey, how ya doin'?" Mr. G. said heartily.

While Michelle complimented him on the roses, Daskivitch turned to Jack. "Hey, did you hear what happened to Billy Kehoe over at the Eight-four?"

"Don't start with the cop talk," Jeannie said. "You promised."

Daskivitch raised his hands in surrender. "You're right. I'll shut up. We're here to relax."

The sky was blue as it could be; the air was dry and cool. Next door, a neighbor's birch tree shimmied in the breeze. Mr. Gardner went inside to his workshop to search out more barbecue implements.

"This is lovely," Jeannie said. "Would you mind if I used your bathroom?"

"I'll go with you," Michelle said.

"Look out," said Daskivitch. "The women are plotting." He watched his wife and her friend go inside. He turned to Jack and bit his lip. "Listen, are you okay? You seemed pretty freaked out the other night."

Jack scratched his nose. "Sorry about that. I guess I've been kind of tired lately."

Embarrassed, Daskivitch looked up at the house. He brightened. "She's nice, huh?"

"Michelle?"

"No. *Mother Teresa.*"

"Yeah, she is. Your wife seems nice too."

"So how'd the big first date go?"

"It was all right." Jack grinned, despite himself.

"You sly doggee."

"It wasn't like that," Jack said. "We had a nice time." He opened a couple of the beers his partner had brought. "Listen, I hate to bring up work, but did you ask anyone at the DOT if someone called looking for Ortslee?"

"I couldn't find anyone over there who remembers anything. You know what it's like, the bureaucracy . . ."

"What about the shoeprint from Ortslee's living room?"

"Crime Scene ran it down. It belonged to some jerkoff EMS guy who answered the first call."

"Shit."

The women returned.

"That's the cleanest bachelor's apartment I've ever seen," Jeannie said.

"How would *you* know?" Daskivitch asked.

Jeannie rolled her eyes and grinned.

While Jack brought out plates and silverware, his landlord kept everybody entertained. Mr. Gardner seemed like a different man. He showed off his fig tree, which he pruned carefully every fall and wrapped tenderly for the winter. He gave a tour of his flower beds — "aside from my name, I'm not really much of a gardener," he joked — held everybody spellbound with an account of his landing on Guadalcanal in World War II, and flirted with Michelle. Jack even felt a twinge of jealousy, until he reminded himself that the man was eighty-six.

They finished Daskivitch's six-pack of Heineken, and then Mr. Gardner went back into the house and came out with a six of Old Milwaukee. Jack brought out a bowl of chips and some onion dip; Mr. Gardner went upstairs and came out with a plate of Velveeta on Ritz.

After they finished the beers, Jack brought out a bottle of California white wine. Mr. Gardner surprised him by bringing out an ancient French bottle of red, some of the best wine he'd ever tasted.

The light dimmed and they all looked up as a little cloud slipped in front of the sun. "What are you gonna do?" said Mr. Gardner with a shrug. "You can't fight City Hall."

Jack sat on a picnic bench next to Michelle. He noticed that her shoulders slumped a little, and her teeth were a bit crooked. He liked her a lot. He watched her eat, watched the way her short skirt rode up over her thighs. Daskivitch and Jeannie grinned at him across the table, and he grinned back.

"I'll go around the corner and get some more beers," Daskivitch said.

"Do we really need it?" Jeannie said.

"I don't know if we *need* it, but we'd *like* it."

"Wait," said Mr. Gardner, a bit loud after many drinks. "Wait." He jumped up, grabbed an empty bowl off the table, and went into the house. He returned a moment later with some beautiful strawberries.

Jack lit a couple of candles; they flickered in the settling dark. Earlier in the party, Mr. Gardner had gathered a few of his roses and stuck them in a beer bottle. Now Michelle plucked some petals and floated them in a stone birdbath.

The table was covered with empty bottles and cans. Jack refilled Michelle's glass, and she leaned back against his shoulder. He could hardly believe his luck. He smelled a sweet, subtle perfume, and he could have sworn that it was her natural scent. He realized that he hadn't thought about Raymond Ortslee or Tomas Berrios for several hours.

"I'd like to propose a toast," said Mr. Gardner. He looked across the table at Jack. "To good food and good conversation," he said. "And to beautiful women in our backyard." They clinked glasses all around. Mr. Gardner stood to raise his glass and nearly fell over backward. "I'm okay, I'm okay," he shouted. "What are you gonna do? You can't fight City Hall."

The candlelight glimmered on the birdbath. Mr. Gardner staggered inside to go to the bathroom.

"Help me carry some plates in, honey," Jeannie said to her husband.

"Where's that bottle opener?" Daskivitch said, fumbling around the table.

"Gary."

She must have pinched her husband under the table, because suddenly he blurted, "Oh. *Right.*" They gathered up some dishes and carried them into the house.

Jack reached up to brush a wisp of hair away from Michelle's face. She let her head drop back and he stroked her cool cheek. Tentative, he pressed his lips against her neck. She twisted around and suddenly they were kissing there in the night.

"Where is everybody?" Mr. Gardner called out, his stocky figure emerging from the back of the house.

Jack groaned.

"I found a couple more beers," Mr. Gardner called out, clunking them down on the picnic table.

Daskivitch and his wife returned. "Sorry, but we have to hit the road," he said.

"Thanks for a lovely night," Jeannie said.

If Jack had been sober, he probably wouldn't have said it, but he leaned forward and pressed his face into Michelle's hair. "Don't go," he whispered. "I'll drive you back in the morning."

He had no idea what she would have said if *she* was sober, but she wasn't. She nodded yes. "I'll get home on my own," she told Jeannie and Daskivitch.

They stood up.

"Where's everybody going?" said Mr. Gardner.

"Don't worry," Jack said. "I'll be right back."

He and Michelle walked Daskivitch and his wife out to their car.

"Are you sure you're okay?" Jeannie asked Michelle. Checking to make sure that she wasn't being taken advantage of, Jack supposed.

"I'm fine," Michelle answered. As if to demonstrate, she slipped her arm around Jack's waist.

"Well, all right, then," Jeannie said. She seemed a little taken aback, but Jack figured she and Michelle could sort it out later.

"You okay to drive?" he asked his partner.

"Jeannie's gonna drive. I was drinking for both of us." Daskivitch winked at him.

They got in their car and left.

Mr. Gardner was fumbling around the picnic table in the dark, gathering up the dirty plates.

"It's okay," Jack said. "We'll take care of it." For once, leaving some dirty dishes for a while didn't bother him.

"You sure?" Mr. Gardner mumbled. "I c'n help." He took a step and tripped over a lawn chair. Jack bent down to find him splayed across the lawn.

"Is he okay?" Michelle whispered.

Jack wasn't sure. He was thinking about old people and broken hips, but Mr. Gardner sat up and laughed. "Just like Buster Keaton," he said.

"Let me help you upstairs," Jack said.

"M'okay." Mr. Gardner got to his feet and set off down the garden path, but he looked like he was about to buckle. He made it up the stairs under his own steam, but Jack followed one step behind to catch him if he fell. "M'okay," he said. "Really."

Jack opened his landlord's door and took the man's arm to lead him in, but Mr. Gardner pulled away. "Okay now. G'night. You gave a good party."

Jack thought about Michelle waiting for him out in the garden. He figured Mr. Gardner could probably make it to his bedroom by himself.

"Sleep tight, Mr. G.," he said. "Don't let the bedbugs bite."

He sat down on the picnic bench and Michelle leaned back against him. He inhaled her soft scent, slid his hands over her silky blouse, cupped the liquid weight of her breasts. She started to tremble.

Ten minutes later they were inside lying on his bed. Jack tried to get her bra off, but the hooks snagged. He gave up for the moment and traced his fingertips down the smooth valley in the center of her back. He thought of the ripe strawberries; pictured her licking the juice off the side of her hand.

He leaned over her and pressed his lips down to hers. Desire surged, and tenderness. He had a vision of a life like this, in which time was something to be savored rather than gotten through.

Michelle raised her head from the pillow and tucked her hair behind her ear. "Maybe you should check on him."

"What?"

"Your landlord. Maybe you should go up and make sure he's okay."

"He's all right." Jack thought of Mr. Gardner mowing the lawn; building the barbecue brick by brick. A strong old man. Vigorous. He reached up again and this time the bra unhooked like magic. He pulled Michelle's panties down over her hips.

A few minutes later he pushed into her, that sweet moment that made this world seem like the perfect place to be. He pressed his face into the sweaty crook of her neck.

Michelle moaned and circled her hips up to meet him.

nineteen

Jack woke at eleven A.M., head throbbing. His mouth felt as if it were stuffed full of socks. He stretched out his arm, but the other side of the bed was empty. He had a vague recollection of Michelle getting up early and kissing him goodbye.

Should he get up? He didn't have to work today; if he wanted to, he could spend the rest of the morning asleep. He rolled over; memories of the night came back and he smiled. Until more memories returned.

He sat up, listening. Usually, at this time of day, Mr. Gardner would have the radio on loud in his kitchen.

Silence.

He got out of bed, pulled on some boxer shorts and a T-shirt. Heart knocking, he opened his apartment door. The hall light was still on. Mr. Gardner turned it off without fail at sunrise every morning.

He stood still and listened carefully: no sound from Mr. Gardner's apartment upstairs. Maybe he just went out, Jack told himself.

He returned to his apartment and stepped into a pair of pants. He went back to the front hall. "Mr. Gardner?"

Silence. Motes of dust settled over a big plastic plant in the corner.

Gingerly, he climbed the stairs.

He paused outside the door. No sound within. He knocked softly.

No answer. The old guy was pretty hard of hearing. He rapped on the door again.

"Mr. G.?" he called out. "It's Jack." No point in giving the man a heart attack by sneaking up on him.

I'll call, he thought. Maybe he's just in the back and didn't hear the door.

Ignoring his own aching head, he jogged downstairs. After he dialed the phone, he heard it ring upstairs. One ring, two rings . . . Six rings . . . Nine.

Panic sheeted his heart. He went out and climbed the stairs again. "Mr. Gardner?" he shouted. He tried the doorknob. It turned easily and the door opened. His stomach dropped. Mr. Gardner would never have gone out and left his door unlocked.

Tensing, he pushed the door fully open.

The kitchen was empty. The air inside was stuffy and warm; the apartment smelled old. He looked around carefully, as if entering a crime scene. There was the massive stove, there was the lazy Susan with the butter cookies, the Tupperware container with the grocery coupons — but there was no sign of the old man.

He stood in the doorway to the back hall. "Mr. Gardner?" His voice sounded hollow and weak.

No answer.

"I'm sorry to bother you," he called out. "It's Jack."

Halfway down the hall, he peered into the living room. There was the the giant old TV, the same one that Mr. Gardner and his wife had probably watched *The Jack Paar Show*

155

on decades before. A flattened pair of leather slippers lay on a throw rug in front of the La-Z-Boy. No Mr. Gardner.

Holding his breath, he turned down the hall toward the bedroom. The house was so quiet he could hear the kitchen clock ticking behind him. He pushed the half-open bedroom door. The dry hinges creaked.

Mr. Gardner was on the floor, half lying, half sitting, propped against the edge of the bed. He had pulled a quilt off the bed and it was clenched in his left hand. His head shifted an inch. He opened an eye and stared up at Jack. He was trying to say something but one side of his face wouldn't move.

twenty

When the phone rang Ben was enjoying a guilty pleasure, watching *America's Funniest Home Videos* on TV when he should have been working on videos of his own. He set down a handful of popcorn, wiped his hand on his pants leg, and picked up the phone.

"Hello?" a man said gruffly.

"Yes?"

"Is this Ben . . . Ben Leetner?"

Every time he got a phone sales pitch, they invariably screwed up his last name.

"It's *Light-ner*. And I'm not interested."

"Is your father named Jack?"

Ben sat down slowly. His father's job was dangerous. His dad had always minimized the risks when he talked to his family, but all the same, in some back part of Ben's mind, he had been dreading this call since he was old enough to think.

"Is he . . . Is he dead?"

The man laughed. "Hey, fellas," he said to someone in the background. "The kid wants to know if his old man's dead!"

"What's going on?" Ben said, angry now. "Who the hell is this?"

. . .

It took almost forty-five minutes for the car service to pick him up and get him to Midwood. Once there, the driver couldn't seem to find the address. They finally stopped a Hasidic man striding past. He seemed irritated by the question, but he pointed the way.

Monsalvo's. With its old Rheingold sign blinking in the window, the bar looked like a dive.

"Can you wait here for a minute?" Ben asked the driver. "I should be right out."

"No problem," the man said, picking up a copy of the *Daily News* from the seat next to him and shifting forward to catch the light from a street lamp.

The door swung shut behind Ben. Even though it was a weeknight, the place was crowded and smoke hung thick in the air. The big, red-faced bartender noticed him looking around anxiously and walked over to the near end of the bar.

"You Jackie's son?"

Ben chewed the inside of his cheek and nodded.

"He's in the back room. Come on, then."

The man came around the bar and led the way toward the back, parting the crowd brusquely.

"How did you know to call me?"

"His wallet was on the bar. Your name was in the wallet."

"Is he all right?" Ben asked as they made it through the last of the drinkers.

The bartender shrugged. "He'll live if he can make it past the hangover. He's in here."

Way in the back, between stacked cases of Rolling Rock and Schmidt's, three steps led up to a little door.

"If he was a stranger, we would have tossed him out, but

158

you father's a friend." The bartender stooped as he passed through the door. Wincing, Ben followed.

A bare bulb illuminated a storeroom packed with cases of beer and industrial-size boxes of pretzels. His father sat on a couple of cases, slumped over a card table. Ben could smell the liquor on him from six feet away. Hard liquor, whiskey or Scotch. He was shocked—he could never have imagined his dad like this. A little old man who looked like a garden gnome sat on a case next to him, evidently making sure he was okay.

"This is the son," the bartender told the old man. He turned to Ben. "Just so you know, he never drinks like this. He nurses one or two beers for an hour, then he goes home."

His father's head rested on his arms. He muttered something.

"What did he say?" Ben asked the old man.

"He's a cop, right?"

Ben nodded.

"He keeps talking about the PD."

Jack Leightner's head rolled back. He raised it a few inches off the table, but he didn't see his son. He had the ugly, twisted face of a man who wants to cry, but can't. "I'm sorry," he mumbled to no one in the room. "Jesus, Petey, I'm so goddamn sorry."

twenty-one

A need to pee woke Ben early in the morning. Squinting, he got up and plodded into the bathroom. When he came out, he headed back toward his bedroom, but stopped in the hall. Listened.

Snoring.

He tiptoed toward the front room. His father was curled up on the futon couch. The sheet that Ben had spread over him the night before was clenched under his chin. His head was smushed down into the pillow and his hair was so cowlicked up that Ben grinned. He held his breath and watched for a moment. The old man didn't look like the tough cop — he looked like a little kid. Ben had always imagined his father as a take-charge guy, surrounded by cop buddies. Giving people orders.

It occurred to him now that maybe his father was lonely too. Living alone. Having a beer after work in an old-man bar.

He went back to bed, but lay awake for a while, puzzling out a new emotion. For the first time in his life, he felt sorry for his father.

• • •

Bright light beyond his eyelids called Jack awake. He cracked an eye to sunlight jabbing in through a window, direct to a pain center in his brain. He pressed his eyes shut, then opened them abruptly. He didn't recognize the window. Groaning with the effort, he lifted his head a few inches off a soggy spot on the pillow—he didn't recognize the room either. He had no idea how he'd gotten there.

He was lying on a sort of couch that felt like it was stuffed full of sand. He looked down, distressed to see that he was wearing all of his clothes from the day before. His watch told him that it was seven-thirty. A.M., evidently.

He pressed his palms against his eyes. He'd been in a bar the night before. Monsalvo's. Christ, he hadn't been drunk in years, and here he was hung over for the second morning in a row. He couldn't remember how the night had ended, but the events of the previous day started coming back. The shock of discovering Mr. Gardner. The guilt he'd felt when he called the old man's son to break the news. He almost never drank on the job, but by the end of the afternoon he'd needed a quick one before his shift.

His shift. He groaned again, and reached down to his belt. His beeper was there, but at some point early in the night he must have turned it off. He had never simply not showed up to work—Sergeant Tanney must be going crazy. He had to get up and find a phone—it would help if he knew where he was.

The room was a mess, cluttered with stacks of books and piles of magazines. It seemed like every inch of wall space was covered with pictures. Paintings, album covers, postcards, photos. Two big film posters dominated the far wall: one for a movie he recognized, *Raging Bull,* and one for a picture he'd never heard of called *The Scent of Green Papaya.*

The posters did it: he'd just realized that he must be in

his son's apartment when a phone rang on the desk. Ben emerged from a doorway, bleary-eyed, in his underwear. The last time Jack had seen him walking around like that, his son had been eight.

"Good morning," Ben said, noticing his father lying awake on the sofa. He picked up the phone. "Yeah? . . . What do you mean? Nobody told me we were working today . . . No, she didn't call me. Are you sure you told her to? . . . Right now? . . . Fuck. I'll be there as soon as I can." He hung up, then stood awkwardly, staring at his father. "You alive?"

Jack nodded, embarrassed. He ran a hand over his head, smoothing down his unruly hair.

"That was my boss," the kid said. "I have to rush in to work."

"What kind of a sofa is this supposed to be?"

"It's a futon."

"*This* is a futon? I always wondered what the hell those things were."

"Dad, are you okay?"

Jack pushed an old blue blanket off himself and gingerly sat up. He considered how to explain.

"My landlord almost died yesterday."

"You guys were that close?"

He grimaced. "You have any aspirin?"

"It's in the bathroom, down the hall. Listen, I'm sorry, but I have to run off to work. There's eggs in the fridge and some bread. You can let yourself out; the door'll lock behind you."

"Do you have a shirt I can borrow?"

"I guess."

"A nice one. I have to go to work."

"I don't own too many business-type shirts, but you can check my closet. Most of the stuff is Salvation Army, but you'll probably find something. I've gotta jump in the shower. Hey, Dad?"

"What?"

"You gonna be okay? I mean, what happened?"

"I'm fine. Don't worry. I don't want you to be late for work. Tell you what — I'll call you later."

Ben turned to leave, but stopped in the doorway. "Do you remember what you were saying last night?"

He shook his head warily.

"I know you don't like to talk about this, but . . . what happened with Uncle Peter?"

Jack blanched. "What did I say?"

"Nothing, really. You just kept saying his name."

"This is not the time. You're going to be late."

"I know. I was just wondering . . . I know a whole lot about Mom's family, but hardly anything about yours."

"Why do you need to know?"

"I don't *need* to know. I just figured it's important to learn about the past. Your history is part of my history, you know?"

"Sometimes it's better to just let things be."

"Maybe, but I think it's weird not knowing anything — "

"Just drop it, goddammit!" He looked up at his son's face and knew he'd spoken too harshly. He was hung over; he'd slept in his clothes, said things he couldn't even remember the next day. Now he was barking at his son . . . He sounded like his own father. If there was any point to life, he should be doing a better job of parenting than the old man.

"Look, I'm sorry, kiddo, I'm just not feeling so great right now. We can talk about this some other time, okay?"

His son looked disappointed, but he nodded.

Jack rubbed his hand over his mouth. "Uh, there's one other thing. I might need a place to stay for a couple of days."

Yesterday, after Mr. Gardner's son had visited the hospital, he'd come back to the house to talk. Jack didn't know Neil Gardner well; they'd only met in passing when Jack visited the Sixty-first Precinct, or on the rare occasions when the clerk paid a visit to his father. Neil was a small-shouldered guy who wore big suits, who teased and patted his black curly hair into a strange puffy unit in an attempt to make it look straight.

They sat in Jack's kitchen, drinking instant coffee.

"How's he doing?" Jack asked. "When I was at the hospital, they said it was hard to guess how much damage the stroke had done."

He'd spent the afternoon in the miserable waiting room of a city hospital while doctors ran a battery of tests on Mr. Gardner. In one corner a homeless man rocked silently back and forth, his rotting body entirely covered in a sheet. Two rows back, a Korean woman held her aching stomach, singing some sort of lullabye over and over for hours in an attempt to soothe her pain.

"We still don't know. It looks like he's gonna have to stay there for a while."

"And then?"

"They said he might never fully recover. It looks like a nursing home will be the best option."

Jack took a sip of his coffee. He squinted, not because of the hot liquid, but what he feared was coming.

"Listen," Neil said. "I don't have a lot of time, because I have important things to take care of. I was looking through my dad's papers upstairs and I didn't see a lease for your apartment."

"We didn't have a lease. We were friends, you know. I just paid him every month and it worked out pretty well."

"Oh," Neil said. "Listen, since you found him and everything . . . I was wondering: if he had the stroke late at night, like they suppose—why do you think he was on the floor instead of in bed?"

Jack scratched the side of his mouth, shrugged.

"He was able to talk a little bit," Neil said. "It was hard to understand him, but . . ."

"He told you about the party?"

"Yeah. Sounds like you all had a pretty good time. Like you gave him quite a bit of alcohol."

"I didn't *give* him any alcohol. I mean, he wanted it." That didn't sound much better.

Neil Gardner stood up. "When I told you about this apartment, I didn't expect you to take care of my father, but this is ridiculous. You should have used better judgment. The man is *eighty-six years old*."

Jack, still hung over, was in no mood for a lecture. "He's a grown man. He had a right to have a little fun, for once."

"What's that supposed to mean?" Neil snapped.

Jack took one look at Neil's face and regretted the comment — the guy obviously felt guilty about never coming around to visit. "All I meant was, he doesn't have a chance to get out much."

Neil pointed at Jack. "Getting out? You give my father a stroke and you call that *getting out!*"

"*Whoa,*" Jack said, his patience run out and his own guilt feeding his irritation. "I've had just about enough of that. All I gave the man is a happy few hours, which is more than you can say."

Neil Gardner drew himself up, livid. "I'll tell you what, Leightner. I want you out of here. *Immediately.*"

"He can't just kick you out like that," Ben said.

"Without a lease, he can do whatever he wants."

"Isn't there a whole eviction process? Doesn't that take a lot of time?"

"I don't know. I think I better just stay out of his way for a few days, and hope the old man gets better."

Jack could have prevailed on a colleague from the task force for a bed for a few nights, or he could have gone to a motel, but he figured this might be an opportunity to finally get to know his son.

Ben chewed on his lower lip. "So you want to stay here?"

"If that's okay with you."

His son scratched his armpit. He didn't answer for a moment. "Well . . . I guess I could clear away some space in here. I think I've got an extra key somewhere." He turned away abruptly. "I better take a shower." He disappeared down the hallway.

Jack got up and stepped over several piles of books on his way to the phone. He called the squad room, praying Sergeant Tanney wouldn't pick up. He was relieved to hear his fellow detective Carl Santiago on the other line.

"Leightner, that you?"

"It's me."

"Man, where the hell you been? The sarge's been going apeshit. You okay?"

"I'm fine. I had . . . a personal problem. Everything okay at the squad?"

"Yeah. It was slow yesterday. You coming in?"

"I'll be there."

He hung up. Pressing his fingers against his temples, he made his way across the cluttered room and looked out the window. Down below, the backyards of the block formed a green courtyard. The sky was a hazy white. On top of a chain-link fence separating two of the yards, a gray cat moved stealthily forward. It stretched out a paw and placed it carefully, as if testing thin ice, sending Jack back to a snow-covered lake and a December day in 1961.

• • •

Christmas was just over. He and his father and Petey crunched through the snowy woods, carrying borrowed skis. The lake was frozen and they were going to glide across it.

The boys walked in their father's footsteps, where he had packed down the snow with his huge oiled leather boots. Petey, husky even at nine, went second, and Jack brought up the rear, stumbling in the deep snow. His stomach was full of delicious slices of glazed ham, fried to a crisp in an iron skillet, and mashed potatoes, and lima beans he ate without protest, not wanting to spoil the unusual peace of the day. They were only staying in the little Catskills cabin for a weekend, but his father was proud that he had been able to bring his family upstate for their first real vacation — in fact, it was the first time they had ever left the city. He was proud that he had learned how to ski cross-country as a boy in Russia, and now he would have the chance to pass this knowledge on to his sons.

The day was chill, but there was no wind and not a cloud in sight. A branch cracked and the sound traveled across the flat white surface of the lake, ricocheted back like a rifle shot.

Petey was singing Buddy Holly: *That'll be the day, when you make me cry/That'll be the day-hay-hay* . . . He'd been singing those two lines over and over for the past three days, driving everyone in the cabin nuts.

At the edge of the lake, they stopped to put on their skis. Across the way, above the rough beard stubble of the winter trees, a plume of smoke uncoiled from the chimney of a neighbor's cabin into the perfect blue of the sky. The snow on the lake was shiny with a frozen crust. Jack and his brother started to argue about who got to wear which skis, but they were stilled by a look from their father. They didn't want to disturb this cheerful mood he was in, heading out with his sons into the wilderness. They clamped on their skis in silence, fingers pink from the cold. Their father took off his red-and-black-checkered jacket and tied the sleeves around his waist. His bushy eyebrows stuck out from under the brim of a thick wool hat.

"This will get the blood movink," he said as he sidestepped heavily down onto the lake. He slid out across the field of white, not looking back to see if his sons were ready. They scurried out after him, short legs pumping double time. The tips of the ski poles poked holes through the crust. They squinted against the glare of sun on ice and snow.

Peter skied out effortlessly, with his usual mysterious ability. Jack scowled as he struggled to keep up the rear. Why, he asked himself for the thousandth time, had God been so unfair? Two brothers, born only two years apart—why would he make one cheerier, handsomer, a born athlete?

Halfway across the lake, their father stopped and reached into his pack to pull out a big chocolate bar.

"You boys aren't gettink tired, are you?" His breath puffed white in the frigid air.

They shook their heads earnestly. Their father gave them each a piece of chocolate, then pulled a metal flask out of his coat pocket and tipped his head back to drink heavily. He'd been taking hits off the flask all morning.

As they resumed their trek, Jack wondered what would happen if he broke through a weak spot in the ice and plunged into the freezing black water, like Tony Curtis in *Houdini*. Sometimes he had nightmares about the scene where the magician escapes from a trunk at the bottom of just such a frozen lake, only to swim up and panic, discovering that he's lost sight of the opening in the ice. What would his father do? Would he dive into the water and rescue his son?

All went well until they reached the far shore. Jack was short of breath, but his father insisted they push on around the bend. His breath turned ragged, and he was afraid that his asthma was coming on, a slowly tightening band of pressure around his chest. He knew better than to complain — his father had heard someone on the radio suggesting that asthma was born in the mind, and since then he had looked on his son's condition as an embarrassing sign of weakness. But Petey heard Jack wheezing and turned back to help — for once their brotherly rivalry was set aside. Jack stopped and bent over to ease the pressure in his lungs.

His father turned around, and it was as though a dark cloud had suddenly drifted out over the picture-postcard lake.

"Come on, Jack, keep going," his brother urged, but it was too late.

His father skied back and grabbed him by his collar, looked down as if he didn't recognize his own son. "Moof," he ordered.

Jack struggled for breath. His father yanked him up. "You little shit. We stop when I tell you."

He knew his father hated to see him cry, but he couldn't help sniffling.

"Moof!"

"My boots hurt."

"This problem, we can solf. Take them off."

He looked up, uncomprehending.

"Piotr, help take his boots off."

His brother gave Jack an anguished look, but their father cuffed him on the ear. He bent over and unlaced the boots. Jack slowly pulled them off.

"Now the socks," his father said.

When his feet were bare, his father yanked him to his feet. "Now we can go beck." The old man skied on ahead,

169

not looking back as they moved across the lake. Jack didn't dare to complain as his feet crunched through the snow. The cabin seemed very far away.

"You all right, Jack?" Petey skied along next to him, his face tight with worry. "Here — let me carry your shoes and the skis."

"He'll get mad," Jack answered.

"I don't care."

Petey gathered up the things and skied clumsily on with his arms full of skis and shoes and poles. Jack had never loved his brother so much.

Soon his feet were purple with the cold. He couldn't help crying.

His father stopped. Just as unpredictably as his dark mood had emerged, it faded. "Put your shoes on, boy," he said, then turned away.

Back at the cabin, his mother stared at Jack, who sat trembling before the fireplace.

"He fell in the side of the lake," his father said. "Silly boy."

Jack was silent. His brother looked miserably down at the broad plank floor.

Their father shouldered the door open and stomped outside.

twenty-two

"You should have called in," Sergeant Tanney said, leaning forward in his desk chair. "If you needed the shift off, I would've been happy to give it to you."

"You're right," Jack said. "I'm sorry." He knew he was due for a dressing-down but he was in no mood for a lecture, especially from such a young supervisor.

"You okay?" Tanney said. "You don't look so great."

"I'm fine."

"Are we back on track?"

"Back on track."

"Glad to hear it. I'm sorry to hear about your landlord. Remember, if you ever have a problem, come to me first."

"You got it. Thanks."

Tanney rose and offered his hand.

Jack left the sergeant's office, surprised at how painless the session had been. His coworkers looked up from their desks.

"He bust your balls?" asked Carl Santiago.

"Not too bad."

"We were worried about you yesterday."

Jack rubbed his jaw. "I screwed up. But I'm fine."

"Back to the salt mines, then."

"Yup."

Sitting at his desk, he called the hospital and was told that his landlord's condition was stable, but that it was still too early to determine the state of the neurological damage from the stroke. Mr. Gardner was not being allowed visitors today, but he could come by tomorrow.

Once you got past the metal detectors, the Brooklyn DA's headquarters was a warren of drab offices and hallways jammed with cardboard boxes of case write-ups dating back before the computer era. Cheap bronze plaques decorated the walls, along with photos of offspring fortunate enough to be able to go to expensive colleges and escape the city bureaucracy.

Jack found Gary Daskivitch sitting on the edge of a desk, chatting with a secretary. "You ready to roll?" he said, cutting into their conversation. He was anxious to get going on the case again.

Daskivitch stood up. "Yeah."

"Have a good meeting?" His partner had come to discuss one of his other cases with an assistant DA.

"It was fine." They walked out into a gray hallway. "Hey, I tried to call you yesterday morning, but you weren't home. Then I got a call from your boss, all pissed off, looking for you. What was that about?"

He frowned. "It was my landlord. He had a stroke."

"No shit? The old guy? Is he okay?"

He shook his head. "Not so good."

"Sorry to hear that. He seemed like a real gutsy old geezer. How *you* doing?"

"I'm beat. I got about four hours' sleep the last couple of nights."

"Maybe you should take a day off."

Jack shook his head grimly. "We've got work to do."

They continued down the narrow hallway.

"Wait a sec," Daskivitch said. He backed up to stick his head in a doorway labeled Narcotics Task Force. "Hey, Richie — how they hanging? . . . Oh, yeah? Give my regards to your wife — tell her I'll be over during the day sometime next week."

A box of envelopes came winging through the door, narrowly missing Daskivitch's head.

Jack pushed a button to unlock a security door. "Who was that?"

"A DEA guy. We did a sweep together when I was with Narcotics."

They followed a group of weary secretaries and attorneys into an elevator. The DA's people were off work, but the detectives were just starting their day.

"You got along with a DEA guy?"

"He was all right — for a Fed."

They walked through the marble lobby of the Brooklyn Municipal Building out into the soupy early evening. The sidewalks teemed with civil servants impatient to get home.

Jack spat on the sidewalk. "I hate Feds. Arrogant sons of bitches. A few years back, we got this call about a shooting in Bensonhurst. Turns out it was a triple murder, a Mob thing. I go out there with another guy from the task force. We pull up, there's two vans parked outside. Unmarked. These guys in suits are not only tromping all over the evidence, they're actually scooping up the bodies and piling 'em into the vans. This guy smiles at me and says, 'Hey, how ya doin'?' I say, 'I'm doing fine, and who the hell are you?' He flashes an FBI shield at me, he climbs into one of the vans, and off they go. Not another word. The dildo actually had the nerve to wave at me as they went by. *Fuck you, NYPD.*"

Around the corner, they settled into his car. He turned the air-conditioning up full blast.

"So where we going?" Daskivitch said.

"Manhattan. Upper East Side."

"What the hell for?"

He filled his partner in on the Romanian maid's story. "I want to talk to her boss." Anybody with an apartment in the Bentley was probably a big wheel; this time Jack was glad of Daskivitch's intimidating bulk.

His partner turned to him. "Your sergeant okay with you spending so much time on this case?"

Jack leaned forward against his shoulder harness. "I don't care how much time it takes."

The dispatcher chattered away on the radio. After a few minutes they joined the line of cars heading up onto the Brooklyn Bridge. At rush hour, it would have been faster to take the subway, but such an undignified option never occurred to them.

"Hey," Daskivitch said. "My wife's been bugging me. She wants to know when you're gonna call her friend Michelle again. Do you like her?"

Jack loosened his collar. "Yeah, sure. She's nice."

"Did, uh, did you have a good time after Jeannie and I left?"

Jack nodded ruefully. "Yeah, we did."

Michelle had been a lot more than a good time. He could see getting close to her. But after the closeness, fights would inevitably come; that was part and parcel of a relationship. He didn't know if he had it in him to ride the roller coaster of love anymore. Maybe he was just too old. Anyway, he didn't deserve to enjoy himself, not with Mr. Gardner in the hospital and Raymond Ortslee in the morgue.

"So?" Daskivitch said. "You gonna call or what?"

"I've had a lot to deal with. I told you about my landlord."

"Is he in intensive care?"

"Yeah. And now his son is trying to kick me out of my apartment."

"That little fuck. I bet he can't wait to sell the house." Daskivitch glanced out the window, down at the East River flowing under the bridge. "You should call her, though. She's not the one-night-stand type."

Traffic stalled in the middle of the bridge. Jack shifted in his seat. He tugged on his shoulder harness — something was wrong with the retractor and the safety belt kept cinching up on him. "Maybe. We'll see."

Down on the East River, a barge bullheaded against the current. Across the way, loading cranes rose over the one remaining shipping yard in Red Hook.

Traffic picked up.

Jack thought about Michelle bucking over him, her long hair whipping around and her back tensing as she came. He thought about his son and hoped the kid didn't think he was some kind of drunk. He pictured Mrs. Gardner inviting him in for a piece of cake; Mr. Gardner sprawled out in pain next to his bed all night; Raymond Ortslee reaching for a doorknob.

He despised himself.

He watched his partner's face as they were ushered through the lobby of Heiser's building and saw his own initial awe and discomfort mirrored there. This time — reluctantly — the doorman showed them to the fancy tenant's elevator in the lobby. The operator, a young man in a braided uniform, kept his gaze fixed on the floor as they rose.

"I hope this is gonna be worthwhile," Daskivitch muttered. "You bug somebody who lives in a place like this, they're liable to gripe about it to One PP." That was One

Police Plaza, also known to cops on the street as the Puzzle Palace.

Jack hadn't actually spoken to Heiser yet. The man was some kind of big real estate developer, head of a corporation called Sumner International. When he called the work number, a snooty receptionist put him on hold, then came back to inform him that her boss was extremely busy and would only be able to speak to the detective at home.

Fuck him. Jack wasn't going to be intimidated. This wasn't Donald Trump, for chrissakes. He'd never even heard of the guy.

As much for his own benefit as for his partner's, he turned and said, "You're a detective now, Gary. You can talk to whoever you need to."

Daskivitch shrugged. "It's your funeral, bunk."

Jack looked up at the numbers as the elevator slowed. Fourteenth floor.

"Which way do we go?" he asked the operator.

The kid smiled wryly. "You'll see."

The doors opened and the two men walked out into a small foyer. There was no question of finding Heiser's apartment — only one door stood ahead. Evidently the man lived on an entire floor.

The foyer was walled in gold-smoked mirrors. Above hung a huge quartz chandelier. To the side, a small gilded table supported an enormous bouquet of white orchids. Jack reached out and fingered the edge of a petal. They were silk, the most realistic fake flowers he'd ever seen. Out of the corner of his eye, he noticed Daskivitch adjusting his tie in the mirrors. He did the same, then pressed the doorbell.

After a moment, he heard a patter of feet on the other side and the door swung open to reveal Marie Burhala's flustered face.

"No, *please*," she said. "You told me there would be no troubles."

Jack patted her shoulder. "It's okay. We're here to talk to Mr. Heiser."

"You won't say nothing about me to the Immigration?"

"Don't worry. This has nothing to do with you. He's expecting us."

She looked doubtful. "Please wait," she said, motioning them into a large entrance hall. "I tell him you are here." She hurried around a corner.

The foyer boasted the 1970s glitz of a casino or a Trump hotel: lots of chrome, more giant chandeliers, smoked mirrors, gold leaf. It was the home of the kind of man who would need to drive a flashy car. Recessed spotlights in the ceiling lit brightly colored paintings, mostly abstract — Jack was no art expert, but it seemed to him that they clashed. What the hell: money didn't necessarily buy class.

"Look at this crap," he muttered, stepping up to a garish painting that seemed to show a huge block of ice melting on a table.

"I'm not too big on art," Daskivitch said. His hands were folded tensely over his crotch — he looked as if he were waiting to be called into the principal's office.

"You know what a jobbee like this would go for?"

Daskivitch didn't move from the entranceway. He shook his head.

"I dunno either," Jack said. "But I bet these paintings cost more than both of us will see in a lifetime."

Marie returned. "He will see you now."

They followed her around the corner and down a long hallway. Other hallways branched off it — the place was a maze. Marie knocked timidly on a grand double door. After a moment, she pushed it open. Jack almost whistled as he walked into a room big enough to serve as a basketball court. It was filled with groupings of couches and armchairs. An Oriental rug covered the floor. The walls were plastered with more artwork that looked as if it belonged in a bad museum. At the far end of the room, a big middle-aged man sat in a leather armchair with his legs stretched out; his tasseled black loafers rested on an ottoman. He held a glass of Scotch in one hand and a telephone in the other. A bit of a paunch showed under his obviously expensive gray suit, but he looked strong and healthy, except for his face, that of a man who liked his booze. His big, nearly bald head was lightly freckled; thin lips, deep-set eyes. He tucked the phone under his chin.

" 'Be right with you," he said to the detectives. He continued a hearty phone conversation, as relaxed as if he were alone in the room. At one point he set his drink down and reached out toward a coffee table. From a large glass bowl he picked up two gray onyx eggs. As he continued the conversation, he closed one hand over the stones and rotated them around with a scraping noise that set Jack's teeth on edge.

Jack edged closer to the window and stared out at the spectacular view. Through a thicket of gleaming glass towers, the East River glinted in the sun. Beyond that, a tiny helicopter whirred out toward the flat sprawl of Queens.

"All right, Tom," Heiser finally wound up. "Have him bring the plans by my office on Monday morning and we'll give it a look-see. I'll fax you my answer by Winsdee." His voice had a Southern drawl to it, but not Deep South. Virginia, Jack guessed.

Heiser put the stones back in the bowl and stood up. He was six two, probably.

"Now," he said. "What kin I *do* for you gentlemuhn?"

He didn't invite them to sit.

Jack stepped forward across the vast carpet and thrust his hand forward. Grudgingly, Heiser reached out his own. Jack squeezed the man's hand and tried to turn it. Not only did Heiser resist, he actually tried to turn Jack's hand the other way.

"This is just routine," Jack said. "We're interviewing the tenants to see if anyone might have any information relating to the death of one of the employees of the building."

Daskivitch shifted from foot to foot at this lie — he knew Jack hadn't talked to any other tenants.

"Oh, yes," Heiser replied. "I heard about that. *Turrible* thing. Shocking. We're going to take up a collection, see what we can do for the man's family." Despite his words, his hard eyes showed no trace of sympathy. Something flickered underneath, though. Jack sensed that he was capable of cruelty. It was an instinctive reaction, certainly not something he could write down in a report, but he didn't like the man.

"Randall," a woman's voice called from a doorway at the back of the room. "Are you dressed yet?" A tall, gangly woman with a sharp chin hurried in. She wore black evening dress and held both hands up to insert an earring. She paused at the sight of the detectives. Heiser's wife might have been pretty long ago, in a stern sort of way — now she just looked stern.

"I'll be right there," he told her. "I'm just finishing up a little business."

She frowned and raised her eyebrows in disdain. "Hurry up. You know we can't be late."

"This won't take a minute," Heiser said.

The woman grudgingly retreated.

Jack cleared his throat. "Did you know Tomas Berrios?"

Heiser shrugged. "I couldn't really say I *know* the custodial staff. I know the names of the doormen, but that's about it."

That didn't answer the question. "Have you had any particular contact with him?"

Heiser touched the back of his shiny head. "Of course we give everyone a nice bonus at Chrissmuss. And we see them around the building all the time."

"He hasn't done any work in the apartment recently?"

"Listen, I was very sad to hear about all this, but as you boys know, this happened in Brooklyn. I don't see what this has to do with the tenants here."

Jack noted the demotion from "gentlemuhn" to "boys."

The phone rang, but Heiser ignored it. A moment later Marie appeared at the door.

"Mr. Heiser, it's —"

Heiser wheeled around. This time he was not so forgiving of the interruption. "Goddammit, Marie, can't you see I'm in the middle of something!"

Like an angry lion taking a sudden swipe, claws extended; the anger was not far from the surface.

The maid flushed. "I take a message, sir." She backed out. Jack felt sorry for her, a young kid having to put up with a powerful, tense boss. Without a green card, she didn't have much choice.

Jack considered pressing Heiser about his recent conversation with Berrios. He wasn't surprised that the tenant would not volunteer that he had been haughty to the victim. If Jack asked him about it, the man would know that his maid had spoken to the police. He would certainly call the poor kid on the rug for that — might even fire her. Besides, sometimes it was wise to withhold a little information. If it ever came down to a real interrogation, he might use it to trip the man up. Jack decided to let it go for the moment — he'd reconsider the matter if Heiser gave any further cause for suspicion.

"Well, now," Heiser said, his brittle attempt at cordiality returning. "If you boys don't have any further questions, I need to change into my evening clothes."

Daskivitch turned, but Jack stayed planted.

"Just one. Do you spend much time in Brooklyn?"

Heiser bent down to a coffee table and opened a silver box. He removed a cigarette, but didn't offer one to the detectives. Jack was tempted to light up one of his own.

"Perhaps you're unaware of the nature of my business," Heiser said. "My company has holdings in Manhattan, Los Angeles, Dallas, Miami. Some of our projects run into hundred of millions of dollars. Brooklyn isn't of much interest, frankly."

"Have you been to Red Hook in the past few months?"

"In Brooklyn? I don't believe so."

Jack folded his steno book and looked at his partner. Daskivitch tilted his head toward the door.

Heiser cleared his throat. "Good luck with your case. Marie will show you out."

"Thanks for your time."

Jack extended his hand. Heiser made him wait a moment before he shook it.

Marie led them out. Just before they reached the front door, Jack stopped. "Do you think I could trouble you for a glass of water?"

"Of course."

Without waiting for an invitation, Jack followed her around the corner. "Come on," he muttered to his partner, who followed reluctantly.

The back hallway was long enough for a bowling lane. It was hard to imagine so much space in an apartment. Photos covered the walls: Heiser sailing, Heiser skiing, Heiser in a tuxedo, smiling with an arm around his wife.

Marie pushed through a swinging door into a kitchen nearly the size of Jack's entire apartment. A tiled island in the center of the room provided yards of counter space. The stove had six burners, like the kind in a restaurant kitchen. Marie reached up into a cabinet for a couple of glasses and then peered inside a giant double-doored metal refrigerator. "Wait here—I get you some Evian," she said, and walked around the corner.

"This guy doesn't feel right to me," Jack said to his partner.

"What? He's rich and he's an asshole—that makes him a murderer?"

"I didn't say that. But something feels hinky to me. Did you notice how he skated away from mentioning that he told Berrios to stay out of the apartment?" Jack saw a door in the back and walked over. It opened into a service stairwell. This was where Tomas Berrios had entered when he paid his visits to Marie.

"You're really hyped up about this case all of a sudden," Daskivitch said.

Jack turned to his partner in exasperation. "Christ, Gary! It's a *murder*. I'm a *homicide detective*."

"There's nothing else bothering you?" His partner's eyes held the same concern and doubt he'd shown on the fire escape outside Ortslee's apartment.

Embarrassment and shame made a twisted braid in Jack's stomach.

"Drop it. I'm *fine*, already."

"Okay." Daskivitch backed up and raised his hands.

Marie returned with a bottle of water and poured two glasses.

Jack downed his water and set the glass in the sink. He turned to the maid. "We'll just slip out the back."

• • •

After a tense, silent ride back to Brooklyn, he dropped Daskivitch back at the Seven-six house and headed on to Midwood to pick up some clothes. He took the Gowanus
Expressway. To his right, New York harbor glinted in the
sun like polished chrome. I should have gotten myself a boat,
he told himself. Should have taken it out fishing like a lot
of other cops. Made the days off more bearable.

At the border between Red Hook and Carroll Gardens,
the elevated expressway crossed over the fetid green worm
of the Gowanus Canal as it slid between the factories and
junkyards of South Brooklyn. Since the canal curved around
a bend, he couldn't actually see the spot where the body of
Tomas Berrios had been found, but he could picture it all
too well. He had a lot of images now, but they stubbornly
refused to flow together into a story.

Why had someone killed the man?

Motive was overrated. On TV cop shows, juries always
had to be told why the perp did the crime. Nice to know,
but unnecessary. If you had good fingerprints or witnesses,
chances were you weren't going to have to go before a
jury, and the perp's psychology didn't matter. Unfortunately,
whoever killed Tomas Berrios had not been considerate
enough to leave evidence or living witnesses behind. Which
left Jack working backward, trying to puzzle out the reason.

Ortslee's follow-up murder seemed to rule out a lot of
possibilities. Berrios had probably not been killed by a jealous lover, or a low-level drug dealer, or someone he'd gotten
into a fight with on the street. The perp here had both or-
ganization and muscle. The only person in the case so far
who might have such power was Randall Heiser, but there
was no evidence of his involvement. You couldn't arrest a
guy for being a prick.

As Jack drove on toward the church spires and green oasis of Park Slope he patted his jacket pocket, only to discover that he was out of cigarettes. The trip to Midwood was a long one and he wished he could light up.

The house was eerily quiet. It might never again hear Mr. Gardner tromping down to his workshop basement, or Mets games playing on the radio in the upstairs kitchen.

Jack made arrangements with a neighbor to feed the old man's cat.

When he got back to Boerum Hill, his son wasn't home. He ate a couple slices of the pizza he'd brought over. At nine, Ben called to say that he'd be working late. It sounded like he was calling from a bar or restaurant, though.

Jack watched TV for an hour, switching back and forth between dopey sitcoms, then stretched out on the futon for a nap.

He dreamt he was a boy again.

He was on the frozen lake with Peter — they were racing to the far shore. Jack was winning, but then a hole cracked open in the ice and he was falling through. And Petey was . . . Petey was stepping on his shoulder, pushing him down into the dark, icy water.

Somehow now it was Petey in the water, instead. Jack searched frantically for a stick or something to reach out with. To save his brother.

Sirens. Cops came, and a crowd gathered. A reviewing stand. The police commissioner wanted to give Jack a medal, or was it a trophy? He looked all over, but couldn't find Peter in the crowd.

Out in the street, a car alarm blared on and off.

He woke, ashamed to find that he'd been crying in his *sleep*.

twenty-three

The next afternoon, Jack had just draped his jacket across the back of his chair and was about to sit down to some paperwork when Sergeant Tanney stuck his head out of his office.

"Leightner, can I see you for a minute?"

He walked over to his boss's office and stood in the doorway. "What's up?"

"Come in for a minute. Siddown, take a load off."

"All right," he said grudgingly.

"Close the door."

Tanney leaned forward in his chair. "Everything going okay?"

Jack nodded.

"You feeling all right?"

"Why?" *Cut to the chase.*

Tanney leaned forward. "If something's going on in my squad, we keep it in the squad. Upstairs stays out of it unless I say so. But I need to know what's going on with the detectives here."

Jack shifted in his chair. "What's your point?"

"I happened to stop by the Seven-six this morning. Your

partner there is concerned about you. And if he's concerned, then so am I."

"What are you talking about?"

"I know you've had some tough news. Your landlord, your apartment. If you need a few days to straighten things out, we can—"

"Hold on. I'm fine. I don't need any—"

"Listen, Jack, I'm gonna say something and I hope you don't take it the wrong way: if you're feeling some stress you might want to consider talking to one of the department counselors."

"You mean a *shrink*?"

"There's nothing wrong with talking to somebody."

"I didn't shoot anybody." Departmental regs required counseling for any cop involved in a shooting.

"I know that, but—"

"And even if I *did* shoot someone, I wouldn't go to a shrink. In my day, if you had to pop somebody, you went to a bar after and some of the guys helped you straighten yourself out."

"Nobody's ordering you to see a counselor."

"Well, that's good. Because I'm fine."

The sergeant rolled a pen around his desk. He considered Jack carefully.

Jack stood up. "Well, if that's all, I've got a lot of paperwork to catch up on."

Tanney tugged at his earlobe. "There's one more thing. I've been reviewing your work on this Berrios case."

Jack sat down.

"You're a good detective, Leightner. Thorough. Strong on the details. You work a case hard."

"Is that a problem?"

"No. Not most of the time. But my job's a little different

187

from yours. I'm not just looking at things case by case. I have to watch the big picture. How we're allocating our resources. Our time. Our energy."

"What? You're saying this isn't an important case? No press, right? Just some poor Hispanic schlub, is that it?"

The sergeant rubbed his hand over his mouth. "Slow down, Leightner. Every victim is important. Though he wasn't exactly the Mexican ambassador, was he?"

"He was *Dominican*." Jack sighed. "Listen, Sergeant: at least half the victims we get are dirtbags. Some of these mutts might as well be running around wearing signs saying 'Kill Me'! But as far as I can tell, this kid was clean. A family man. A good worker. He didn't deserve to be trussed up like a hog, to have his face bashed. To get stabbed in the, in the fucking *heart*."

"Of course not. But the question is, how much time do you need to spend on this? And do you need to go knocking on doors all along the Upper East Side?"

Jack smiled fiercely. "Oh, *okay*. Now I see where we're going with this. Heiser. That son of a bitch went and complained to One PP. They're busting your balls."

"It's not like that."

"How is it? Some rich prick doesn't feel like answering a few questions, you're gonna yank my chain?"

"If you have so much energy, how about helping with some of our priority cases? Santiago could use a little help with this Cobble Hill thing I have to read about in the papers every goddamn day."

"You're saying that Tomas Berrios wasn't as important as some Cobble Hill yuppie? And it's not just him—what about the Ortslee murder?"

"We don't know for sure that there was any connection. Look—all I'm saying is that we don't need to stir up problems unless there's some concrete reason."

Jack stood up. "You want me off this case, I want an order in writing."

The sergeant sat back in his chair and swung from side to side for a moment, considering Jack. "I'm just asking you to use your best judgment, Detective."

Jack glared at his boss. "That's what I get paid to do."

In the Seven-six squad room, Daskivitch was at his desk, his head down as he shuffled through some paperwork.

"Hey, bud," Jack said as he walked in. "Everything good with you? 'Cause everything's *great* with me."

Daskivitch looked up, his guilt in his eyes. "I didn't go to the sergeant—he came to me and asked me how you were doing. I was worried about you. You haven't been sleeping, you seem all riled up—"

"Listen, you're a good kid. But what you did—*not good*. This is not how a cop fucking behaves. You have a problem with me, you bring it to me."

"Come on, Jack. I don't have a problem with you. He thought you might want a few days off. That's all."

"Number one: the last thing I need is the sergeant on my back. Number two: mind your own goddamn business. *Capisce?*"

"I was just trying to be—"

"Fuck you. Okay? Just fuck you."

A female clerk turned from a filing cabinet in the corner of the room and stared.

"Fuck *you* too," Jack told her. Daskivitch started to get up but Jack pushed him back into his seat.

"Leave it alone, kid. I'm not gonna tell you again."

He strode out of the squad room.

• • •

He found a café on Court Street to sit in, a yuppie place with tiny, expensive pastries and fancy coffees. At least it was air-conditioned. At the wrought-iron table next to him, two young mothers discussed the speed of their Internet connections as their little kids ran around and whined that they wanted to go home.

It took half an hour before the rage inside him ebbed away, and then he was just left with shame. Sometimes it seemed that Daskivitch was more like a son to him than his own son — and he couldn't seem to get right with either one of them.

He resolved to go home and talk to Ben. The kid was getting to be a man now — maybe they could finally bury the hatchet and meet on a new level. Get to know each other after all these years.

But his son wasn't home. Was he avoiding his father, or just busy with work?

twenty-four

Before his next shift, Jack stopped off at the hospital to see Mr. Gardner.

A beleaguered clerk at the front desk told him that unless he was immediate family, visiting hours for the intensive care unit were not due to start for another forty-five minutes. He held up his detective shield.

Upstairs, a pretty young Filipina nurse led him through the ICU, a loud demented frog pond with its constant unsynchronized beeping and booping, its bubbling of liquids and hissing of gases. She pulled back a curtain to reveal a small oasis in the whirl of activity. Mr. Gardner looked shrunken, like an elf sleeping amid a tangle of intravenous tubes, hoses, electrical cables, and hanging bags of bright liquids. A compressor chugged, feeding air into the tube which branched into the old man's nostrils.

Jack looked up at the four jagged green lines surging across the monitor over the bed. "How's he doing?"

"He's stable," the nurse said. "But if he's a witness or something, you won't be able to talk to him today. He's very weak."

"Do you know what the prognosis is? What are the chances of a good recovery?"

"I'm sorry, but it's too early to tell. I can give you the name of his doctor so you can check back later."

"Thank you. Do you mind if I sit here for a minute?"

The nurse shrugged. "I'll come back." She stepped out and drew the curtain closed.

Jack set down the box of chocolates he'd bought at the newstand in the lobby and prayed that Mr. Gardner would be well enough to eat them before they went stale. He stood next to the bed and held on to the metal railing.

"I don't know if you can hear me, Mr. G., but it's Jack. I just want to tell you that I hope you get better soon. And"—he swallowed—"and that I'm sorry this happened."

In the corner, the air compressor chugged on. "I been screwing up a lot recently," he confided to the sleeping man. "I don't know what's wrong with me."

Somewhere beyond the curtain a small alarm trilled.

He sat for a few minutes watching the sheet over Mr. Gardner's chest slowly rise and fall.

He leaned over and murmured, "I'll come back when you're feeling better. You fight City Hall, okay?"

He spent the morning helping one of the other task force members canvass an apartment building in Flatbush. It was the kind of work no one wanted: going door to door, floor to floor, in a place where just about everybody hated you for being a cop. And then you had to spend more time typing up the Fives. *3B—no answer. 3C—tenant at work at time of incident. 3D—tenant watching TV with grandmother at time of incident* . . . Normally, a team of uniforms would have been assigned to the duty, but on some sensitive cases the detectives did the work themselves—patrol rookies didn't have the experience to analyze the subtle undercurrents of an interview.

He'd just returned to the task force office and sat down to his lunch, a meatball hero, when a call came through from Gary Daskivitch. The young detective sounded breathless. "Can you come over right away?"

"What's up?" Jack said curtly, peeling a hot string of mozarella off the sandwich's foil wrapping.

Daskivitch cleared his throat. "When I'm not too busy here, I keep an eye out for what comes through the Eight-four." That precinct was in Brooklyn North, just over the line from the Seven-six. "Last night they brought in a kid named Ramon Aguilar."

"So?" Jack said around a mouthful of steaming meatball.

"He was one of Tomas Berrios's bicycle buddies."

"What did they bring him in for?"

"Attempted assault. With a knife."

Jack almost choked on his sandwich. "Hot damn!" he said. He slapped his desk and grinned like a proud father. "You know what, kid? You're not as dumb as you look."

There was a silence on the other end of the line, then Daskivitch said, "Thanks . . . I think."

They met at the Seven-six house and then the young detective drove them north, through Carroll Gardens, on past the genteel brownstones of Cobble Hill. At Atlantic Avenue, in the middle of a strip of Middle Eastern grocery stores, they sat waiting for a long red light. A couple of Arab women veiled from head to toe were slowly crossing the intersection.

"Just use the siren and go on through," Jack said impatiently.

"I don't want to hit those women. They must be boiling inside there," Daskivitch said. "What a strange way to go through life."

Jack nodded distractedly. His heart lifted as the car

picked up speed and swung around onto Atlantic. He remembered Tomas's buddies, remembered one particularly lippy, sharp-faced kid, the one who'd made some dumb joke about the Mod Squad. He hoped this was Ramon Aguilar.

Daskivitch careened left onto Boerum Place, just next to the massive barred monolith of the Brooklyn House of Detention, where—God willing—the Berrios/Ortslee killer would soon take up temporary residence. Daskivitch swerved into a side lane and zipped past the traffic waiting to go across the Brooklyn Bridge.

"Speed it up," Jack said.

They ran up the steps of the Eight-four house and slipped around three laughing patrol cops coming out the door.

A young sergeant with a weak mustache glanced up from behind the front desk as they rushed in. "Hey, Gar'," he said. "What are you doin' over here?"

Daskivitch hunkered down over the desk. "I need to know who brought in a kid named Ramon Aguilar last night. Attempted assault."

The sergeant consulted a computer printout. "Let's see . . . that was Tony Ruiz."

"Did they take the kid to the House of D yet?"

The sergeant swiveled in his chair and called out to an office next door. "Hey, Nootsie, did Ruiz leave with that Spanish kid?"

"They're still upstairs," said a voice from the office.

The sergeant turned back with the news, but the detectives were already on their way up.

Ramon Aguilar paced back and forth in a holding cage at the back of the squad room. Jack recognized him as the wisecracker of Tomas's little crew. The kid walked up to the bars and scowled. "Oh, shit, it's the Mod Squad again. What's your problem? You lock *me* up, but you can't even find the guys who killed Tommy."

Jack grinned. "Oh, yeah? Maybe we got lucky today. Maybe we got a two-for-one."

"The fuck you talking about?" sputtered Ramon, but Jack and his partner moved on to find Tony Ruiz, a handsome detective with the on-the-balls-of-his-feet stance of an ambitious young riser in the department. They stepped into the squad lounge, another drab little room with crappy furniture, to give him the background on the Berrios and Ortslee stabbings.

Ruiz frowned at the grave direction his case was taking. "The complainant's a kid named Carlos Fulgencia, twenty-three, also Latino. He says he was walking with his girlfriend and one of her friends in the Fulton Street Mall last night. Says they passed Ramon here, and our friend made a comment about his girl's ass."

"Did the guys know each other?" Daskivitch asked.

"Yeah. He said they used to be friends, but apparently last year there was a falling-out—something about a bike. Anyhow, the Fulgencia kid said he challenged Ramon, and our guy pulled out a knife. They were tangling when a mall security patrol came by and broke it up."

"Did Ramon cut the kid?"

"Nope. He just pulled the knife out in the middle of the scuffle and waved it around."

"You have witnesses?" Jack asked.

"Well, the two girls backed up Fulgencia's story. My partner's down at the mall trying to find others."

"Did they recover the weapon?"

"Yeah. We got it downstairs."

• • •

The clerk in charge of the evidence room, a very pregnant young Italian-American woman, unlocked the cage and waddled back among shelves crowded with tagged brown bags. A minute later she waddled back with a small sack.

Jack eagerly opened it and reached in to lift out a plastic bag.

The detectives frowned. The bag contained a folding hunting knife with a blade about four inches long. It was certainly big enough to cause mortal damage, but had no hilt.

"Maybe he has more at home," Daskivitch said. "At least we know he likes blades."

Ramon glared across the table at Jack and his partner. Tony Ruiz leaned against the closed door with his arms folded across his chest: *to get out, you have to go through* me.

Ramon turned to look back at the detective from the Eight-four. "I told you already, man—yeah, I said something about his girlfriend, but he's the one who got all up in my face. And it wasn't my fuckin' knife! She was carrying it, in this little Hilfiger backpack."

Jack leaned forward and set his palms flat out on the table. "Let's forget about this for a minute. What I wanna know is: if Tomas Berrios was such a good friend of yours, why would you stab him? How could you do that, Ramon?"

Ramon groaned and grabbed the sides of his head. "You're fuckin' crazy, cop. I never had nothin' to do with that. Me and Tommy din't have no problems."

Jack lowered his voice. "What knife did you use when you stabbed him?"

Ramon squirmed and glanced back at the door. "This is fucked up," he moaned. "You got the wrong guy. I never even been arrested."

This was true: the kid didn't have a sheet.

"Where were you on the morning Tomas was killed, then?"

Ramon pointed at Daskivitch. "I already told this guy! *I work in a bodega on Hoyt Street. I was there all day.* Why don't you just call my boss?"

Jack turned to his partner. "Did you check this alibi?"

Daskivitch shrugged. "I never thought he'd be a suspect."

Jack turned back to Ramon. "All right, kid, what's your work number?"

Daskivitch got up to make the call.

Ramon kept shaking his head dramatically, muttering, "I can't believe it! This is so *wrong*, man."

Jack crossed his arms over his chest and settled back to wait.

A knock came at the door. Tony Ruiz admitted a big man with the look of an athlete gone to seed — an overweight bull. Ruiz introduced his partner to Jack and then stepped outside to confer with him. When he came back in, he was frowning. "Ramon," he said. "I want you to go talk to Detective Carlucci out there."

Ramon sullenly rose to his feet and walked out.

"What's goin' on?" Jack said.

Ruiz sank sheepishly into a chair. "Looks like we screwed up. My partner found a busboy who was working in a Wendy's on Fulton Street where the fight went down. He says he watched it through the front window and that it happened just the way Ramon says. The girlfriend pulled the knife out of her backpack. When Fulgencia waved it at him, Ramon tried to grab it away. An Arab guy selling incense at the curb tells the same story."

Ruiz frowned. "The girlfriend's friend broke down and gave us some background: it turns out Fulgencia is some kind of Army/Navy store freak—he's got a collection of brass knuckles, nunchuks, knives . . ."

It was Jack's turn to groan. And groan again: a minute later Daskivitch returned to say that the bodega owner had confirmed Ramon's alibi.

Jack closed his eyes and rested his face in his palms for a moment. He'd been overeager—he should have thought it through. Ramon might have killed his cycle buddy due to some sort of rivalry or moment of anger, but how would he have moved the body all the way to the canal? And how would he have tracked down the barge captain?

"This case is a pain in my ass," he muttered. Abruptly, he stood up. Many cops wouldn't have bothered with what he was about to do.

"Where you going?" Ruiz asked.

"I'm gonna go out and apologize to that jerk kid."

twenty-five

Ben Leightner came up from the subway onto Steinway Street in Astoria, Queens, struck as always by the neighborhood's bustling mixture of Greeks and other immigrants. Within a couple of blocks, you could buy a souvlaki sandwich, a sari, or a plate of pierogis.

Steinway Books was a tiny used-book shop, tucked between a Dunkin' Donuts and a Korean nail salon. Ben ducked his head to miss the low doorway and squeezed in amid the crowded, disordered stacks. At the counter in the back, nearly hidden by more piles of paperbacks, he found a gaunt, disgruntled-looking man whose long, frizzy white hair was tied back in a ponytail.

"Hi Avery," he said. "Is my mom around?"

The aging hippie couldn't be bothered to answer. He looked up at the ceiling and picked up a battered telephone. "Louise," he muttered into it, "your kid's down here."

Ben's mother lived over the shop. She'd moved there from Brooklyn several years after the divorce. The jumble of books reminded Ben of the house he'd grown up in. His mother had never been a fanatical housekeeper, but after his father left she almost completely gave it up. She'd do the laundry, but leave piles of clothes on the couch, the stairs, the kitchen table. She stopped cooking, and the two of them lived off TV dinners. She withdrew from all of her social contacts, and spent most of her time doing crossword puzzles or reading.

Avery picked up an open book; he didn't make small talk. Despite his distinct lack of charm, Ben's mother kept him on because he was the only employee who understood her Byzantine filing system. He understood it better than she did—once he'd saved the store during an IRS audit.

Ben browsed while he waited for her to come downstairs. Ironically—considering his father's occupation—the largest section was given over to mysteries. Mystery readers were among the most devoted of buyers, but that wasn't the only reason. During the first hard years after the breakup, his mother had become an avid consumer—she preferred the "cozies," books set in quaint English towns where some feisty little spinster always set the chaotic world to rights. For years after the divorce, Ben worried she'd end up a spinster herself. During his senior year of high school, he was both relieved and dismayed to find that she'd taken on a "boyfriend."

"Is everything all right?"

He looked up to see his mother standing halfway down the narrow staircase in the back of the store; she peered over the top of her glasses. She wore purple sweatpants and an Emily Brontë T-shirt. After his dad left, she'd put on a shocking amount of weight, but after Ted came into the picture, she lost it all, thanks to endless laps in the local YWCA pool.

"You're looking good, Ma."

His mother shrugged. She came down the stairs and gave him a quick peck on the cheek—she wasn't the demonstrative type.

"You wanna come up and have something to eat?" Another mother might have made a big deal about how skinny he looked—she went right for the practical.

They tromped up to her apartment, which was bright and airy, with hanging plants everywhere, suspended in macramé holders. She lived alone, even though she and Ted had been going out for years. They both valued their privacy. "How about a sandwich?" she said, opening the refrigerator. He was still surprised to see how well stocked it was with fresh vegetables and fruit, after the years of junk food.

"I'm okay," he said, leaning on the counter.

"How's work?"

He snorted. "The usual excitement. Yesterday, I had to listen as these corporate clients went on for hours about how the slice of pizza we were shooting wasn't 'glistening' enough. We had to brush more oil on it, then I had to reset the lights about ten times."

He watched his mother cut up a peach; he was impressed by her swimmer's muscles.

"Jesus, Ma—you're getting pretty strong these days."

She didn't respond, but smiled, pleased by the compliment. She dropped the peach slices in a blender. "I'm making us a fruit smoothie. So, how's the filmmaking going these days?"

He toyed with a can opener he found lying on the counter. "That's actually one reason why I came over. I've been working on a project about Red Hook."

"Really? Why Red Hook?" His mother asked the question evenly, but he knew she'd see behind it.

"It's an interesting place, with all of the history, the shipping, you know . . . I wanted to throw some family stuff in there too."

"Have you talked to your father? You could go see him."

He spun the can opener around. "Actually, he's been staying in my apartment for the past couple days."

His mother raised her eyebrows. "He's *staying* with you? Why?"

"His landlord had a stroke, and the son wants him to move out."

She shrugged. "I hope you have better luck living with him than I did."

These days his mother didn't talk compulsively about his father, the way she had after the divorce, but the bitterness remained.

"Have you asked him about Red Hook?" she said.

"You know what he's like."

"I'm afraid I do. What do you want to know?"

"I don't know . . . It just occurred to me the other day: it's ridiculous, but I don't even know his parents' first names."

"His mother was Doris. His father's name I think was Maxim, but in this country he was just called Max."

"And he was from Russia?"

"From somewhere near Leningrad. Or whatever they're calling it these days."

"Did you know him?"

"Not much. His father was a mean man. When we were dating, Jack never took me around to Red Hook. The old man died just a year or so after we got married."

He stopped spinning the can opener. "Do you know what happened to Dad's brother?"

His mother pressed a button and they had to wait a moment for the blender to stop whirring.

"Why do you ask?"

"Like I said, background for the film. Also, I was thinking that if I ever have kids, it'll be weird if I can't tell them about their own history."

His mother looked up quickly. "Kids? Is there something I should know?"

He blushed. "No. Nothing like that. But what about Dad's brother?"

She lifted the pitcher off the blender and poured two creamy drinks. "Your father was never very communicative, even at the best of times. All I know is that his brother was killed. Some sort of accident."

"Jesus—all he ever told me was that his brother died young. If I try to ask more, he always tells me to drop it."

His mother shrugged. "Don't expect too much from him. He's not a happy man."

Ben wrinkled his nose. "When you started going out, you must've thought better of him. I mean, weren't you in love?"

She shrugged. "I *thought* we were. But I don't know if he's really capable of loving someone else."

Ben felt the same way he had as a little kid: he was impressed that his mother told him such grown-up things, but he wished she wouldn't always cut his father down. Especially since his dad never turned the tables, never said a bad word about her.

He realized that his mission today was fruitless—he wasn't going to get the truth about his father from his mom. He was only going to get *her* truth.

twenty-six

Silence was at the heart of the job.

On TV detectives ran around waving guns, cars screeched and flipped over, bad guys shouted and jumped fences. In real life there was violence and noise during the crime, and there would be crying and confusion after, but in these first moments of discovery, the scene was still as a painting.

The condo was expensive and freshly painted, the few items of furniture new and pricey, but the place was a mess. Dirty clothes lay in heaps around the bedroom and the hall, beer cans and junk-food wrappers spread like confetti in the living room, crusty plates were piled in the kitchen sink. As usual, Jack was afflicted by the desire to start tidying up, to make some sense of the disorder; as usual, he refrained. A few posters provided the only decor: a Bud Light ad; a *Sports Illustrated* swimsuit model over which someone had pasted Hillary Clinton's head; the ghoulish made-up face of some rock star called Marilyn Manson. The magazines on the coffee table—*Money, Entrepreneur, Playboy, GQ*—were addressed to one Bruce Serinis, who was currently splayed out on the living room carpet, DOA.

Jack had caught the fresh case so soon after his talk with Sergeant Tanney that he suspected his boss had tampered with the sacred rotation order. He was angry, but realized that little would be gained by a fight. Not until he had a solid lead on the Berrios case.

For now, he had this job in Park Slope. Most Brooklyn homicides took place in rough areas like East New York, which saw scores of drug-related slayings and simple diss murders — citizens popped just for looking at their neighbors the wrong way. But the Slope was a bastion of yuppies with baby carriages, health food stores, renovated brownstones. The rare homicides on the eastern side of the seventy-eighth Precinct were likely to be the result of a mugging gone wrong, not this sort of inside job.

It was a busy Saturday night — the usual crew of Crime Scene techs and other interested parties had not arrived yet. The local detective, one Tommy Keenan, was a clothes horse: cream linen jacket, red silk tie, gold bracelet on one wrist, a Rolex or a damn good imitation on the other. The linen jacket was not a great sign, Jack thought — it didn't indicate any eagerness to get in close to the blood and guts of the job. And Keenan was a rookie.

Even so, he'd evidently been on the job long enough to become blasé about the sight of a murder victim. He seemed more interested in a photo of a half-naked woman than in the body of the late tenant. He whistled and held the picture up in a rubber-gloved hand. "Check it out. This is that chick from the new *Star Trek*. You know, the one who plays the shrink on the *Enterprise*?"

"That's very exciting," Jack deadpanned. "Make sure you include it in your Fives."

It was clear from the get-go that drugs might be involved in the case — they'd found a professional scale on the counter separating the kitchen from the living room, a tin of silica gel packages in a drawer, seven boxes of sandwich-size Baggies in a cupboard, a stack of wax-paper squares for wrapping grams of coke. If that wasn't enough, there were pot seeds in the crease of the Grateful Dead double album — an LP, historical relic — on the coffee table. An empty bong lay on the carpet next to a foul-smelling stain. Apparently the vic had been hit while sitting on the couch, then sprawled forward, knocking over the pipe.

"Thank God for AC," Keenan said. Serinis might have been dead for a couple of days, but the apartment was so chilly that he hadn't started to smell much — or at least not worse than the bong water.

"I remember the first DOA I ever caught," Keenan said. "This guy's neighbors smelled something bad coming out of his apartment — and it was the middle of a heat wave. We break down the door and there's this old guy laid out on his kitchen floor; he'd been dead a long time and he was blown up like a parade float. My partner gives me a couple cigarette filters to put up my nose. I see this half-empty bottle of roach killer lying next to the vic. One of the neighbors walks in. 'Oh, shit,' she says. 'He just come home from the clinic last week. They told him he had *roaches of the liver*.' "

Keenan dug a finger in the back of his collar. "Can you believe it? *Cirrhosis of the liver*." He laughed, a ghastly booming noise, then moved closer to the body. "How do you see this? I mean, there's no forced entry, so the vic probably knew the killer. Some customer comes over to make a buy, figures why give old Brucie the money when he can just take it, instead?"

"Maybe," Jack said. "But it looks more personal than that."

Keenan bent down for a closer look at the dents in Bruce Serinis's forehead. "I guess you're right." The perp could have come up behind Serinis when he was cleaning the seeds out of his Maui Wowee — knock him over, take the money, get out. But this was a facial assault, which often meant that he had something emotional against the vic.

Keenan yawned. "Those Crime Scene guys are taking their goddamn time. You wanna watch the tube? He's got cable."

"No. Go ahead if you want."

Jack's new partner didn't move toward the TV. Instead, he perched on a stool, careful not to disturb anything on the counter. The clock in the kitchen ticked loudly. The refrigerator hummed. Keenan shifted on his seat. "You remember the first time you saw a body?"

"A body?" Jack said. A chill flicked the base of his spine.

"Yeah. Not at a funeral—I mean, out on the street."

Jack looked down and pinched some carpet lint off his knee. "I don't know," he lied. He had been fifteen years old. November 14, 1965. One o'clock in the afternoon.

"I guess when I was in the Army," he said instead.

"You saw somebody get shot in Nam?"

"No. It wasn't a gunshot. And it was in Germany. I was stationed there for a few months before I got shipped to the Philippines. It was winter, and we had to go walk guard duty—it was so cold that sometimes our feet would literally freeze. We'd start up a jeep, then take off our boots, sit on the back, warm our feet in the exhaust. One night this grunt was doing that and some hot dog swung a personnel carrier real fast into the compound, crushed him right into the back of the jeep."

"*Oof.*" Keenan grimaced.

Jack wandered over to a sleek black answering machine. The counter said three messages. He pulled on a glove and then pressed play.

"Bruce, it's your mother. Your father and I were wondering if you'd like to come up for the weekend. You can bring a friend if you

want. What was that nice girl's name—Laurie? Anyhow, call us. We might have a barbecue on Sunday." Beep.

"Serinis, you stud-muffin, it's Alan. That chick looked pretty wasted by the time we left. What a cow. So, did you fuck her? Let me know—I'm at work." Beep.

"Yo, Brewster, man, it's Dingo. Can I come over and get something later? Like around midnight? I've got the cash right now. Call me at home. Thanks." Beep.

Jack turned to his new partner. "Could be our perp right there. If some cokehead was dumb or stoned enough to leave a message like that, he might have been dumb enough not to erase it after he did the murder."

"We need to find old Dingo."

"Let's look for an address book."

"Hold on." Keenan walked over to a desk in the corner, where animated tropical fish swam across a computer screen. He nudged the mouse and the Desktop blipped into view. He sat down and clicked on various icons.

"I've got an address list," he said after a minute. "No 'Dingo,' though."

He returned to his clicking and scrolling. "Wait a minute. Here we go. Boy, he did a great job of hiding the file—he called it 'Cheech and Chong.' Phone numbers, even addresses. And here's our friend Dingo."

"Tell you what," Jack said, sitting wearily on a stool. "If you want to go pick up our boy, I'll wait here for the Crime Scene guys. Get some backup before you go over there."

Keenan grinned. He made a quick call to request that a couple of patrol units meet him at the location.

"I'll let you know how it goes down. Thanks, Leightner."

Jack sat in the silent apartment, remembering a victim in Germany. And another one in Red Hook.

To shut out the past, he went over and stared down at the present vic.

Bruce Serinis was dead. He wouldn't be attending the Princeton alumni reunion marked by the invite on the coffee table. He wouldn't watch any of the programs listed in the *TV Guide* for the rest of the week, would never again call any of the customers in his computer file. But Jack could watch the TV and he could pick up the phone. That was one of the strange lessons of the homicide squad: a life could be snuffed out in an instant, but the world went right on.

Serinis lay in a twisted, awkward position. The side of his face was smashed into the carpet and his mouth sagged slack. Human life was a battle to stand up, take steps, fight gravity. With a blow or gunshot —*bang!*—gravity suddenly won. Every crime scene was a testament to that victory.

Looking at the slumped, wasted bodies, Jack found it hard to believe in an afterlife. It was difficult to look at Serinis and consider him more than just blank flesh. And he didn't feel his usual curiosity about the victim. That was partly due to an instinctive distaste: he didn't like the rampant sense of irony in the apartment, from the posters to the victim's T-shirt, which read: Welcome to New York. Now Fuck Off. He didn't like the sound of the friends on the answering machine; didn't like the picture of a shallow and slobby life. He had dealt with all sorts of mutts as victims, but they didn't have the opportunities this kid had had. It was one thing to sell drugs if you were trying to break out of the ghetto, but this graduate of an Ivy League school should have made better use of his head start.

Maybe it wasn't the victim. Maybe he was just getting burnt out on the job. Sick of all the corpses. He'd seen plenty of old workhorses who didn't give a shit anymore, who just plodded toward their pensions. The Homicide beat didn't foster an optimistic outlook. Dive bars and casual sex didn't help. He had to cast far back to find moments — making love with his new wife, holding his infant son for the first time — when he'd been certain that the body was filled with a spirit.

The clock ticked on. He picked up the copy of *Playboy* from the coffee table and flipped through a pictorial. The July Playmate of the Month had tits that were perfectly round and so freestanding that they had to be fake. And she had one hand between her legs. Christ. He remembered *Playboy* from the days when he could really get excited about it, at thirteen, fourteen. Back then the models had big tits but they were real and slightly droopy. And the women were modest, wearing negligees coyly placed to conceal even the slightest trace of bush. He'd been thinking a lot lately about whether life tended to get better or worse — this seemed like a crazy way to mark the progress.

He remembered a stack of magazines in an old shed, a clubhouse where the more streetwise Red Hook kids smoked cigarettes and speculated about sex. He'd been initiated into the club after he boosted a carton of smokes from a five-and-dime. That was a time when, despite his father's heavy hand, Jack had started taking pleasure in small acts of rebellion. His brother followed him to the clubhouse one day, but Jack told him to buzz off, to come back when he was older. If only he could take back those moments — if only he could go back in time and invite him in.

Peter, who left this world before he really lived in it. Who never saw men land on the moon. Never watched the Beatles turn hippie. Never knew that Nixon became president. Or Ford or Carter or the rest. Never used a computer, VCR, or fax machine. Never even had a chance to make love to a woman.

Jack sighed, then stood up. His heart was heavy, but he'd been carrying this weight for thirty-five years.

Out in the hallway a uniform kept guard, a beefy Irish kid. He held one hand to his belt in the stance of an aspiring gunfighter, but his eyes were dull with the boredom of the job.

Jack pulled the door closed. "Don't touch anything in there, okay? If the Crime Scene guys show up, tell 'em I just went out for a cup of coffee."

"Yes, sir," the kid replied.

Jack pulled out a cigarette. He coughed as he took the first drag. A little voice in his head said, *Those are gonna kill you someday.* Another voice answered: *Everybody dies.*

The sidewalks of Park Slope buzzed with couples and hungry singles, crowds streaming across Seventh Avenue against the lights. A group of yuppies in rumpled business suits spilled out of a bar and swaggered around Jack without a single "excuse me;" the air was thick with alcohol and testosterone.

Happy faces floated past, but he was sinking. He thought of calling Michelle — he *wanted* to call Michelle — but her image in his mind was blended with a picture of Mr. Gardner lying helpless upstairs. Was that the only reason he didn't call? No, he dug deeper into his heart and hit ice: he was afraid.

And tired: he hadn't slept well in a week.

There was always Sheila. He hadn't spoken to her since his last drop-in; now here he was considering a call. What a sad sack.

He could fall into a bar instead; he was in plainclothes, so who would be the wiser? He wanted to bury himself — in flesh, in alcohol, it didn't matter.

Go home, he told himself. Go talk to your son.

He was afraid of that too.

Instead, he walked. Off Seventh Avenue, the side streets were quiet save for a few dog walkers and couples promenading in the warm night air. He turned a corner outside a church. Through a tall iron fence, a group of little white statues gleamed amid some dark ivy. A shepherd. A wise-faced little lamb. The Virgin Mary, sad and sweet.

He paused, weary. He supposed he should get back to the crime scene, but he was sick of the smell of bong water, sick of searching the remnants of Bruce Serinis's wasted life. What was he doing? he wondered. A Jewish man standing in the dark outside a church? He didn't have to be Christian to be moved by the Virgin, though. She had the face of any mother grieving over her murdered son.

"The meeting's down there," someone said in the darkness.

Jack spun around. Under the little bit of light that filtered down from a street lamp through the dense trees, a man sat on the steps of the church, smoking. The stranger leaned over the railing and pointed. A flight of stairs led down below street level to a door. "It's okay. It hasn't started yet. Go on in."

"I think you've got me mixed up with someone else."

The man sat back and took a deep drag of his cigarette. "Whatever. It's an open meeting."

Jack stepped away. He looked at his watch and realized that he'd only killed ten minutes. Chances were that the Crime Scene team hadn't even arrived yet. On impulse, he turned back and walked down the stairs.

He felt awkward entering the church, even if it was only the basement. When he was a kid in Red Hook, some neighborhood boys had dared him to go inside Visitation Church. They told him he'd be hit by lightning because he was a Christ Killer.

He walked down a corridor to a large fluorescent-lit basement hall. Rows of people sat in folding chairs facing a low stage with a faded red velvet curtain and an American flag on a stand. It reminded him of his elementary-school auditorium. Out of old habit, he found a seat near the back.

A lanky red-haired man casually mounted the stage and sat behind a card table. "Okay, let's get going," he said. "If this is your first time here, you should know that we have a regular meeting every night, and on Fridays we have a special Step meeting after that."

Jack glanced around and noticed small red-lettered signs on the walls which proclaimed One Day At A Time and Take It Easy. His eyes widened at a big scroll headed The Twelve Steps. He'd stumbled into an AA meeting. Would it suddenly stop when they noticed the arrival of an impostor?

Flushed, he was about to jump up, but when he looked around no one seemed concerned about his presence. The forty or so members sat calmly, many of them with arms folded across their chests. He'd never been to such a meeting before, but he'd imagined they'd be full of old men with stubbly beards, wearing dirty raincoats. *Alcoholics*. It hadn't occurred to him that they might look like this, these people who might have walked in off a busy downtown street. People in suits and ties. Normal-looking people.

Nowadays his own father would probably be called an alcoholic, though he hadn't drunk steadily through the week. Paydays were the worst, when the old man would go on a bender, spinning like a tornado through the row of waterfront bars. But back then, you were simply a "drinking man" or "dry," and there weren't many of the latter down on the docks.

On a bulletin board at the Homicide Task Force office, someone had posted a flyer for ACOA meetings. Adult Children of Alcoholics. Jack scoffed at the notion. Meetings, steps, counseling—it all seemed riddled with weakness. So

213

what if he'd had a tough childhood? Who didn't, down in the Hook?

The red-haired man glanced at his watch. "Okay, let's start with our qualifying speaker."

A young woman in the front row stood and walked up on stage. She sat and cleared her throat.

"Hi, my name is Janet, and I'm an alcoholic and an addict."

"Hi, Janet," everyone around Jack replied. Startled, he looked around, thinking that someone was sure to notice his silence.

"I'm going to talk for a while," Janet said. "Then we'll open this up to anyone who wants to share."

She wore a businesswoman's suit with a skirt and a silk bow, and her blond hair was pulled back into a neat ponytail. She looked as though she belonged in some suburban country club. She was pretty, Jack noticed—he glanced under the table and saw that she had great legs. Inwardly, he snorted—what hard-luck story could she tell? That she sometimes drank an extra glass of white wine after a tennis match?

"I had my first drink when I was twelve," she said. "I was a chubby girl. My parents were always pushing me to join different groups or take classes after school, but I never felt comfortable with other kids. I didn't want to go to school at all because I was so scared of talking to people."

"My parents went out a lot to social events, political fundraisers and things. We got left with this baby-sitter who would fall asleep right away. My dad kept his liquor on a little side table in his den. There was this green bottle sitting there; I was curious, because my father always drank some when he came home from work. One night I went in and poured a little bit into the cap, like mouthwash. I swallowed it in one gulp. It tasted terrible. I swallowed a couple more capfuls and — this may sound strange — I realized immediately that I had found something I could be good at. I could be good at drinking."

Jack shifted his weight, trying to get comfortable on the hard metal chair. He glanced around. The other listeners sat back patiently, half of their attention focused on the speaker and half directed somewhere deep within themselves. A couple of them nodded their heads sympathetically.

"Before, when I went into a room full of strangers, I was so scared I felt like I was going to pass out, but I found that if I drank a little first I could deal with it. It wasn't that hard to get ahold of the liquor. My parents ordered a lot and they didn't keep track of it. And drinking helped me to start making friends with other kids at school. We'd sneak off during free time and get people to buy us some Boone's Farm or André cold duck."

The listeners chuckled, remembering their own drinking days.

"When I was fourteen, I got shipped off to prep school up in New Hampshire. I don't remember much from those years because I was so drunk most of the time. Or high. A lot of the kids had really good pot. Or quaaludes. We had ways to get into town and get adults to buy liquor for us. There were a lot of fucked-up kids there, kids whose parents were famous, or psychiatrists, or whatever. These were sophisticated kids: they didn't drink cold duck. We had Amaretto drunks, Drambuie drunks . . .

"I don't know how I managed to graduate. I guess you had to do something really terrible to get kicked out of that school.

"In college, it was easy to drink. It was even encouraged. I joined a sorority and we used to make the rounds of all the frat parties. We'd get wasted on grain-alcohol punch. It tasted like Kool-Aid."

"The second semester of my sophomore year, I went to this Halloween party. I must have blacked out. When I woke up I was in a storage room full of old bedframes and stained mattresses, and this guy was on top of me. He might have been raping me, or maybe I started it. I couldn't remember. The next thing I knew, there were a couple of his friends in the room. They gave me some shots of bourbon with Coors chasers. Boilermakers. And then they took turns fucking me. One of them even threw up on me."

Jack looked around. He felt uncomfortable listening to this raw confession, but the others were impassive, still. It seemed incredible that someone would stand up and say such things to a group of strangers, and nearly as incredible that the strangers would calmly listen.

"I woke up the next day," she continued. "Somehow — I have no idea how — I got back to my dorm room. I should have felt horrible, but I didn't let myself feel anything. I took a couple of quaaludes and went to this bar in town and drank three pitchers of beer.

"After college I went to law school. To this day, I can't imagine how I got in. Maybe the interviewer thought I looked cute. I was sort of conventionally pretty by then, and of course I was blond. I used my looks a lot. On the inside, I felt like I was really ugly, that I was just *shit*, but guys were always coming on to me, so I used it.

"I was still a functioning alcoholic. I was able to do my schoolwork during the day and party just at night and on the weekends.

"The pressure that first year was really terrible, with such a heavy course load, but I met this guy in the library who turned me on to speed. I started getting into coke too, into freebasing. I remember one time I went home for Thanksgiving and I was so wired that I almost ground my teeth completely down. My mother asked what was wrong, and I just told her that I was under a lot of stress with the studying. They didn't know, my parents. They were too fucked up themselves. Five o'clock cocktails.

"I hardly ever went out anymore. I'd just stay in my room, 'base, drink. I didn't eat. I spent all the money my parents sent me on staying drunk, staying high. I would even drink in lecture classes. Take an orange soda and pour out half the can, fill the rest up with vodka.

"The school finally kicked me out. I told my parents I was taking a semester off. I started hanging out with some really bad people. I would black out a lot, but somehow I always made it back to my apartment. I'd get phone calls, people telling me that they'd found my purse somewhere. I'd pass out on trains, get shaken by cops at the end of the line. Sometimes I'd wake up, and I'd have pissed all over myself. Or worse."

Jack winced. He looked around, but no else seemed to be judging the speaker. The others sat and listened, some of them nodding or shaking their heads ruefully, as if they knew exactly what she was talking about. A man sitting next to him quietly got up and went to a table in the back of the room, where he poured himself a cup of coffee. When he came back, he offered Jack a chocolate-chip cookie. Jack shook his head.

"I started living with a man," the speaker continued, "but I wasn't in love with him. I'd never been in love with anybody, because I was afraid that if they got too close they'd freak out when they saw what a disaster I was inside. We hardly ever went out or even had sex — we'd just sit in the apartment and drink.

"Sometimes I'd go out drinking with this woman, Lee-Anne, the only friend I had left over from college. I think I really loved her — not in a sexual way, but because she was such a mess, and I didn't have to hide anything from her.

LeeAnne had shot smack, whatever. She would try anything. She was the only person I could really talk to. We
cried together a lot.

"One day she told me that she'd gone to a meeting and
decided to get clean. I laughed and gave her shit about it.
She stopped going out, but I'd call her up: *Come on, we'll just
have one beer. Don't be such a fucking goody-goody.* She avoided
me. I was pissed off that she'd abandoned me. I was so
angry that I even . . . one time when she finally agreed to
come over, she asked for a Seven-UP and I took a can of
Bud and put it in one of those foam insulator sleeves so she
couldn't see the label. She must've smelled the alcohol, because she didn't drink. She was so upset she refused to see
me after that.

"She was sober about four months.

"And then one afternoon—I was living on Boylston
Street—this dealer named Henry came by and told me she'd
OD'ed. One day she was going to meetings, the next day
she was just *gone*. I was scared shitless. I was able to think
clearly enough to wonder what would have happened if I'd
given her a little support."

Jack shifted again in his chair—not from restlessness, but
because he felt his eyes watering.

"One day," Janet continued, "I was passing a community
center near Inman Square. I saw these people walking up a
stairway and I just followed them in. I think in some sub-
conscious way I knew where they were going. I don't know
if it was God or fate that led me there, but I do know that
if I hadn't gone in, I'd be dead now.

"That was my first meeting. I've got seven years sober."

"Before I wrap up, I want to talk about Steps Four and
Five."

She picked up a booklet and read. " 'We made a searching
and fearless moral inventory of ourselves.' " And, " 'We ad-

mitted to God, to ourselves, and to another human being the exact nature of our wrongs.' "

She picked up a water glass and took a sip. "I was doing okay in the program for the first year, but those two steps scared the hell out of me. Nobody could make me do them, no way.

"After I got my first year, my sponsor helped me work up the courage. I did both steps together in one weekend. I spent a whole Sunday morning in her apartment, telling her everything, even things so horrible that I always thought I would take them to the grave with me. Just talking about LeeAnne, I thought I'd die.

"And you know what happened? I *didn't* die. All of those things I was so terrified to say, even to myself—since then I've talked about them from podiums, I've shared them in meetings.

"Though I can try to make amends to the people who are still alive, I know I can never go back and change the past. But at least I don't have to pick up a drink tonight. Thanks for listening."

She stood up and returned to the front row.

Other people took turns sitting behind the table. They thanked Janet and told her they identified with her feelings of being different and isolated. They joked about their own blackouts and lost wallets. Jack was nervous that someone would ask him to get up to speak, but he was too stunned by the confessions to leave.

One man didn't respond to Janet's speech—he seemed too wrapped up in his own problems. He identified himself as an alcoholic and a sex offender. He said he felt bad because he'd spent the past weekend "acting out with pornography," but that thanks to the program he had resisted the impulse to drink or to follow up on his "other urges."

Some of the other people in the group looked slightly

uncomfortable, but no one criticized the man. Jack was amazed: it seemed that there was nothing a person couldn't say in front of the group.

When the meeting wound down, he got up quietly and slipped out. He suspected that the session would end with the members gathering around to chat with each other and he didn't want to be there.

Out on the street, he lit a cigarette and strode off, his mind whirling. He went back and spent another hour dealing with the crime scene. And then, the next thing he knew, he was sitting on a stool in a yuppie bar on Seventh Avenue, ordering a Bass ale.

"You want a pint?" the bartender asked.

"No, a short one will do it."

Do what? He didn't plan on any heavy drinking. He just wanted to feel the frosted mug in his hands, to savor that first cold sip going down. He thought of all the people in the meeting, tormented by the one drink they couldn't have.

He remembered a joke he'd heard once sitting on another stool in another bar, a joke that seemed to explain a lot of stupid behavior.

"Why does a dog lick its balls?"

Because it can.

twenty-seven

The morning brought good news.

First, Jack called the hospital and found out that Mr. Gardner had been moved out of intensive care to a semi-private room.

Then, he was at work at the task force when a call came in from Tommy Keenan at the Seven-eight: the "Dingo" on Bruce Serinis's answering machine had turned out to be one very jittery cokehead. After less than half an hour of interrogation, he broke down and confessed to the Serinis murder.

"Incredible," Keenan said. "The mook actually left his message on the machine."

Jack wasn't surprised. He knew of more than one perp who'd accidentally dropped his wallet in flight from a crime scene. Another criminal genius lost an inscribed gold bracelet, then had the further brilliance to return and ask a uniform guarding the scene if he could look for it.

He celebrated with a fresh cup of coffee from the supply room, then sat down with renewed energy to review his files on the Berrios/Ortslee killings, hoping to tease out some new angle or approach.

He made a call to the Department of Transportation, trying again to find someone who might have been contacted as to the whereabouts of Raymond Ortslee. The call was forwarded deeper and deeper into the labyrinth of city, state, and federal bureaucracy, bouncing him like a pinball from the Coast Guard to the Maritime Administration office to the Port Authority. End result: zilch.

On a hunch, he tried some background checks on Randall Heiser, the real estate hotshot who lived in Berrios's building. Sergeant Tanney wouldn't approve of further interviews, but the boss wouldn't know if he made a few routine calls.

He ran *lugs and tolls*, a check of phone-company records to see if Heiser had made or received any calls from Tomas Berrios or Raymond Ortslee.

No luck there.

He called a friend at the Department of Motor Vehicles.

Three minutes later, brimming with excitement, he set down the receiver and grabbed his jacket.

Daskivitch was behind his desk inhaling a jelly donut when Jack walked in to the Seven-six squad room. The young detective looked up sheepishly. "Want one?" he mumbled.

"No, thanks," Jack said. "I'm watching my figure."

"Wanna siddown?"

Jack nodded and pulled up a chair. He grinned. "I got something you might be interested in."

Daskivitch wiped some sugar off his chin. "Like what?"

"I decided to dig a little deeper on that guy Heiser we talked to the other day."

Daskivitch glanced around the squad room and leaned forward. "Quiet, okay? My boss busted my chops about our little visit to Manhattan. I guess that rich jerkoff must have griped."

"Don't worry about him," Jack said. "The thing is, I checked lugs and tolls and came up short: Berrios never phoned Heiser from his home, or vice versa."

"That's very exciting. But you shouldn't have come all this way—"

Jack held up a hand. "I also called the DMV. Turns out our friend Heiser has several outstanding parking tickets. His last one was a summons issued on May eighth for a right on red. On Van Brunt Street. In Red Hook."

"Holy shit. He said he hadn't been there recently." Daskivitch paused to consider the implications. "Do you think we should bring him in?"

"Not yet. With the flak we're getting from above, I want to figure out what he was up to before we call him in. Let's keep this between us for now. If we get some evidence on the bastard, they won't be able to pull us off him. In the meantime, I'll buy you lunch."

"Actually, I'm in court this afternoon, but I'll work with you as soon as I get past this other case. Great job, bunk. Let me know if you get anything else."

Jack stood up to go. "You better believe it, kid."

Carroll Gardens had once been part of Red Hook, until the Gowanus Expressway sliced the neighborhood in half. While the waterfront side had deteriorated over the years, the Gardens had maintained its strength as a tight-knit Italian community. As Jack drove down Court Street, he passed little family stores advertising fresh mozzarella and ravioli. The neighborhood had a low burglary rate because every block had its grandmothers leaning out the windows—and because the Mafia *soldieri* didn't tolerate any crime on their quiet side streets. As Jack got out of his car, he heard the Righteous Brothers singing "Unchained Melody" on a radio somewhere, and a grizzled old man who could have been an extra for *Goodfellas* trudged by pushing a baby carriage.

The front yard of Cosenza's Funeral Home looked like a

patio in front of a pricey Italian restaurant: well-trimmed hedges, cherubs spraying water in a little aquamarine fountain, a four-foot-high statue of the Virgin Mary standing with open hands. The interior — dim table lamps, plastic-upholstered pale green couches, and sprays of orchids in marble urns — was gloomy, but Larry Cosenza was not. As Jack entered, he rose from his desk, a handsome, broad-shouldered, white-haired man who wore his tie loose at the collar, indicating how comfortable he was as the unofficial mayor of the neighborhood. He was also the local historian, philosopher, and community activist — in the 1960s, when hundreds of middle-class families were fleeing South Brooklyn for the suburbs, he'd organized to keep his neighborhood intact.

"Jackie Leightner! Haven't seen you around here since Artie Benvenuto's funeral. How long ago was that?"

"I dunno. Maybe four, five years."

"You look tired. Hey, how's the family? I hope this is just a social visit."

Jack loosened his own collar. "Not really, Larry. It's a work thing. I need your advice. You have a few minutes?"

"Sure. I'm having a slow day here."

"Why don't we go for a drive?"

Jack stopped for a red light at the edge of the Red Hook Houses. Scraps of trash dotted the dried-out lawns between the buildings. A group of young toughs glared at the car, then melted into the interior of the projects.

"Jesus, things sure have changed since our day," Jack said, glancing at a flashy sports car double-parked at the curb. Even through the closed window, he could feel the angry bass of the car's stereo thumping out into the world.

Larry chuckled. "Remember Mr. Anselmo, with his withered arm, shouting at us to stay off the lawns?"

"He swung that arm at Pat Spillane. Knocked him on his ass. Nobody gives a shit about the lawns now."

"That's not true," Larry said. "There are a lot of good people in the Houses. I've been spending a lot of time in there."

"What, are you kidding?"

"You remember when those three white kids from the Gardens beat the shit out of that black kid last year?"

"Yeah, I remember. Some of those kids were *connected*."

"Well, that's what I'm working on. The kids in the Houses see most of us in the Gardens as racist mobsters, and a lot of people in the Gardens think everybody in the Hook is a ghetto hood. I'm trying to set up programs to get kids from both sides together."

Jack whistled. "Good luck. The place is a mess."

"Maybe—but you can understand how it happened."

"Yeah, a lot of people discovered that it's easier to sell drugs than to do a real day's work."

"Work? What work? There are no jobs. You know how many longshoremen we had in Red Hook before the Second World War? Over ten thousand. You know how many were left by the mid-sixties? About a hundred."

"If people want work, they can find work. Look at my old man. He came to this country hardly speaking English, without a dime in his pocket."

"Hold on," Larry said. "Your father and my father came to this country because the government let a certain number of foreigners in to do the shit work—dig the ditches, build the railroads, unload the ships. Now most of those jobs are gone."

The light changed and Jack drove on past the Houses, toward Van Brunt Street and the waterfront.

"Everybody acts as if the poor were just dropped here by God," Larry said. "As if it's just a fact of life. We don't look at the history."

Jack watched two teenage boys on a corner shoving each

other around in a mock fight. "I know, I know. Slavery and all . . ."

"That's not what I'm talking about. After World War Two, Big Agriculture was wiping out the small farms down South, so we had millions of blacks moving north, looking for jobs. And Puerto Ricans. By the time they got here manufacturing was dying out, the docks were fading. All those people couldn't find work and they weren't allowed to train for the new industries. That's when you get into welfare and drugs and the rest of this mess. It's not a mystery how the neighborhood ended up this way."

Jack shrugged; he had more pressing concerns. They parked in front of the city tow pound on Conover Street and walked down to the tiny Garden Pier.

"We're trying to build some new parks here," Larry said. "There's almost no place left where the public can get to the water these days. We want the city involved in getting this neighborhood going again. Did you hear they're finally cleaning up the Gowanus? It's gonna take a lot of work to get all the sludge and poisons out of there. This may sound crazy, but I think that one day it could be like San Antonio, with restaurants and parks all along the canal."

They sat on a bench and watched the Staten Island ferry chug out across the bay.

"Listen, Larry—you probably know more about this place than anybody. I need to know why a big Manhattan real estate guy would be interested in such a fucked-up neighborhood in Brooklyn."

"What's the guy's name?"

"Randall Heiser."

"Never heard of him."

"He keeps a low profile. Have you heard of a company called Sumner International?"

"Can't say I have."

"What's been going on around here, real-estatewise?"

"The neighborhood's been on an upswing in the past few years. Since that school principal got shot, your buddies in Narcotics have been running sweeps in the projects and we get more patrol cars on the street these days. Some artists and yuppies have been moving in, buying up old houses. But that's penny-ante stuff, not something a big shot would be involved with."

"What else?"

"A guy in the neighborhood's been buying up some of the old piers. He's turning them into artists' studios, homes for small businesses. If you're still with Homicide, though, I guess you're looking for something a little more sinister."

"Sinister enough to kill somebody over. Let me come at this from another angle. What could some Manhattan real estate developer be doing over here that he'd want hushed up?"

The funeral-parlor owner considered the question as they watched a couple of seagulls struggle against a stiff shore breeze. He pointed out across the water. "That might be your answer right there."

Jack leaned forward, staring. "What?"

"You can't see it from here, but I'm talking about the Fresh Kills landfill over there on Staten Island. It's the largest dump on earth and the biggest thing ever built by human hands. The city sent most of its garbage there."

Jack sighed. "That's great, Larry, but what does this have to do with Red Hook?"

"Fresh Kills finally got too big. Hey, pretty good name for a murder investigation, huh? 'Fresh Kills'?"

Jack groaned *"Larry."*

"The point is, the city just closed the place down. Which raises the question of where is all that trash gonna go? They wanna send most of it away somewhere, but first it has to go to waste transfer stations."

"What does that mean?"

"That's where regular garbage trucks transfer the stuff to bigger trucks so they can haul it out of town."

"What does that mean for Red Hook?"

Larry tossed a pebble into the water. "If you're the government, and you have final say over where these stations are gonna go, how do you decide? Red Hook already has a lot of property zoned for heavy industry, and it's missing the most important obstacle."

"What's that?"

"Voters. There are only about eleven thousand people here now. And most of them are black or Latino, and poor. They're not organized and most of them don't even vote. If they manage to scrape together some money, they get the hell out of the 'hood as fast as they can."

Jack frowned as he stared out across the water. *Garbage.* If the two men attempting to dispose of Tomas Berrios had been Mobbed up, it wouldn't be a surprise to hear that garbage was involved. What was it with the Mob and its attraction to such elemental industries? Concrete. Gravel. Trash. They were playgrounds for brutal, primitive men who liked to use their hands. The city had done a major crackdown on Mafia involvement in the trash-hauling trade, but that hadn't necessarily finished it off.

"So the city can just go ahead and put the station here?"

"Not so fast. You got me and a group of other people who are gonna make a hell of a noise if they try. We've already got petitions going, and we're holding meetings. If they put a big station here after all the work we've done to turn the neighborhood around, we're screwed. How many people are gonna want to buy a house here if you've got hundreds of stinky garbage trucks barreling through the streets? The neighborhood has taken a lot of hits over the years, but this could be the last nail in the coffin."

Jack imagined the Hook finally dying under a heap of trash. Burying all of the good memories along with the bad. He felt helpless again.

"What could you do?"

"If they want to put it on city property, we can hold all sorts of public hearings, maybe tie them up in the courts."

"What if they put a transfer station on private property? What if a private contractor runs it?"

"Now you're asking some good questions."

Jack stared out across the harbor. "Larry, can you do me a favor?"

"Anytime."

"I need you to look into some real estate stuff for me, but you gotta be real low-key about it, 'cause it could be dangerous. Ask around and see if you can find out if this Sumner International has bought up any chunks of property in Red Hook recently. They'd probably have done it under some other name — it might be a company called, hold on a minute" — he pulled out his steno book and flipped through the pages — "P and L Enterprises. They own a garage at Seven Coffey Street. That would be a big help to me." He turned away from the water and looked back to Red Hook. "And maybe it could be a big help to you too."

"I'll be glad to do it," Larry said, "but why don't you just run this through your NYPD research people?"

Jack bent down and picked up a pebble, shook it in his cupped hand. "I would, but I've been told not to stir up trouble. You know how it gets when you start dealing with rich people." He squinted. "Speaking of which: this transfer station — would there be much money in it?"

Larry Cosenza stood up and brushed off the seat of his pants. "Fresh Kills received thirteen thousand tons of garbage every friggin' day. *You* do the math."

twenty-eight

The night skittered by in uneasy dreams: a corpse crying in a closet, a rumbling mountain of trash, a knife wound like a little red mouth.

As the first light filtered in through the window, Jack heard his son tiptoeing through the living room. He rolled over blearily. "Hey, kid. You on your way to work?"

Ben nodded. "Sorry. I didn't mean to wake you."

"S'okay."

His son navigated around the futon and several piles of books. He lifted a canvas bag and a tripod off the desk, then continued on toward the front door. His hand was on the knob when he stopped and turned. "You gonna be around later? Like around six or seven?"

Jack yawned. "I dunno — why?"

Ben scratched his little tuft of beard. "I was thinking maybe I'd make some dinner. If you were gonna be around."

Jack was eager to get back to sleep, but he was awake enough to notice that the kid was making an effort to be more sociable. He squinted with one eye open. "Okay. Sounds good."

Ben nodded and went out.

Jack rolled over and burrowed as best he could back into the hard futon.

He had the day off; he managed to sleep in for a couple more hours, then got up and went out in search of food. Under normal circumstances, he would have asked Sergeant Tanney if he could come in to work, but his boss was clearly not in favor of pursuing any small leads against Randall Heiser. That was okay—the trail would still be there when he returned to the office. There was no concrete evidence that Randall Heiser had anything to do with the murders, but the man had lied about being in Red Hook. It was a loose thread—and the key to good detective work was having an eye for such threads. You never knew when you'd pull one and the whole mystery would unravel.

If—to play with a possibility—Heiser had been involved in the murder, what was the motive? What could Tomas Berrios have done to set him off? Had he re-entered Heiser's apartment? What could he have messed with inside? The man's wife? Jack doubted that. Was Berrios sleeping with the maid? That didn't seem like a reason for homicide, unless perhaps Heiser also had a thing with the Romanian girl. No—if he was having an affair with Marie Burhala and then caught her with the porter, he'd hardly have kept her around after.

Just before the day of his death, Berrios had hinted to both his wife and his large-headed friend about a financial score. A drug deal? A robbery? Considering his reputation and lack of a serious criminal record, neither scenario seemed probable. Could Berrios have been involved in some sort of shady deal with Heiser in Red Hook? That also seemed unlikely. Why would a big real estate mogul need the services of a humble porter?

Maybe the score was based on some sudden opportunity. Maybe Berrios had seen something valuable in Heiser's apartment and grabbed it. Or could he have seen something he shouldn't have and decided to blackmail the tenant? It was all pure speculation. There was still no proof that Randall Heiser had committed any crimes greater than arrogance and dishonesty.

The day was already shaping up to be a scorcher. A couple of blocks past his son's apartment, Jack walked by a wizened man sitting on a folding chair in the shade of a store awning. On the sidewalk stood a wheeled cart lined with bottles of syrup in Day-Glo colors: blue, orange, red, yellow.

The little man peeled back a piece of burlap from a block of ice. "You want?"

Jack hadn't even eaten breakfast, but he was in unusually high spirits. He nodded and pointed, curious what flavor blue would be.

The vendor scraped shavings into a little paper cup, poured syrup over it.

Jack stood on the corner in the sun, savoring his snow cone. Mint. Soon he was squeezing the last cold slush out of the bottom of the cup, wondering if his lips were stained blue.

Tomas Berrios might have bought cones for his kids at this same stand.

Recina Berrios sat out on her stoop. She wore a faded housedress; Jack noted the dark circles under her eyes, the way she looked thinner in just two weeks. She watched him listlessly as he walked up to the gate.

He held out his gold shield. "Do you remember me, Mrs. Berrios? We talked at the funeral."

Her face came alive. "Did you find him? Did you find who did this to my husband?"

Jack scratched his head. "I'm sorry, ma'am. We're still working on it. Believe me."

Her face turned off and her gaze returned to some vague middle distance.

The bedroom was small, with barely enough room to walk around the queen-size bed with its shiny silver comforter. Several diamond-shaped mirrors were set into the black-and-white headboard: Art Deco, purchased cheap. Studio photos of the kids covered the walls; they posed stiffly in their Sunday best, little pastel suits and dresses. A wooden crucifix hung over the bed, Jesus looking sadder than ever.

Recina stood in the doorway. "He didn't have nothing to hide. No drugs, no guns, nothing like that."

"I know," Jack replied. "But that piece of paper you found with the address might have been important. Maybe he left something else like that around."

The wife shrugged. "You can look. I'll be in the kitchen."

Most people would never have trusted a cop to pry around their bedrooms alone, but she seemed past caring.

The children were shopping with their grandmother, so the apartment was quiet, a museum of humble treasures.

Left to himself, Jack surveyed the hot little room — no air-conditioning here. The Crime Scene crew had already searched the apartment, but they hadn't necessarily known what to look for.

The job took longer than it might have, for two reasons. First, since this was not a forced search, he had to be careful to return everything to its original state. Second, he kept pausing to muse about Tomas Berrios's life.

Checking out the mattress, he wondered if this was where the little boy and girl were conceived (such sacred sex, when you knew you were making a child). As he ran his hand underneath the box spring, he wondered if the children had run squealing in the room mornings to leap on the bed and wake up their father with a game of hop on Pop (as Ben had when he was a little boy). It was not uncommon to find hidden pornography, even in a married man's bedroom, but there was none of that here. He did find writing on the plywood back of the dresser, a newlywed couple's pledge: *"Tomas + Recina para siempre. Jan. 4, 1993."*

Tomas Berrios had a wife who loved him. Children who depended on him. A family and a home. He was not important enough in the world for his death to draw the attention of the media, but in his own way he had been a rich man.

Tossing a white-collar home was time-consuming: you had to scan stacks of paper — business files, personal records, letters, computer data. But Tomas Berrios's home was nearly devoid of reading material, save for a Spanish Bible, a local weekly newspaper, and some photo-comics. The search was an inventory of mute objects.

Jack explored the front room, the kitchen, the childrens' bedroom, even the bathroom, without success.

On impulse, he returned to the bedroom. A place for private things. Secret. He opened the clothes closet and scanned the small collection of cheap suits and dresses. He dragged a chair over and stood on it to run his hand over the top shelf. Nothing but dust.

He sat on a chair, his shirt sticking to his skin in the hot, humid apartment, and looked around idly until his gaze fell once more on the local newspaper, which lay on top of a cheap laminated-walnut dresser. It was in English — aside from a *TV Guide*, it was the only English-language text in the house. Why?

The front page held articles about a proposed new mall on Atlantic Avenue and a vandalism problem in Park Slope. He kept going, past an article about a movie shoot disrupting neighborhood parking, a review of an Italian restaurant, a story about a school board scuffle. In the middle of the paper, a jagged space marked where an article had been torn out.

He took out his cell phone and called the number listed on the masthead. A receptionist referred him to the assistant editor, who found a copy of the paper and read him the missing article.

The headline was "Red Hook Residents Vow Garbage Fight." It began:

Recent speculation has local residents concerned that a new waste-management transfer station is coming to Red Hook. At last Wednesday's meeting of Community Board 6, a large and vocal group of residents and community activists pledged that any such plan would be met by protest marches and legal challenges, saying that the increased truck traffic and bad odors would threaten the revitalization of the neighborhood.

Jack went out and found Recina Berrios in the living room. He held up the open newspaper. "Do you know who ripped this article out?"

She looked at him blankly. "I don't know. Are you going to find my husband's killer?"

Jack folded the paper and slipped it in his pocket. "I'm going to try, Mrs. Berrios. I'm going to try as hard as I possibly can."

Out on the sidewalk, he tucked his sports coat in the crook of his arm and walked away, convinced he was on the right track. When he returned to work, he would double his research into Randall Heiser's business dealings.

In the meantime, though, he had an afternoon to kill. He paused on a corner at Smith Street, considering where to go.

An old couple approached down the sidewalk, the man a little sporty gent in a polo shirt and fishing hat, the woman in a tan overcoat despite the summer heat. They bickered. He threatened to walk away and leave her behind; she snapped, "Go ahead—see if I care!" They ventured out across the street, a cat and dog tethered together for life. They didn't like each other, but at least they *had* each other. Jack's maternal grandparents had lived like that: they argued and fought every minute of their lives together, and then his grandmother died. Without his sparring partner, his grandfather had been desolate, inconsolable.

Another couple strolled by, hand in hand, content in each other's company.

He stopped at a pay phone and searched his wallet for Michelle Wilber's phone number.

A little white puff of a cloud drifted out across the blue sky, following Ben as he set off toward Red Hook.

An old Italian guy in an apron was sweeping the sidewalk outside a bakery on Sackett Street, crooning along in a cracked voice with the radio, Paul Anka and "Put Your Head on My Shoulder." Up the block, a tiny East Indian kid was riding a broomstick, whacking himself on the butt with one hand, whinnying and galloping around like a snorting little pony.

Ben pulled out his video camera and collected a few shots, then continued on across the highway into Red Hook. He headed for a quiet back street called Imlay, home to the

TIME Moving and Storage Company. During the day, the company's fleet of small white trucks dispersed throughout the five boroughs, but at night they all returned here to park on the street like pigeons coming home to roost. Ben liked to film them, especially at night. In fanciful moments, he imagined that the company was the secret source of time itself, which the trucks delivered to the city.

Today he found a driver sitting in one of the few vans that remained at the headquarters. The old guy was reading the paper, leaning back with his feet up on the dashboard, a Yankees cap cocked high on his head. He looked mournful, yet content.

"Excuse me," Ben said, "would you mind if I take your picture?"

"What for?" the man said warily, revealing a mouthful of crooked teeth.

"I'm making a film about Red Hook."

"Suit yourself." The man folded his paper, sat up, and posed stiffly.

Ben ran off a few feet of videotape. "Can I ask you a question?"

The man shrugged.

"I've been wondering—does it ever seem strange to you that your company is named after the one thing you can't really move or store?"

The man didn't show any surprise or amusement. He simply tapped the side of his head. "Whaddaya think this is for?" he said dryly. Then he opened his paper again and settled back to read.

Ben chuckled, then walked on, considering what to buy for dinner. That was the easy part—the hard part was thinking of something to talk about with his dad. What was it with fathers and sons, that weird, uncomfortable silence they couldn't seem to escape? It must be a bummer to be a dad, he mused: one day you've got a cheery, talkative five-year-old who's thrilled to play with you, the next you've got a sullen, uncommunicative adult on your hands.

He resolved to try harder. His father wasn't going to be around forever. He rounded a corner, then stopped in the middle of the street. He'd started out with a hazy plan to make a film about the history of Red Hook. Then he'd realized that he was searching for his father's history. Now it occurred to him that what he was really looking for was an explanation of himself. Maybe there was a reason why he was often lonely, why he felt estranged from other people. His father seemed to be the same way. Maybe it had something to do with his grandfather. Maybe the answer lay somewhere in Red Hook.

Tonight he'd find a way to interview his dad about the neighborhood. Set up the tape recorder without making a big deal of it. Say it was an "oral history."

On the way back, he stopped in Carroll Gardens to shop for food. That was the great thing about the neighborhood: even in an age of giant supermarkets and convenience foods, it still had little mom-and-pop stores: butcher shops, a fruit and vegetable stand, bakeries, places where you could buy homemade pasta and olives by the pound.

He bought a bottle of wine and ingredients for the only fancy dish he knew how to cook: vegetable lasagna. It didn't occur to him until after he was home that he'd gotten the recipe from his mother. He hoped his dad wouldn't have some sort of flashback to his failed marriage after the first bite.

Jack had arranged to meet Michelle at five-thirty in a Greek diner in Park Slope. He arrived half an hour early with a copy of the *Daily News;* he figured he'd sit casually, sip a cup

of coffee, and read, and that's how she'd discover him —
relaxed, carefree, mildly apologetic.

The problem was that he couldn't focus on even the short-
est articles. He looked up every time the door opened. As
the clock over the grill parceled the time out in endless
minutes, he was surprised and then alarmed by his level of
eagerness and anxiety. As he thought about his short time
with Michelle, it wasn't the lovemaking he remembered
most, but the fun they'd had on that first date. He was sad
to think how long it had been since he'd known that light-
ness of spirit, that sense of adventure in his life.

Finally, Michelle walked in. She frowned as she set her
purse down and slid into the booth.

"Hey, thanks for coming," Jack said. "I just wanted to
tell you — "

A sad-faced middle-aged waitress bustled up. "What can
I get you folks?"

"I'll have a cup of coffee," Michelle said.

"I'll just have a refill," Jack added.

The waitress pointed to a folded card on the table. "We
have a three-dollar minimum per customer after five
o'clock."

"It's too early to eat," Jack said. "We just want coffee."

"I understand that, sir, but we have a policy here."

He pulled out his wallet, yanked out a ten-dollar bill,
threw it on the table. "Here. Why don't you buy yourself a
personality?"

The waitress drew herself up. "There's no call for that kind
of talk." She left the bill lying on the table and walked away.

"I was a waitress once," Michelle said. "It's a tough job."

Jack sighed. "I've had a rough week. I'm sorry."

"Don't tell me — tell her."

He put his hands up in surrender. "You're right."

When the waitress walked by again, he apologized.

239

"Don't worry about it," she said gruffly. She walked over to her station and poured them some coffee.

Michelle leaned forward as soon as the waitress left. "I want you to understand something: maybe you got the wrong impression, but I don't do that."

"What?"

"What we did. One-night stands. Maybe you think that's the kind of person I am, that you don't have to call again."

"Whoa, wait a minute. I just called you, didn't I?"

"Jack—it's been a week."

"I've been going through a lot. I figured Jeannie would have told you. My landlord had a stroke."

"She told me and I'm sorry. He seems like such a nice old man." She was silent for a moment. "But that's not enough."

His eyes widened. "What do you mean?"

"You could have called and told me directly. Don't you think I would have cared?"

He didn't respond.

"There's more to it than your landlord," she said. "Isn't there?"

He picked up a spoon and rolled it in his fingers. "I don't know. Look, if you want the truth, I haven't been very good with women since my divorce. Sometimes I think I might be too old for this dating business."

"That's not good enough."

He sat up. "*What*'s not good enough?"

She pushed her coffee away. "Listen, I was really hurt when you didn't call. And I'm sorry to be so blunt, but I think you just want to be let off the hook. You figure maybe if you admit that you're nervous, some woman is going to come along and say, 'That's all right, honey.' Well, it's not all right. Everybody's scared—the question is, what are you going to do about it? I don't need another fifty year-old man who doesn't want to grow up."

"Hold on — I wanted to apologize. I just . . . I wanted to talk to you."

She looked down at her lap for a moment, then raised her head. "There's a problem."

"A problem?"

"I'm sort of seeing someone. There's a guy at work, a sales rep, who's been asking me out for a while. After I didn't hear from you for a few days, I accepted his invitation. He's very nice."

"Nice? This is what you want — *nice?*"

"He may not be the handsomest man in the world, and he doesn't have some glamorous job like *homicide detective*, but he's not afraid of a little responsibility."

Jack put up his hands. "Look, I just wanted to see you again. I know I should have called, but I thought we had something special the other night. Are you all committed to this guy, or what?"

She pulled some bills out of her purse and set them down. "I'll see how it goes. Who knows? If it doesn't work out, maybe I'll give you a call."

Jack whistled in disbelief. " 'Maybe' you'll call me. Jesus, you're a tough cookie, aren't you?"

Michelle slung her purse over her shoulder and stood up. "The dating business hasn't been much fun for me either."

Jack stayed at the diner, moping. He couldn't believe how hurt he felt. Evidently you never got too old for heartbreak. When the waitress returned to check up on him, he absently ordered the meat loaf special, which he then pushed around the plate for half an hour.

Out on the sidewalk, the heat was finally draining out of the day. He took a walk, joining the flow of pedestrians along Seventh Avenue.

He had the nagging sense that he was supposed to be doing something, but he couldn't force it into his consciousness. After a while, he looked up a side street and saw a familiar church. He turned off the avenue and descended the stairs into the basement meeting hall. He felt a strange thrill — as if he'd been given the password to a nationwide secret society, a subterranean world.

A speaker was just finishing, a twenty-something kid with a muscle shirt, a gold chain, and a thick Long Island accent.

"I didn't tell my girlfriend I was in the program," he said, " 'cause I wasn't sure I could stick with it. But then I finally broke the news. You'd think she'd be thrilled, 'cause all we ever did the whole time we were going out was sit on the couch all night, staring at the tube and drinking and getting high. You wanna talk couch potatoes — we were a couple of *mashed* couch potatoes."

Even though this was only his second meeting, Jack had noticed that the horrific AA stories were often accompanied by a dark humor. The cop in him approved.

He turned around to find a small, hunched man staring directly at him. At last, he thought, someone is on to the fact that I'm an impostor. The man's heavy-lidded eyes blinked slowly and then he pulled his chin in and looked away.

"And then," the kid continued, "I was telling her, hey, let's get out, you know, do stuff, go to concerts, whatever — like I was realizing how pathetic our relationship had been. And you know what she did? *She broke up with me.*"

The kid paused, stared down at the floor, shook his head. "And I just can't . . . I can't get my mind around that. Like, instead of having a real boyfriend who wanted to take her out, she'd rather have me sitting on the couch like a vegetable. And it makes me so angry that I just want to drink, or snort up a big fat line. And that's why I'm glad I'm in the program, 'cause I can come here and

be pissed off and I don't have to pick up a fucking bottle."
Jack turned around. The hunched man was gone.

After the kid finished, others got up to sympathize and trade similar stories. Jack looked around and realized that they shared a deep pool of experience, a profound bond. He was sitting in the middle of a bunch of alcoholics—and he was jealous.

A woman told how hard it had been for her to go home for the Fourth of July and be surrounded by her drinking family. A man got up to say that he was starting a new job, and he was afraid, and tempted to drink to quiet his fear. And Jack sat and listened to the stories, soothed by the rhythm of their voices, these people who looked so calm but spoke of such incredible turbulence in their lives. He was startled every time someone stated, "I'm so-and-so, and I'm an alcoholic." He watched their faces, revealed under pools of light. He was so used to people lying all the time, lying about the most trivial things just because it was their habit to lie—he didn't know what to make of all these people struggling to reveal their most uncomfortable truths.

Priests were probably used to such stories. Many times he'd wondered what it must be like to sit in the dim booth of a confessional, whispering. But Jews didn't have confessionals.

Cops did, though. Half the job was calling people in, trying to get the truth to surface. Contrary to popular belief, force was rarely used. The pros, the hard cases, knew enough to shut up, but a lot of perps—miserable, tired, guilt-ridden—seemed as if they had been praying for the chance to spill.

After the meeting, he wandered into a local Irish bar.

At six-thirty, Ben opened the wine and poured a glass before chopping the mushrooms. He had another glass while the lasagna was baking and felt guilty because there wasn't much left for dinner. He cleared the kitchen table of a pile of film magazines, grant proposals, and other crap and set out the silverware and plates. He checked to make sure that the batteries in his Walkman were good, popped in a blank cassette.

By the time the food was ready, his dad still hadn't arrived. Ben sipped more wine and watched a dopey sitcom, listening with one ear for the front gate to clang shut.

By nine o'clock, he was so hungry he sat down and ate.

By ten, he was so pissed off he was ready to clock the old man over the head with the wine bottle.

At eleven, he called the dive bar, Monsalvo's, where he'd rescued his father before. The bartender said he hadn't been in all night.

He was in bed just drifting off when he heard his father unlock the front door. "Thanks a lot," Ben muttered, and fell into a restless sleep.

When Jack returned to his son's apartment, the place was dark. He banged his shin on a chair, but was able to pull out the heavy futon bed without making too much noise. As he undressed, the urge to call Michelle again weighed powerfully on him and he wondered if it was like an alcoholic's thirst.

twenty-nine

When Ben got up, his father was sitting in the kitchen eating a bowl of granola.

His dad made a face. "This tastes like something you'd feed pigeons. Don't you at least have any sugar to sprinkle on it?"

"No. I'm allergic to sugar."

"Allergic? Whaddaya mean?"

Sugar made Ben's skin break out, but he didn't want to share that particular secret this morning. "What happened to you last night?" he asked instead.

"Last night? Why?"

"I made dinner. I told you I'd cook."

His father clapped his hand to his forehead. "Oh, shit. I'm sorry, kid. I was at a meeting."

"A meeting? What meeting? You said you had the day off."

His father didn't answer the question. "Look," he said, "I'll make it up to you. How about we go get lunch somewhere, my treat. Someplace fancy."

"I'm not in the mood." Ben turned to the fridge to get some milk.

"Come on, we'll get a great lunch, that'll cheer you up.

How about Peter Luger's over in Williamsburg? Best damn steak in the city."

"*Dad!*"

"What?"

"I told you: I don't eat meat."

His father looked startled. "You don't? Since when?"

"Since about five years ago. Don't you hear a word I say!"

"Hey—don't bite my head off just because I offered to buy you lunch. We'll get spaghetti. Vegetables. Whatever you want."

They went to a fancy place down by the base of the Brooklyn Bridge. Ben didn't say a word during the whole drive, even about his father smoking in the car. He was so quiet he scared himself: his silence mirrored his father's long silences when he was growing up. A red burst of anger flared up in him. His film project was no use. Nothing was any use. It didn't matter what the deep psychological reasons were: he was going to turn out just like the old man. A turtle.

As usual, his dad ate his lunch section by section: meat, vegetables, starch. Watching him was torture.

His father had some cheesecake for dessert. "This is great," he said. "You want some?"

Ben groaned. "That's it. I can't take it."

His father looked bewildered. "Take what?"

"What did I tell you? This morning, when we were in the kitchen?"

"Oh, damn. I'm sorry—you're allergic to sugar."

He stared at his father in disgust. "I could have told you I had *cancer* and you'd hardly have noticed."

"Whoa, come on, kid. Don't be like that. I'm sorry. Really. I've been crazy busy these past couple of weeks."

"You're *always* so wrapped up in your own business." Ben

noticed his voice rising into an embarrassing higher register. "What you have to do is so much more important than anything else." His voice cracked, as if he were regressing to childhood. "More important than being a father. Or a husband." *You Left!* he wanted to shout. *I Was Only Eight Years Old! How Could You Do That If You Really Loved Me?*

"Now hold on—" his father started to say, but Ben cut him off.

"No wonder Mom got so disgusted." Something inside him spiraled out of control. "No wonder she calls you a loser."

His father's eyes widened. "She said that? I mean, she told *you* that?"

"I'm fed up." Ben's voice cracked with anger. "I'm fucking fed up. Why do you even bother calling me anymore?"

"Hey. Come on. I know I could've done a better job with you guys. I know that. And I'm trying to do better now."

Ben sighed. "Forget it. It's not worth it." He stood up, just wanting to get away. When it came to fight or flight, his family was much better at the second option.

"Where you going?"

"I'm going out to do some shooting."

"Shooting?"

"Filming. It's what I do—remember?"

"Wait up," his father said. "I'll give you a ride."

Ben clenched his fists. "I'll walk."

Jack watched his son stride out of the restaurant. By the time he settled the bill and went outside to look for him, Ben was gone.

He walked down toward the East River, the massive stone anchorage of the Brooklyn Bridge hanging over his head. He crossed a cobbled street and stepped out on a sun-baked plaza. Across the water, tourists crowded the terraces of South Street Seaport. The metal-and-glass towers of Wall Street and the World Trade Center glinted cruelly in the afternoon sun. He stared across at the moneyed towers of Manhattan as he had stared years ago as a poor kid growing up in a poor housing project on the wrong side of the river.

Disgusted. Loser. His son's words rang in his head. He couldn't believe it: he'd never once raised his hand to the kid—how could the boy have turned out so angry?

He remembered one time when he'd taken Ben swimming—the kid must've been about six years old. "Look, Dad!" his son kept shouting in his little voice, craving attention, proud as only a kid could be of his splashy dog paddling. Jack went out into the middle of the pool and asked his son to swim over to him. But he'd gotten distracted for a second when the kid was about halfway there. When he looked down, the boy had swallowed some water and he was panicking, beating the water with his little fists, desperately trying to stand up in water over his head. Jack scooped him up—that panicked, hiccupping little kid— reproached by his son's look of disbelief that his father could let him down, *would* let him down.

No father could protect his son from the harshness of the world, but it was easier for a kid to put the blame close to home.

He spent a few minutes wandering around by the river feeling sorry for himself, then turned back to his car. Maybe he couldn't win at love or parenting, but there was one thing he still had a chance to get right.

thirty

Jack signed the day log, glad to be home in the task force office again. The phone rang.

One of his fellow detectives swiveled in his chair. "You've got a call, Leightner. Some guy named Larry—he says you'll know who he is."

Jack reached across his desk for the phone.

"You got something for me, buddy?"

"Yeah," Larry Cosenza said. "I asked around the neighborhood, real low-key like you said. About that Sumner International company: last year they bought up a couple of big lots on the Red Hook waterfront, just across from Governor's Island. Another thing: they own P and L Enterprises and that garage over on Coffey Street."

Jack whistled. "Jesus, Larry, I owe you big-time. Tell you what: when I'm ready to kick, I'm gonna order the fanciest casket in your place."

He walked into the supply room and paced. Randall Heiser had just been promoted from interviewee to suspect. If the man had been less prominent, the next step would have been to ask him to come in for questioning at the Seventy-sixth Precinct, screw with his head for a while in hopes that he'd break or let something slip. Legally, suspects were not required to come in unless they were formally charged with a crime, but thanks to TV cop shows many still thought they were supposed to make the trip. But someone as well placed as Heiser would immediately call his attorney, who'd tell him to simply clam up.

There was another option, though. If he could charge the man with some other, minor violation—failure to pay his parking tickets, say—then he could bring him in.

Sergeant Tanney got up and closed the door to his office. He turned to Jack. "We're not going to arrest the man for three *parking tickets.*"

Jack gripped the arms of his chair. "He lied to me. He said he wasn't in Red Hook."

"He wasn't under oath when he talked to you. He could just say he forgot. Why are you still on this? Didn't I ask you to move on?"

Jack took a slow breath. "It was a direct lie."

"You know what I think, Detective? You're being a bit overzealous here."

"Overzealous! Unless—by some incredible coincidence—Berrios and the barge captain both got randomly knifed in the same couple of weeks, we're looking at two connected murders."

"Do you have any direct evidence that Heiser was involved?"

"No, but I've got lots of good reasons to believe he was."

"Such as?"

"Number one: he told Berrios to stay away from his apartment just a month ago. Number two: his company owns the garage, the address Berrios had in his pocket the day before he was killed. Three: Heiser himself was in Red Hook on at least one occasion recently. Four: he lied to me about that and said his company couldn't be bothered with Brooklyn. Now it turns out they bought property there recently."

"None of those brings us close to charging the guy with anything, not even conspiracy. Anything else?"

"I've been on the job long enough to know when somebody is not *right*, and the second I met the guy my Not-Right Meter started swinging off the scale."

"I respect your judgment, but that's not good enough. I want you to leave this man alone unless you have a concrete reason to charge him."

Incredulous, Jack forced himself to take a deep breath. He raised his hands. "Okay. Listen—how about we at least get a warrant and send a forensics team over to the garage? Then we can get Alvarez and the Crime Scene people to analyze Berrios's shoes. Maybe we can definitely place him there on the morning he died."

"I told you already: we have more important cases to deal with right now."

"We're looking at a double murder, Sergeant. With a conspiracy to commit. If that isn't a media case, I don't know what is."

Tanney's face tightened. "Are you threatening me, Detective?"

Jack sighed. "No, sir. I would never have kept my shield this long if I was the kind who would talk to the press."

"Let it go, Jack. I want you to help Santiago with the Cobble Hill thing, full-time."

"You're ordering me off the Berrios case?"

"That's right."

"You're just gonna drop it?"

"No, I'll put Mickey on it. I need you for the more pressing case."

• • •

Jack got in his car and rolled down the window while he waited for the AC to start blowing cold.

Take a minute to make sure you're doing the right thing, he told himself. As a detective, he knew that he had a lot of power and he was conscientious about not abusing it. He didn't like Heiser on a personal level—could that be why he was so convinced the real estate man was guilty?

Hell, even if a detective was biased somehow, that didn't make the suspect innocent.

He pictured the knife wound in Tomas Berrios's chest. Pictured a terrified Raymond Ortslee holding up his hands as the knife slashed down. And he pictured Red Hook, abandoned, stinking with trash. That filled him with the righteous rage he needed.

"You don't need to stir up problems unless you have some concrete reason," Tanney had said. Randall Heiser had told several direct lies to a member of the Homicide Task Force. Any self-respecting cop could see that that was an insult. And reason enough.

Traffic was bad. Going over the Brooklyn Bridge, it slowed until everything was funneled through one tight lane. Then it stopped altogether. Jack sat and watched the temperature gauge rise.

He'd thought of calling Gary Daskivitch, asking him to ride along. (The Berrios case officially belonged to his partner.) But if the shit had to hit the fan, he wanted the young detective safely out of the way.

Finally, the cars began to crawl forward. Near the Manhattan end of the bridge, the reason for the delay became apparent: a dented utility van with tinted windows had slammed into the back of a yellow cab, sending the taxi skidding into a guard rail. Shattered glass glittered on the roadway and paramedics swarmed over the accordioned cab. The right lane was clear and traffic should have been moving, but everyone was slowing down to rubberneck, hoping for a glimpse into the glass-toothed mouth of the cab's rear window. Hoping for blood.

Sumner International was headquartered in a fancy new skyscraper on Fifty-second Street. Jack emerged from the elevator to find two sleek-looking women with telephone headsets sitting behind a huge circular teak desk in the reception area.

One of them, a beautiful young woman in a canary-yellow suit, held up her forefinger as she finished with a call.

"May I help you?" she said.

"I'm here to see Randall Heiser."

"Do you have an appointment, sir?" She raised her finger again as another call came through the switchboard.

Jack veered around the desk and picked a direction.

"*Sir*," the receptionist called, "you can't go back there."

He headed down a hallway full of people in cubicles clacking away at keyboards. Everything was plush, modern, expensive. The computers looked brand-new.

The receptionist called out again, louder this time.

He hurried on. He turned a corner and leaned over a cubicle. "Hey, which way is Heiser's office?"

A harried secretary was immersed in her computer screen. "Down the hall and to the left. It's the corner office—you can't miss it."

Sensing that she might have been too free with this information, she looked up. "Is he expecting you?"

Jack was already moving. "We're old friends," he said.

He pressed on, ignoring the anxious voice of the receptionist who was now following behind.

He found the corner office and wrenched the door open. A floor-to-ceiling tinted window dominated the far wall. Across a huge plush carpet, Randall Heiser looked up from his desk in surprise.

The receptionist burst in behind Jack. "I'm sorry, sir — I asked him to wait, but he just — "

"It's okay, Helen," Heiser said. "Perhaps the gentlemuhn is in the market for a little real estate."

"Not exactly. I'm doing a little follow-up on the murder of your porter, Tomas Berrios."

Heiser waved a hand and the receptionist withdrew, closing the door behind her.

"You just happened to be in Manhattan? That's a long way from Coney Island, isn't it?"

"Yes, sir, it certainly is." He wondered how the man knew that the Brooklyn South Task Force was based near Coney. That wasn't a secret, but it was hardly common knowledge.

He walked across the carpet and gazed out the huge window. Forty-nine stories — the only time he'd seen Manhattan from this high up was when he'd visited the Empire State Building. Down below, tiny pedestrians marched past the red-and-yellow umbrellas of hot dog stands. Strings of taxis flowed up Park Avenue like blood cells pulsing through a vein. The air-conditioning system whispered softly.

Jack pulled out his steno pad. "I don't want to waste your time. Does Sumner International own a garage on Coffey Street in Red Hook?"

Heiser leaned back in his massive, padded leather chair. "I have no idea."

"Excuse me?"

"We're the parent company to a number of real estate and development companies. All told, Sumner owns well over a hundred properties. Many of them are significant, but our companies manage all sorts of small buildings. Surely you don't expect me to have memorized every one."

Across the river stretched the flat plain of Queens; farther south, Brooklyn disappeared into a haze. From this high up, homes and streets and stores were just part of tracts of land. Sites for development. Like Robert Moses before him, Heiser wouldn't have to care about what might happen to the people so far below. If Red Hook was buried under thousands of tons of trash, the smell would never waft up here.

"Is there some problem, Detective? Something I can help you with?"

"Maybe. The last time I talked to you, you said you hadn't been to Red Hook recently. Can you remember the last time you were there?"

"I travel constantly, all over the country. No offense, but a visit to Brooklyn would not constitute the most mem'rable occasion."

Never the direct answer. Jack decided on a more forceful approach. "Were you in Brooklyn on May eighth of this year?"

"I don't remember," Heiser snapped. "And I have no idea why you've come barging into my office to ask me such an irrelevant question."

"You got a traffic ticket in Red Hook on that date. Let's try another one: were you in Brooklyn on July twelfth of this year?"

The real estate mogul narrowed his eyes. "That was the day that poor man was murdered. I think you've gone far beyond the bounds here, Detective. I don't know what your problem is, but if you have further questions, you'll need to direct them to my lawyers. Tell me something: do you enjoy working for the city?"

Jack weighed the implied threat. "Yes, sir, as a matter of

fact I do. And it would take quite a lot to stop me from doing my job. You can complain all you want."

"If you keep badgering me, you can be damn certain I *will* complain." Heiser stood up abruptly. "Goodbye, Detective. I wish you the best of luck. This seems to be a difficult case for you—you might need it."

The man's smug manner infuriated Jack. He knew he was going too far, being outrageously unprofessional—he could hear himself saying the words but couldn't stop them: "I don't think I'll need luck. Do you really think you can commit murder and walk away? You screwed up, dirtbag, and I'm gonna nail your rich little ass to the wall."

Heiser started to sputter something about his lawyers, but Jack turned on his heel and walked out.

On the drive back from Manhattan, his beeper went off. Sergeant Tanney's number, at the Homicide Task Force office. Urgent code. Jack shook his head: Heiser certainly hadn't wasted any time.

He thought of turning his beeper off and pretending he hadn't gotten the page. He thought of staying in his car and driving until he ran out of highway. Canada. Or Key West.

He headed back to Coney Island.

"Close the door behind you," Tanney said.

From the grim expression on the sergeant's face, the man might as well have been holding a cane. Jack sat down.

"Do you remember what we discussed the last time we talked?" the shift commander asked. "Just a couple of hours ago?"

"Yes, sir, I do."

"I know that I haven't been here long, that you haven't gotten a chance to know me very well, but tell me: do I look like an idiot to you?"

Jack didn't answer.

Tanney sighed. "Look — I'm not here to break anybody's balls unnecessarily. I try to leave that to One PP." He stood up, walked around his desk, and looked up at the left wall. An acetate-covered chart ran the length of the office, bearing a list of victims. Each name was written in black if the case was closed, red if it was still open. The primary detective's initials were attached to the right of each victim's name. Jack knew what the board told the sergeant: not only was his shift running behind in the ever-continuing race to clear away the red, but Jack's name was attached to fewer cases than most of his colleagues.

Tanney turned. "I told you to give this case a rest. Next thing I know, you're running in to Manhattan to flog it."

"That prick complained again, did he?"

"Why do you have such a hard-on for this guy, Leightner? If there was some sort of tangible evidence, maybe I could understand your behavior."

"The man lied. Don't you want to know why?"

"One thing you should know about me, Detective, is that I don't talk just to feel my lips flap. We don't need to discuss this any more. I want you to take some time off. To rest up and think about the priorities of the squad."

"No, thank you. *Sir.*"

"I'm not asking you — I'm telling you."

"You're suspending me?"

"That's right. For 'willful disobedience of a lawful order.' Until further notice."

"But you can't — "

"I can't afford to have a loose cannon rolling around these

decks. If you want, you can appeal through the union. That's all, Detective. Put your gun and your shield on my desk, and leave the door open on your way out."

"So don't say hello," called out Mary Gaffney from behind the desk downstairs.

Jack thought he detected a look of pity on her face, even though he knew that was impossible; the news could not have spread through the building that fast. He ducked his head and jogged past her, just as he had avoided his comrades in the task force squad room.

He missed the weight of his detective's shield in his pocket. For almost twenty years he'd carried it off duty and on. It was his armor, his flag, his totem of power.

A blast of heat met him as he pushed through the back door of the building. He was used to striding through that door with a sense of purpose, but now he didn't have anywhere to go. He stood still, heart twisted with anger and shame.

His son's voice echoed in his head: *loser.*

Out in the street beyond the parking lot, a couple of kids were having a contest, seeing who could ride his bike the farthest on a wheelie. The air was so humid that already Jack could feel sweat soaking his chest. He took off his jacket and slung it over his shoulder. One of the kids came down hard on his front wheel and swerved, narrowly missing a car. The other kids hooted and laughed.

Jack took a deep breath and set out across the sweltering blacktop toward his car.

thirty-one

Down beneath the seawall, the waves slapped green-stained, mossy rocks. Jack sat on a bench on the Red Hook Garden Pier, drinking from a pint of Jim Beam and watching the late afternoon sun hit the bay in fierce jangly diamonds of silver. Rusty old tankers plodded past the Statue of Liberty, out to sea. To the left a rocky promontory stretched a hundred yards out into the water; big wall-size slabs of concrete from an abandoned Red Hook construction project lay jumbled on it, someone's well-ordered plan knocked down like a house of cards. In the harbor, a distant buoy rang a mournful note.

The distant shorelines of Staten Island and Jersey were half smothered by a hot white haze, but Jack could still make out a forest of loading cranes over the busy Jersey ports. And he could see the Verrazano-Narrows Bridge arcing across the water to the far south. Why had Tomas Berrios cared about that bridge? Maybe it seemed like a promise: of escape, of life going on somewhere besides these crappy streets. The kid's bicycle hadn't carried him far enough.

Berrios was beyond all cares — it was himself Jack needed to be concerned about now. He frowned. After all these years, he hadn't managed to make a much better job of life than his old man. Another father who wasn't ready for the job. Maybe it was bad blood.

His father hadn't been all bad, though. He got mean mostly on paydays, when the booze took hold. Other times, he showed a different side. One Fourth of July Jack and his brother had bought some cheap fireworks out of someone's trunk. Their mother and father stood on the sidewalk in front of the Red Hook Houses to watch as they crouched down in the street to light them. One of the little fountains tipped over as soon as the fuse reached the cone and it spun out across the street like a crazy whizzing top, chasing an ornery neighbor halfway down the block. Jack expected another explosion from his father, but instead the old man laughed so hard he sank down onto the sidewalk and lay gasping on his back.

Another memory, this one a photo, his father's pride and joy, a yellowed clipping from *Life* magazine. The photographer had climbed a lamp post to snap a crowd of World War II soldiers packed into a European square, grinning as they waved newspapers with a huge one-word headline: "PEACE." As a boy, Jack had loved to scan the faces in the photo until he found his father looking up at the camera with a small, enigmatic smile. His father, the victor, staring across time and space.

Now his own son was calling him a loser. And why not? He'd failed at marriage, failed at parenting, let another good woman go. And without his job, he was nothing.

He threw the half-empty bottle out into the water. He could hear his brother Petey shouting, laughing, as he swam away from these same rocks.

He rubbed his weary eyes. Didn't he deserve to see his life go wrong? Wasn't it in the Bible? *If a man is burdened with the blood of another, let him be a fugitive unto death. Let no one help him.*

A cloud crept across the sun and its bright phosphor mirror died on the water like a fish's scales gone gray. He stared out into the expanse of sea and sky. What difference did he make to the grand picture? He was just a speck — if he was gone, the ships would still plod out to sea. The waves would lap, the buoy would ring. Perps would still commit murder, and other detectives would catch them or not. If he removed himself from the world, who would care? If a whole neighborhood could bow out, why couldn't he? He could do it the slow way, fall into the bottle. Or he could eat his gun — go out with a bang and a whimper. No: he'd seen too many gunshot victims to want to damage himself that way. He stood and moved to the metal railing, watched the gentle waves. Maybe drowning would be more peaceful.

He thought of the missile bay on Santiago's son's Navy ship, imagined an alarm sounding as the air thickened with a mist so dense a man could drown in it. Maybe it would be good to breathe it in and let everything go.

Thirty-three years before, a scared kid on a Navy ship bound for Europe, he'd looked down at the ocean and wondered what it would be like to drown. If you fell overboard in the night in the middle of the Atlantic, with thousands of miles of icy water in every direction, you were a doomed man. An old salt told him the best thing was to just give up and fill your lungs with water, but he couldn't imagine that. He had promised himself that, if such a moment came, he'd set out swimming.

He chewed a stick of peppermint gum, hoping it would cover the alcohol on his breath. The speaker, a fat little man in a business suit, was up on stage telling a long, sad, and funny story about the disintegration of his marriage, a story that—judging from the few sentences Jack could focus on— he would normally have found compelling. In the middle of the tale, he glanced up and noticed a mirrored ball hanging from the basement ceiling; he stared at it for a while. He was exhausted but wired, as if he'd drunk a pot of bad coffee after a double tour.

Several volunteers made the trip to the front of the room. A young Irish kid said that he'd felt nothing the day his father shot himself—he'd been too drunk and stoned to care. A housewife cried when she told how she had been drunk so often that she'd missed the high points of her children's lives.

"Would anyone else like to say anything?" a woman behind the desk asked. "Do we have anybody new to the program?"

Jack's hand rose as if by its own accord.

The woman pointed to him and nodded. Her wan face looked kind.

And then—he didn't remember getting up or moving forward—he was sitting in front of the group. He looked out on the rows of people sitting calmly around the room. He looked down at his lap. He was trembling so hard he couldn't speak.

"It's okay," the last speaker said from her seat in the front row. "You can do it."

He wanted desperately to get up and bolt, but his legs wouldn't cooperate. He pushed his palms over his thighs as if to wipe them clean.

"My name is Jack," he finally mumbled. When he didn't add "And I'm an alcoholic," he expected the group to rise up and cast him out. He hoped they would.

As one, they cheerfully called out, "Hi, Jack!"

He pinched the front of his shirt; his wet undershirt clung to his ribs.

"I don't . . . I've never . . ."

He stopped and cleared his throat. A silence. He glanced at the faces in the room, recognized the woman who had spoken at that first meeting. Jill? *Janet*. And there was the kid with the gold chain whose girlfriend had ditched him when he sobered up. Their faces were sympathetic. Interested.

"I grew up in Brooklyn," he said. "I don't know if you know Red Hook. It's just past Carroll Gardens. Near the water. My father worked the docks. When I was little, he'd take me and my brother Peter down the docks to visit the ships. There used to be so many. That's one reason we won the war. World War Two, I mean. We built great ships."

He paused.

"I don't know what I'm talking about here. I don't . . ." He took a deep breath. "Things used to disappear off the ships. You had the ILA, the longshoreman's union, and you had the Mob down there. From every load, between the ship and the trucks, a lot of stuff disappeared. Liquor, clothes, tools, whatever. It was *normal*."

The bourbon sat raw and fiery in his stomach. He reached out and poured himself a glass of water. "Excuse me. I guess I'm rambling. The point is, I had a brother. In nineteen sixty-five he was just thirteen years old. Petey was such a funny kid. He could imitate everybody in the neighborhood: the barbers, the longshoremen, the people in our building. He was a natural at sports. A great shortstop. People used to say he'd grow up to give PeeWee Reese a run for his money. Everybody liked him. He was such a good-natured kid. And I was . . ."

He stared down at the table as if hoping to find more words there. He hadn't mentioned alcohol even once. Surely

263

it was only a matter of time before the others caught on. Before they stopped him.

"I wasn't as good as Petey—I used to act up. And I wasn't as popular as him, especially with the girls. Maybe sometimes . . . I was a little jealous. I loved him, though. He was my only brother.

"One day in November of that year it was really warm. Indian summer. Me and Petey were playing hooky; I was going through this thing where I was trying to act like James Dean, or something. My old man insisted that we finish high school, because he never had the chance. He always said we should never end up working on the docks like him. But we didn't give a damn about school.

"We went down to the water for a while. Chucked rocks off a pier. Stupid shit. We tried to catch a seagull. We got tired of that pretty quick—let me tell you, no matter how hard you try, you'll never catch a seagull."

A chuckle passed through the room. Someone shifted; their chair squeaked on the linoleum.

"We walked up Sullivan Street. Petey was singing "Help Me, Rhonda," which was a big hit that year. He was always singing. There was a vacant lot there, with a trailer in the back. And we're walking through the lot, and Petey's bouncing a rubber ball. A Spaldeen, that's what we called it in the old days. And we're walking by, and it takes a bad bounce. Under the trailer, which was up on blocks. Petey's digging around, searching through the weeds, and all of a sudden he stands up. 'Jack,' he says. 'Get a load of this.' And he drags out a wooden case. We crack it open and it's filled with bottles of Scotch. We figured it was swag, boosted off some ship."

He imagined the other people in the room telling themselves, *Aha, now we finally get to the booze.*

"Normally, I would have said, 'Don't mess with it,' 'cause

either the longshoremen or the Mob might have been involved. Only they would never have hid it in such a stupid place — it would have been sold right away to some bar or social club. We argued about what to do with it, and finally I said, 'Let's take it.' Not home — my father would have killed us — but up to Richards Street, to this friend of mine named Joe Kolchuk, who could keep it in his basement. So Petey throws his jacket over it, and we take turns carrying it up the street."

He stopped and licked his lips. Nobody in the room moved; they didn't even shift in their chairs. He could feel his throat tightening, feel his voice going flat. He'd told the story before, to his parents, to the police — but never the whole story.

"We were about two blocks away from Joe's house, walking down Richards Street, when these two black guys came up behind us. They were older than us, maybe sixteen or seventeen.

"They said, 'Hey!'

"I said, 'Hey what?'

" 'You got something belongs to us.'

" 'Oh, yeah?' At that point I was carrying the case. Under my breath, I told Petey to keep walking.

" 'You found that under the trailer,' one guy said. 'Give it up.' He was wearing an old army jacket. Had an Afro. He was bigger than me and Petey and so was his friend.

"We could have handed it over and probably that would have ended it. But I knew they weren't from the neighborhood, and because they were Negroes, I knew that no way were they with the Mob. And just then, about three blocks down, I saw a police car turn the corner. They were rolling right toward us. I knew all the cops on patrol in the Hook. I got cocky.

" 'Yeah?' I said. 'You gonna make us?' "

"One kid grabbed Petey by the neck and slammed him up against a wall. I guess he didn't grab me 'cause he didn't want to risk breaking the bottles.

"Petey gave me this scared look. He said, 'Just give it to them, Jack.'

"I held on to the case.

" 'I'm not gonna ask you again,' the guy said.

"The patrol car was coming closer.

"I smiled. 'Fuck you, nigger.'

"They looked like they couldn't believe I said that, including Petey.

" 'What did you say?' one of the guys asked me.

"I said, 'Fuck you and your nigger friend.' It wasn't like I had anything against black people. I mean, I used to run with black guys from the project. Puerto Ricans, whatever . . . I just wanted to piss them off. And I knew that patrol car was comin' up the street.

"The guy who had Petey up against the wall pulled out a flick knife."

" 'Whoa,' I said. 'Look, I'm gonna hand it over.' The whole thing was going wrong, but I saw the cops were only about a block away. I started to put the case down on the ground, and I looked up the street, and . . . and . . ."

He paused and wiped the side of his mouth. He took a deep breath and continued.

"The patrol car had stopped on a corner, outside this diner called Bud and Packy's . . . I guess they went in to get a cup of coffee. Petey started to struggle. I jumped toward him, but it was too late. My brother started to throw a punch, but the guy opened the knife and stabbed him. Just once, under the ribs."

Jack pressed his right hand to his stomach. The same spot where Tomas Berrios had been stabbed. The same exact spot.

266

"Petey grunted and we all stared at him. The black kid looked like he couldn't believe what he'd just did. Petey put his hand under his shirt and it came out all covered in blood. He looked at me like he was confused, and then he fell down to his knees, fell on his side like a . . . like a . . ."

He couldn't finish the thought. "He died almost instantly. Heart failure."

He fell silent. Outside, a car horn bleated.

"The other guys hightailed it out of there. They never got caught. We didn't have all the resources we have these days, the computers, the coordination . . . They just disappeared.

"I told everyone that we got mugged. I never mentioned the things I said. I testified that they came up to us out of the blue, jumped us for the booze."

The room was deathly quiet. Jack took a sip of water from a glass on the table.

"After that, I was so shook up, I couldn't stay in the neighborhood. As soon as I could, I lied about my age, joined the Army, got shipped to Germany. That was a blessing. I didn't have to look my parents in the face anymore. Sometimes I hoped I'd get killed. I volunteered to go to Vietnam, but I got sent way behind the lines, to a supply base in the Philippines."

His face crumpled, but he pulled himself together enough to finish.

"What can I say? It was my fault. We should have just handed it over. What was it? A goddamn case of booze. I was his big brother. I should've looked out for him. Protected him. But I was jealous of him. I was jealous."

He stared down through his open hands. And then he cried.

thirty-two

Ben rose at midday. He'd stayed out most of the night drinking with a couple of buddies in the East Village because he was too embarrassed to deal with his father again. When he stumbled out into the living room, he was relieved to find the old man gone.

He went back into his bedroom, changed into his most nonyuppie clothes—old jeans, a faded black T-shirt, work boots—and emptied his wallet of all but twenty bucks. Then he packed his least expensive camera and set out for the Red Hook Houses.

If anybody tried to jump him, he planned to just hand over the twenty quickly and split. His canvas shoulder bag was old and frayed; he removed anything he didn't need. Despite these precautions, his stomach knotted as he crossed the Brooklyn-Queens Expressway and headed straight into the projects. The day was overcast and foggy.

He wasn't sure what to expect. Kids flashing gang signs, crack dealers screeching around corners firing Mac-9s? At the least, some poor black and Latino teenagers who would not be happy to see a white guy from the other side of the tracks invading their turf.

Maybe he was secretly hoping for a little excitement. Not

to get mugged, certainly, but a chance to put his photojournalistic skills to the test. A documentary report from the front lines, Robert Capa during the Spanish Civil War. It was hard capturing violence on film. With street trouble — a car crash, a punch-out — he usually only saw it out of the corner of his eye, a wild, jagged flash.

As it turned out, no one in the projects seemed to care much about him. People just went about their business: mothers pushed strollers, kids goofed around on bikes, men in green uniforms roamed the grounds picking up trash.

He shot a few minutes of video, but there was little to get excited about.

He wandered east toward the water. As he moved away from the projects and potential danger, his other worry was free to resurface like an ache in a back tooth. Part of him was glad that he'd managed to finally vent some deep, long-standing complaints about his father, but he couldn't help picturing the crushed look on the old man's face. He'd been too harsh. Maybe cruel, even. And he hadn't even been accurate. His mom had never used the word "loser." What was it she'd said? Something about not being sure if the man was capable of loving anybody. Was that better or worse?

Either way, he felt he ought to apologize.

He thought of heading back to see if his father would come home after work, and he squirmed.

Down on the waterfront, he filmed a tugboat pulling a garbage barge; soon it disappeared into the mist. The Hook today reminded him of the old photographs and he half expected to see tall sails gliding out of the fog.

Later in the day, the sun broke through the clouds. He roamed for hours, enjoying the solitude of the back streets, the beauty of the rust and aging brick. At one point he looked up to discover a white crescent of moon in the blue sky.

As he set out for home, the whole neighborhood glowed honey-orange in the sun's last rays, and the hush of evening settled down over Red Hook.

thirty-three

The house looked like a three-story brownstone, but the stone was white. In the tiny front yard a flowering tree, willowlike, sprayed down over the iron gate; the street lamp above lit its delicate white blossoms, made them translucent and waxy in the warm night air.

A young couple strolled past, the man's hand pressing the small of the woman's back, casually slipping lower. She laughed and knuckled him in the shoulder. They didn't notice Jack sitting paralyzed in his car, peering up through his windshield at a bay window on the second floor.

Go up already, he told himself. *Go up, unless you want to make a career as a lurker.* He got out, the car door thumping hollowly in the canyon of row houses, a tranquil street in Prospect Heights. He stared up at the flower boxes hanging beneath the bay window and hoped the window and the light belonged to Michelle Wilber.

The gate clanged shut behind him as he made his way up the walk.

He located her name next to a buzzer; he ran his tongue over his teeth to make sure they were clean. He glanced at his watch: almost ten-thirty. Late, but not terribly so. He cleared his throat and pressed the buzzer.

A crackle. "Hello?" Her voice.

He cleared his throat again. "It's Jack. Jack Leightner." He was prepared for the jig to be up right there and then. If she didn't want to talk to him. If, God forbid, Mr. Salesman from her office was up there right now, reclining smugly in her bedroom with his arms behind his head. He stared at the mute circle of holes in the intercom for what seemed like minutes.

The lock buzzed open.

He stared at the door in confusion and disbelief, then dove for it just as it click-locked. Sheepish, he buzzed again.

Michelle stood at the top of the stairs. "Well," she said dryly, "look what the cat dragged in."

He couldn't read her expression well enough to tell if she was kidding.

"Come on up." She didn't wait for him to reach to the top of the stairs, but moved out of sight.

On the landing, he turned and saw an open door. And then he was in her apartment, but where was Michelle? He felt like a suspect ordered down to a precinct house, left sitting by the front desk. Make 'em feel like they're not important, let their nerves fray and sizzle.

He gathered quick impressions: a small Persian carpet, lots of plants, a peach-colored sofa, interesting paintings on the walls. (Unlike the ones in Sheila's place, these didn't make him worry about the emotional stability of their owner.) The apartment wasn't fancy, but she had a real sense of style, an eye that tied together the colors and textures. Class.

"I'm in the kitchen," she called.

He followed her voice.

Halfway down the hall, he turned through a bright doorway. Michelle stood on tiptoe, reaching up into an old yellow kitchen cabinet.

"I'm packing my lunch for tomorrow," she said. "I'm not much of a morning person."

He watched as she took down a roll of tinfoil and wrapped a sandwich. She wore flip-flops, cut-off blue jeans, a spaghetti-strap T-shirt that revealed her bra straps. A simple rubber band held back her hair. A woman going about her own business.

She took out a plastic bag and tried to open it from the wrong end. For the first time, Jack realized she might be nervous too.

She dropped the sandwich in the bag, placed it in the fridge. Finally, she turned to look at him. "How did you know where I lived?"

"Where there's a will . . ."

She weighed his answer. "Was it some sort of cop trick? Isn't that illegal?" He thought he saw a hint of a smile.

"Would you mind if I sit down for a minute?" he said. "It's been a very long day."

She looked at him, unreadable again. "Sorry. Here." She pulled a chair away from a mahogany table, the wood burnished to a fine dark gloss. "You want something to drink?"

"Just some water," he said. "Please."

He watched as she took a pitcher out of the refrigerator, tried not to stare at her as she reached up into another cabinet for a glass. He looked at the back of her neck, imagined wrapping his arms around her, pressing his lips there.

She handed him the drink but remained standing; she leaned against the edge of the counter, arms folded across her chest. He couldn't help thinking of an interrogation, where every move had its own meaning, its own purpose. He considered standing up himself, to level things out. He could make it look casual, as if he wanted to check out the view out the window, or the collection of antique postcards taped to the fridge. He could make them out from where he sat: old tinted photos of Coney Island, back in the days when it had been a place of wonder. Steeplechase Park. Luna Park. Dreamland.

"Do you ever go out to Coney?" he asked.

"Sometimes." She looked at him coolly. She didn't seem to be in a hurry to find out why he was sitting in her kitchen.

"Where's Mr. Nice Guy?" he couldn't resist asking.

She shrugged, conceded a small grin. "I hate to say it, but you were right. Nice isn't everything."

He sipped his water, taking this in. Perhaps the field was clear, but she wasn't exactly bounding into his arms. If he was going to be allowed to make progress, he'd have to start out on his knees.

She smoothed a hand along the counter and looked at her palm, as if checking for crumbs. Judging by the neatness of the kitchen, he doubted she'd find any. She wore pale nail polish but it was chipped; that made him like her even more.

"So," she said. "Where are you coming from? Work?"

"No," he said. "Not work."

"Where, then?"

He pinched his lower lip. He looked toward the window, then back to her. "I've been thinking."

"Oh?" She didn't seem to care enough to ask more.

He stared at her until she returned his gaze, until the silence, the looking, became unbearable. He pushed his chair back and stood up. "Look, it's late. You have to work tomorrow."

She didn't answer.

He took a deep breath. "I wanted to see you. I wanted to tell you that I'm ready for you."

"Why?" she asked. "What's changed?"

He reached out, and smoothed his palm against her cheek. "I'm ready," he repeated, and stood there, shivering, until finally she turned her head toward his palm and closed her eyes.

Later, they lay in bed, letting the sweat evaporate off their warm bodies. She laughed. "You weren't really going to just get up and go home, were you?"

"I would have," he said. "I mean, I didn't *want* to. But I didn't want to assume anything. I don't want you to think I came here for sex. I mean, I'm glad we did this, but it's not why I came." He groaned. "I'll just shut up now."

"I'm going to brush my teeth," she said. He lay in her bed and watched the warm light hum out of the bathroom doorway. After a moment, he got up and padded inside. He stepped behind her, wrapped an arm around her stomach, and hugged her to him as she brushed her teeth. Together they stared into the mirror, a naked man and woman, grinning.

They settled back into her bed, bathed in the street light flowing in from the window, floating in it. He thought he didn't deserve such happiness, but he was ready to accept it.

As a test, he willed himself to picture Randall Heiser's face. He probed his heart to discover that it wasn't filled with anger and frustration anymore. Maybe his colleague Mickey would bring Heiser down. Maybe he wouldn't. Or maybe he was just plain wrong about the man. Maybe it was time to stop being obsessed with crime and criminals, time to retire and get a job where his clothes didn't smell of the slaughterhouse at the end of the day.

Maybe, after all these years, he could recognize the difference between the devil without and the devil within.

He felt bad about Red Hook, though. What if the neighborhood was turned into a garbage heap? He shrugged. Maybe he should just let the memories go, like Mr. Gardner burning photos of his wife.

Suspects had a million ways to lie, but all veteran cops knew one almost infallible sign of guilt. If you threw a guy into a holding tank and left him there for a while, and when you came back he was asleep, you knew you had your perp. Any innocent person taken into custody would be shaken up: anxious, wired, unwilling to even sit down. But a perp, especially a novice, might have already been juiced for days after the crime. By the time he got arrested, he'd be burnt out from waiting for the hand on the shoulder. If you put him in a cell, you could often watch him fall into a deep sleep, even with an arm handcuffed to a wall. There was a certain peace in knowing that the worst was over.

Jack thought about that for a moment. He thought about his father, standing in a crowd of soldiers holding up a sign that said Peace. And then he wasn't thinking at all—he sank into his first full sleep in weeks.

A chirping woke him. Groggy, he opened his eyes, disoriented until he remembered he was at Michelle's. The red LCD of a clock on a bedside table told him that it was 1:37 A.M. He'd been woken by his pager. He turned to his right: Michelle was sleeping soundly. The page was probably just a misdial. But he hadn't told Ben he wasn't coming home—what if his son was worried? Maybe the boy felt bad about what he'd said. Jack was ready to forgive him.

Maybe now that the kid had gotten the poison out, finally, they could come to a new and better understanding.

He reached over the side of the bed for his pants and turned the pager toward the light coming in through the window. An unfamiliar number — a misdial. He set the pager down and pulled a pillow over his head.

A few seconds later, as he was falling into a rich, sweet sleep, the chirping tugged him back. He pushed the pillow away and reached for the pager. Same number.

Cursing under his breath, he swung his legs over the side of the bed. He had to pee, anyhow.

Down the hall, he stopped off in Michelle's bathroom, admiring her respect for cleanliness and order. (Unlike Sheila's bathroom, which had always been a disaster area of used cotton balls and wadded-up, lipsticky tissues.) He clicked off the light and continued down the hall to the kitchen, where he found a phone, slumped in a chair, and dialed the mystery number.

"Detective Leightner?" A man's voice, muffled, nervous. It sounded familiar, but he couldn't place it.

"Speaking. Who's this?"

"You wanna know who killed that Berrios kid?"

He sat up straight. "Yeah, I do."

"I can't discuss this over the phone. Can you meet me in a few minutes?"

"Where?"

"The corner of Imlay and Commerce. You know where that is?"

"In Red Hook."

"That's right. And Detective? One more thing: come by yourself. I'm afraid to think what he'd do to me if he saw me talking to a bunch of cops. All right?"

"Yeah."

The line went dead.

Wide awake now, he dialed the Homicide Task Force. The call was answered by Scott Cooney, one of the detectives on the night watch.

"Scotty, it's Jack Leightner. Do me a favor, will ya? I need an address for this phone number." He squinted at his beeper and read it off. "I don't know if it's residential or commercial. Could be a pay phone."

"You got it."

While he waited, he rubbed the sleep out of his eyes and poured himself a glass of water.

"Sorry," Cooney said. "It took me a minute to find it. You're right, it's a pay phone."

"Where?"

"Brooklyn. Corner of Van Brunt and Commerce. You need anything else?"

He debated whether to tell Cooney about the call. He considered asking for backup, but he knew that it would get back to Sergeant Tanney that he was still working on the Berrios case. It was better to be suspended than fired outright.

"Nah," he said. "Thanks, Scotty. I'm good."

thirty-four

Deep in the heart of Red Hook, Imlay Street was home to the New York Dock Company, two huge block-long warehouses with a Moorish architecture. Widely spaced streetlights cast pools of light along the dark cobblestones and made the metal-capped curbs gleam. Above the lights, the upper floors of the warehouses floated up into darkness.

On the other side, the street was lined with vacant lots overrun with weeds and little ailanthus trees. At this late hour, the street was so quiet that Jack could feel his heart beating over the quiet purr of the engine.

A block ahead, at the corner of Commerce, a lone gray car was parked on the right side of the street. A big car from the seventies, a Chevy Malibu, he guessed. He stopped for a moment, opened the glove compartment, pulled out his own personal .38 — to hell with Tanney — leaned forward, and tucked it into the back of his belt.

He drifted up behind the Malibu and pulled into a regulation stop: his car not directly behind, but staggered to the left, so that when he got out it would provide him with partial cover. He left the lights on for further protection, to dazzle the other driver.

There was only one person in the other car, a man who

kept his hands in plain sight, gripping the steering wheel. Something about the set of the man's head seemed familiar. He sneezed.

The manager of the Coffey Street garage.

Jack's heart rose. This was the icing on the cake. He'd nail Randall Heiser, get his job back — it would be Sergeant Tanney's turn to apologize.

He got out and walked up to the other car.

"How you doing tonight, Mr. Greenlee?"

The manager's head dipped down out of the deep shadow inside the car. "How'd you know it was me?" He sneezed again. "Oh."

"Thank you for coming forward."

"Thanks for comin' down so late. You didn't bring anybody, right?"

Greenlee opened the door warily and eased his bulk out from under the steering wheel. He wore a baggy brown suit. "You can't be too careful," he said. "He'd kill me if he knew I was talking to you."

"Don't worry."

"You're not wearing a wire or anything, are you?"

Jack shook his head.

"You mind if I make sure?"

"Go ahead."

The manager reached inside Jack's jacket and patted his chest and sides.

"So what do you have for me?" Jack said.

Greenlee sneezed. "Excuse me," he said, and reached into his baggy jacket. Expecting a handkerchief, Jack saw metal. Immediately, he stomped down on Greenlee's instep. At the same time, he grabbed the hand holding the gun and bent it back fiercely. In a second, he had the manager down on the cobblestones and was jamming his arm up behind his back. With his free hand, he reached back for his .38.

A fierce pain exploded in the back of his head and then he was lying facedown on the cool cobblestones himself. Someone grabbed his hands roughly, yanked them behind his back, and trussed them together. He winced at the splitting pain in his head, but twisted to look up. The nimbus of a streetlight blinded him, but he could just make out the dark figure of a stranger standing at its center.

Greenlee pulled the gun from Jack's waistband. He stuck it in his own jacket pocket.

"We're wasting time out here in the open," the stranger said. "Let's get him in the car." He looked down at Jack and shook his head. "If *I* was such a hotshit detective, I would've had the brains to call for some backup."

thirty-five

They forced Jack into the passenger seat of his own car, and then the stranger drove it slowly down Imlay Street, holding a gun below the level of the dashboard. He didn't say a word. When he turned slightly to make sure Greenlee was following in the Malibu, Jack glanced over: the man was his own size, perhaps fifty, drawn cheeks, liverish complexion. He wore a dark windbreaker over a black polo shirt. The passing streetlights played over his deep-set eyes. He worked a piece of gum as if rolling a pebble on the tip of his tongue, calm as a truck driver on a long night drive. Unlike Greenlee, he was clearly a professional.

They didn't pass a single soul during the dark ride. They turned onto Coffey Street. As they neared the garage, the stranger turned off the headlights. Behind, Greenlee also extinguished his lights. The little house next door to the garage was completely dark.

Through the windshield, Jack watched Greenlee come around and open the garage door. The stranger pulled into the dark left-hand bay. Greenlee pulled the Malibu into the right. The manager got out and the sliding door rattled down behind them.

Greenlee turned on a small caged light in one of the work

pits. Above, a car perched on a hydraulic lift like a guardian lion. The shadowy cave was full of wrenches, crowbars, and other potential weapons, but with his hands tied, Jack knew he wouldn't be able to use them. Greenlee opened Jack's door and the stranger nudged him out. The manager held up a gun while the second man pulled out a couple of surgical gloves and worked his hands into them. Jack flinched at the rubbery squeaking.

Greenlee jabbed the gun against Jack's temple. "Don't you move," he said, all jocularity gone from his voice.

The stranger picked up a roll of duct tape, used his teeth to tear off a couple of lengths, and stretched them over Jack's mouth. Then the two men force-marched him around the pit and across the oil-stained concrete toward the back of the garage. In the dim light, the *Playboy* pinup grinned coyly from the wall. Greenlee clicked off the light. Jack stood still, trying to adjust to the darkness. A door in the back opened, Greenlee stepped out, and the other man pushed Jack forward.

It was dark outside, but a new moon gave just enough light for him to make out a yard filled with junk. The men led him through a narrow passage between heaps of twisted metal and trash cans spiky with scraps of wood. The murky form of a dog detached from one of the heaps with a low growl, but Greenlee kicked it in the ribs and it slunk away.

At the back of the lot, the manager hauled aside a huge metal Coke sign leaning against a fence. The sign covered a gap in the chain links. Greenlee ducked through first, then the stranger pushed Jack's head down and guided him on, into another dark yard.

As soon as Jack was through, he dodged around Greenlee and ran. Five yards on, something snapped against his thighs and he flipped over. Sprawled on the rough asphalt, he realized he'd run straight into a low-slung chain. He moaned into the duct tape and took quick pained breaths through his nose.

The manager trotted up, snickering. "Well, *that* was cute." The men yanked Jack up off the ground and shoved him, stumbling, on.

Ahead rose the abandoned warehouse; a sheet of metal glinted dully from each window frame under the faint moonlight. At the back, under a fire escape, a set of concrete steps led down below ground to a door. Greenlee forced Jack down into the stairwell and then, cursing the darkness, he produced some keys and fiddled with a hasp lock.

Inside, a musty, pitch-black space. From the close sound of their breathing, Jack guessed they were in a hallway. The floor was hard and smooth: more concrete. He tried to go slow, wary of what he might bang into, but one of the men grabbed his elbow and hustled him along. They stopped. Metal scraped. Someone turned Jack to the side and gave him a shove.

A bright bare light clicked on overhead, revealing a low-ceilinged room empty save for a card table, several folding chairs, and a rusty bedspring propped up against a plaster wall damp with rot. The room was eerily quiet — no traffic noise, no radios or voices, just the ragged cycles of their breathing.

On the floor in front of the bedspring spread a rust-colored stain. Jack took a deep breath — and gagged at a sickly-sweet odor he knew all too well. Up to that point, he'd been more confused than scared. Now he was seized by a deep, demoralizing panic. Was this what cows felt as they were forced through the final chute in a slaughterhouse?

The manager shoved him down into one of the chairs. Greenlee sneezed violently, then shuffled around behind the chair to tighten the knot binding Jack's wrists.

"Too tight?" he asked.

Jack nodded.

"Good." Greenlee sneezed again. "Shit!" he said. "I hate it down here."

Jack closed his eyes for a moment. The back of his head was pounding; he felt a warm stickiness that was probably blood. He opened his eyes again. He couldn't believe that when he first met the manager, the man had not raised his suspicions at all. So much for a veteran's intuition.

"Go make the call," the stranger told Greenlee. "I'll keep watch."

After the manager went out, the man pulled a chair over by the door, sat down, and leaned back till the chair tilted against the wall. He set the gun down on the card table and folded his arms coolly over his chest. After a few minutes he pulled an orange from his jacket pocket, peeled it, and ate it, watching Jack the whole time with a muted professional interest. He wiped his hands on his pants. Bored, he picked at the scraps of peel on the table. He grabbed a piece, took out a cigarette lighter, then squeezed the peel in front of the flame. The vaporized oil flared up. The man smiled.

With his arms strapped behind him, Jack's shoulders ached as much as his bruised thighs. He wished he'd had the sense to call Daskivitch and tell him where he was going. The dust in the room made his nose itch. What if it got stuffed up and he couldn't breathe? What if he got an asthma attack? He struggled to shake his head clear of such thoughts. He looked down at the red stain on the floor, then closed his eyes and tried to even out his breathing. His hands tingled with loss of circulation. They hurt till he lost all feeling in his arms.

This was what it was like to be a vic.

• • •

How long had he been down here? Half an hour? An hour? He had no idea. The back of his neck was caked with drying blood.

A faint noise sounded above and the stranger rose from his chair.

Muffled voices outside the door. The door scraped wide and Greenlee entered, followed by Randall Heiser, wearing a charcoal-gray suit. Heiser's habitual scowl brightened at the sight of Jack.

Another man moved into the doorway. His short, massive arms hung wide of his body as if he'd left a coat hanger inside his black satin baseball jacket. The kind of crew-cut, pig-eyed weightlifter who might delight in working as a club bouncer—he was big enough to throw a dead body over a fence all by himself. He stood just inside the door with his meaty hands folded over his crotch and stared in a very odd way—Jack wondered if he was the one who liked knives.

Jack's captor scowled at the new arrival. "Who the hell is this?"

Heiser pulled out a handkerchief, dusted off one of the folding chairs, then sat with a smug smile. "He's my new friend. Don't you worry about it. Ah thought it might be nice to have someone watching my back."

The first stranger's mouth worked as if he had just bit into something bitter. "You don't trust me?"

Heiser shrugged. "Mistakes have been made. I need to make sure you boys do this one neat." He pulled a small bottle of spring water from his suit pocket; Jack watched jealously as he cracked the top, took a long pull, and set the bottle down under his chair.

"Free up his mouth," Heiser told Greenlee.

The manager moved forward and ripped the tape away. The skin around Jack's mouth burned. He drew several deep breaths. "Are you out of your mind? I'm a New York

City police detective—do you realize what kind of trouble you're in right now?"

Heiser nodded at the sallow man, who stepped forward and calmly punched Jack in the mouth.

He decided it might be a good idea to shut up.

A phone trilled. Heiser pulled a tiny cellular out of his jacket, got up, and walked across the room. "I'll be home soon. Yes . . . No . . . Don't wait up. An hour and a half, two at the most." He hung up and grinned. "Time to go—can't keep the wife waiting."

Jack licked his lip—it was wet and salty where the blow had split the skin. "Tell me something," he said. "I know why you had Ortslee killed, but why get rid of a harmless kid like Tomas Berrios?"

"Don't you think it would be a bad sahn if I answered that?" Heiser said. He paused to let the implication sink in, then grimaced. "Since you asked, that greasy little wetback invaded my privacy. Just as you've done."

"He went into your apartment?"

"That's right."

"What did he do? What did he find?"

Heiser's eyes narrowed. "He had no right to enter my home. To go into my *den*."

Jack shook his head. Every killer he'd ever met had some "justification" for his crime. He prodded the man on. "I know what you're up to. I know all about the garbage."

Heiser's eyes narrowed. "I think it's time to wrap this up."

"What was it? Was it the plans for the waste transfer station?"

Like a confused animal, Heiser considered Jack. "He took my blueprints," he finally muttered.

"What did he want?"

Heiser snorted. "It was *puhthetic:* he asked for fifty thousand dollars. You know what he said?"

Jack waited.

"He said fifty thousand dollars to him was like only fifty dollars to me." Heiser picked a piece of lint off his pants leg. "I told him I wasn't interested in having my money translated into greasy wetback dollars. But I did say that I'd pay him. I asked him to meet me right here, in fact." He looked down at the bloodstain on the floor and nodded.

Jack sat up straight in his chair. "All right. Maybe you could get away with killing a porter and an old barge captain. But you won't get away with making an NYPD detective disappear. Every cop in town will be on the case."

Heiser grinned. "It might raise a ruckus if you just vanished. But what if you had a bad car accident tonight? What if you'd been drinking? You've had some problems with the booze recently, haven't you, Detective? Going to AA meetings and all."

Jack stared. He remembered a strange hunched man checking him out at one of the meetings.

Heiser took a pint bottle of liquor out of his pocket and unscrewed the cap.

Jack turned away and clenched his mouth shut. Heiser nodded to the first stranger, who went around behind Jack, grabbed him by the throat, and clamped a hand firmly over his mouth and nose. He struggled until he almost fainted. When the man finally removed his hand, Jack gasped for air. Heiser stepped forward, upturned the bottle, and rammed it into Jack's mouth. He couldn't help inhaling a gulp of fiery whiskey. He choked and sputtered. Heiser and the stranger repeated the harsh procedure until he had downed half the bottle.

"We should get going," the goon in the baseball jacket said, standing over by the door.

"Good idea," Greenlee said, rubbing his eyes. "This dust is killing me."

Heiser looked at his watch. "All right. Let's get it done."

It was the first stranger who stepped forward. He reached down under the bedspring and pulled out a strange black canvas roll. He set it on the card table and untied it. Jack's stomach dropped: it was a chef's knife kit. The man spread it open, examined his options, and pulled out a small, thin, hooked blade. Fillet knife.

Jack couldn't suppress a low moan. He thought he might pass out.

The goon in the baseball jacket gave a nervous glance at his boss. "I thought you said we were gonna smash up his car."

"Why wait?" Heiser said. "He doesn't have to be alive for that."

"You're making a big mistake," Jack said.

"*Hush,*" Heiser said. He nodded at the stranger. "Let's show the detective what happens to people who interfere with my business."

The man calmly poured some oil on a whetstone and sharpened the weapon; each pass made a scraping noise that reminded Jack of Heiser sitting in his fancy apartment, grinding his onyx stones in his closed palm. The stranger hefted the knife and took a step.

Jack lurched to his feet and staggered forward.

Startled, Greenlee grabbed the gun from the card table and fired. The shot popped hollow in the bare room. Jack jerked back as if pulled by a giant hand. He stumbled over the chair and crumpled onto the damp floor.

The goon in the baseball jacket reached into the back of his waistband. He pulled out a small stubby gun and shot the knife man in the back. Greenlee wheeled around, but the big man raised his gun and shot him in the face.

Jack thought he was hallucinating.

The big man spun around. "Get down, motherfucker!" he

screamed at Heiser in an odd high voice. "Lie down! Hands behind your head!" He tucked his head down toward his chest and shouted, "Move in, move in! We're in the warehouse next door!" His eyes were wide and he was hyperventilating. "The back! We're in the back! Downstairs!"

Greenlee lay on his side in the middle of the room. He sucked air through what was left of his mouth. All Jack could see of the knife man was his legs sticking out from under the card table. Bitter smoke hung in the air.

Holding his gun in both hands, the man in the baseball jacket bent down over Heiser. "Don't move an inch, shithead!"

He turned to Jack. "It's okay!" he shouted. "I'm a federal agent. Fuck—we told you to stay out of this." He knelt down and felt Jack's neck for a pulse. "Ten-thirteen!" he shouted into his wire. "Ten-thirteen!" The most urgent police code. *Officer down.*

Jack struggled to lift his head: a puddle of blood had soaked through his shirt and pooled on his chest; it fountained up.

He thought of his brother. He thought of his son.

The world died.

epilogue

On such a beautiful fall day, it would have been easy to forget that Green-Wood Cemetery was a place for the dead.

The burial grounds covered almost five hundred acres. Ben Leightner walked up a steep rise near the northern edge. He'd followed many twisting lanes to get here, all paths with soothing names: Jasmine, Cypress, Lily, Laurel . . . Hoping for a view of Manhattan, he climbed higher. The cemetery was all hill and hollow, forested with trees, stone angels, and obelisks.

From the top, he saw only more marker-covered hills. On this crisp day, the sun flooded the trees in a bright glory of red, orange, and yellow.

After he entered the cemetery, he'd seen a guard in a security car and a couple of orange-vested workers raking leaves, but in the past few minutes he hadn't seen anyone. The few sounds were pleasant ones: the crunch of leaves beneath his feet, the wind sighing in the trees, a hint of traffic so far away it sounded like a softly rushing brook. It was so peaceful he could hardly believe he was in the middle of Brooklyn.

• • •

He had received word of his father's shooting early the next morning through a phone call from his dad's boss, one Detective Sergeant Tanney. The sergeant offered his sympathies, but very little information.

The official story was released two days later, when the police commissioner himself announced that Detective First Grade Jack Leightner had gone down in the middle of a valiant attempt to arrest the murderer of two Brooklyn residents.

The real story didn't emerge until several days after that, when an anonymous tip to the *Daily News* opened up a very different account. It turned out that Randall Heiser had been under covert investigation by the FBI for two years. Though the Feds should—in hindsight—have moved against him after the Berrios and Ortslee murders, they argued that they'd lacked any direct evidence of Heiser's involvement. They claimed that a shaky indictment would have jeopardized a much broader investigation into racketeering in the national real estate and development markets. In their defense, they pointed out that following the murders they had assigned an undercover team to monitor the man around the clock.

Two senior FBI managers and an NYPD lieutenant were suspended from duty pending the conclusion of a full investigation into the matter.

Ben heard a noise and his heart iced over, but it was only a squirrel skittering through the leaves. He tromped down the hill, retracing his footsteps. At the bottom he crossed an asphalt lane called Linden Avenue and climbed another ridge, this one thickly wooded, the trees shading ornate marble mausoleums. Even in death, the rich had grander homes.

The view opened onto a sunny clearing below. His father

stood there, leaning on his cane in front of his brother Peter's humble tombstone. The cane was a recent luxury after two weeks in intensive care, a month in a private bed, then a month in which he shuffled around with a walker. At first, before the true story came out, the city had tried to lawyer out of full coverage for the medical bills — they argued that his father had been officially suspended before the incident, that he'd acted outside the department's jurisdiction and responsibility — but his boss, Sergeant Tanney, threatened to quit if they didn't do the right thing.

The doctors said his father might never be fit enough to qualify for active police duty again. Ben was surprised to discover that the old man didn't seem to care. A week ago, he'd gone to visit his father at the apartment in Midwood. (The landlord was doing relatively well upstairs with the help of a home-care attendant and he'd brushed off his son's demands that Jack move out.) Much of the conversation was still awkward, but at least this time they had more to talk about.

The old man had been down there by the grave site for almost an hour. Ben was about to step down the hill, but he saw his father's lips moving. Embarrassed, he turned away to give him more time.

These days his father seemed *lighter*, somehow, which was kind of weird, considering that he'd been shot, and all. Maybe it was the therapy. His dad would never have admitted that he was seeing a shrink, but Ben had accidentally come across a bill on the old man's kitchen counter. His father *did* say that as soon as he got better, he planned to go back to school for a certificate — he wanted to try for a new career as a drug and alcohol rehab counselor.

Maybe it was the romance. It was pretty weird seeing his father with a new girlfriend. In the hospital, Ben had been grumpy with her out of loyalty to his mom, but Michelle turned out to be nice, and she seemed to really care about his dad.

His father called out for him.

"I'm up here," Ben shouted.

Jack looked up, shielding his eyes, to locate his son among the shady leaves. He rested his hand on the tombstone for a moment, then slowly set off up the path.

Ben pulled out a camera and began to film. Someday, if he had a son, the kid would be able to see what his grandfather had looked like when he was still a relatively young man.